Merry-Go-Round
and
Other Words

Published by The Alchemy Press

Astrologica: Stories of the Zodiac

Beneath the Ground

Doors to Elsewhere

In the Broken Birdcage of Kathleen Fair (ebook)

Invent-10n

Rumours of the Marvellous

Sailor of the Skies (ebook)

Sex, Lies and Family Ties

Shadows of Light and Dark

Swords Against the Millennium

The Alchemy Press Book of Ancient Wonders

The Alchemy Press Book of Pulp Heroes

The Alchemy Press Book of Pulp Heroes 2

The Alchemy Press Book of Urban Mythic

The Komarovs (ebook)

The Paladin Mandates

Where the Bodies are Buried

www.alchemypress.co.uk

Merry-Go-Round

and

Other Words

~

Bryn Fortey

Introduction by Johnny Mains

The Alchemy Press

ISBN 978-0-9573489-6-7

The Alchemy Press
Cheadle, Staffordshire, UK

www.alchemypress.co.uk

CONTENTS

**For
Maddalena and Jim**

**With special thanks to
Johnny Mains
&
My daughter Maria**

INTRODUCTION
by
Johnny Mains

Forteyfication: a collection of Bryn's stories that is as solid as a military stronghold.

I'm obsessed with horror anthologies. And I'm obsessed with the people who write for them. Growing up, I always wondered why so many authors, who were to all intents and purposes anonymous, who featured in the seminal series and one-off anthologies in the 1970s and '80s, producing such sterling works of fiction, did not have novels flooding the shelves of John Menzies or have countless films adapted from their works.

Stories of horror, written by seemingly faceless people. But they all had lives, families. They loved, they lost. Being a writer was not their main job – they wrote because it was their passion. It was a hobby with benefits. It brought in a few quid that might have paid for a holiday or helped to fix the boiler.

Bryn Fortey was one of those faceless people, an author whose work I was familiar with and enjoyed – but someone I knew nothing about; a producer of words that made sense because they were all written in the right order.

For twenty-seven years Bryn worked for the same company. In steel. A hard, unforgiving job. The last seven years of his working life were spent on night shift. He has much in common with another once-faceless author, Conrad Hill, a hard-working, chainsaw-wielding man of the land who turned his hand to earning money writing for the *Pan Book of Horror Stories*. One can imagine Bryn coming in from a long shift, then sitting down to write such macabre masterpieces as those you are about to read in a collection that has been decades in the making and is arriving in Bryn's twilight years. But what a collection!

My journey with Bryn *really* started with several sheets of photocopied paper sent to me by Mary Danby in 2007, editor of the *Great Fontana Horror*. On these sheets were the names and addresses of everyone from whom she had commissioned stories. Even the more famous names. The stalker in me rejoiced, but I soon calmed down and slowly started crossing out those who had died. Bryn Fortey's name stood out. A quick internet search revealed that, yes, he had written for a few anthologies, but nothing more. His address? Was it an old one? Was it still current? Perhaps the greatest tool invented, BT Lookup, soon told me that Bryn was living in the same house from all of those years ago since he was writing for Fontana, and would I like his phone number?

Five minutes later I was speaking to the gentle-sounding Bryn. We chatted about his time writing for the anthologies and about Mary Danby. I was furiously scribbling down as much of the information he was giving me. And then, very softly, he told me about his son James, who had been stabbed to death only a few months before by a paranoid schizophrenic. His story was heart-breaking and I sat dumbstruck at my desk as it unfolded. Yet I didn't think it odd that he was telling a complete stranger this; to Bryn I wasn't a stranger; I was connected to him in the same way we had been connected the very first time I picked up a book including one of his stories. It was a long phone call and afterwards I wrote down his phone number on the photocopy of his address, and was sure that I was going to call him again.

And then, as with every bit of paper in my office, it got lost. I became distracted with something else, another project – which would turn out to be *Back From the Dead* and my biography of van Thal. When I did think to phone Bryn I searched high and low for that piece of paper. Couldn't find it. I felt bad and it's still a regret I carry that I didn't look harder, or at least search around on the internet.

And then 2011 came around. I was trying to gather the *Fontana Horror* authors together. I had edited Mary's debut collection, to be launched at Fantasycon. I thought that it was only right that some of her authors should be there to meet her, so I started going through the files again (they're always in a mess) and I found, through some stroke of luck, that scrap of paper with Bryn's phone number, hidden away between the pages of a copy of *Pieces of Mary*, one of the greatest fanzines published in the '80s.

I phoned Bryn again, and it was as if the previous phone call was only the day before. We hit a kind of rhythm and I invited him to Brighton for the book launch. He then told me that it would be good for him to get out because his wife Maddalena had died just a couple of months earlier. As before, I was at a loss for words. If anyone was ever going to believe in fate, that there was a reason for me to phone him, out of the blue, so close to his deep, deep losses, then I'm going to sign up for it. There had to be purpose, not just a sad coincidence.

Bryn arrived in Brighton and we had a chat and he met Mary. It was excellent seeing her with all of *her* authors, and I haven't lost touch with Bryn since then. We phone each other regularly and I helped him to get in touch with David Sutton who was reprinting his excellent Sphere anthologies which included Bryn's tales; and I suggested to the publisher of this book, Peter Coleborn, that he should do this collection. That it needed to be done.

And Bryn's writing again. He blames me for it. I'm happy to be blamed.

He's on Facebook – I think I may have persuaded him to get a computer. We message each other, mainly about music – we share a passion for jazz, blues, great tunes by artists no-one born in the last twenty years would know.

Now to the stories herein – and are you in for a treat! Not *just* stories, there are poems aplenty too, and with Bryn's expertise they come alive; their wordplay is par excellence and you will get a lot out of reading and re-reading them.

This is a *collection* in the truest sense of the word.

In his first published story, "Prison", Bryn shows how nasty he was willing to go, and this story does have a touch of the Charles Birkin about it. Birkin at his awe-inducing best. In "Merry-go-Round", David Morgan is tricked into murder by Jane and then goes on a bit of a spree before topping himself. And what occurs is a classic *Groundhog Day* scenario where he finds himself back in the past on the very night he met Jane. Do you think things will end up the same or will he have a chance to redeem himself? Read it and find out.

"Daddy" is the most affecting story in this collection, written after the passing of his son and wife, and it is a tale that will strike at your very heart. It's an incredibly moving piece and one that found me with tears in my eyes as I read it.

Bryn's newer work shows that he's still at the top of his game with stories such as "Ithica or Bust" and "The Flier", showing a more playful side to his writing. "Skulls" is a neat concept, expertly written, that reminds me of the *Ghost Rider* comics; and "Nasty" is another firm favourite of mine.

The crowning glory is the brace of stories that top and tail this collection, "Shrewhampton North-East" and "Shrewhampton North-West". The former was written for David Sutton's *New Writing in Horror and the Supernatural 2* and the latter written at my insistence. I loved the original and wanted a sequel and thus I pleaded with Bryn to write one. He did and it sums up what kind of writer Bryn is. Not afraid to revisit the past, yet constantly pushing himself forward and re-inventing his own wheel.

David Sutton and Mary Danby need to take a step forward and take a bow, for without them using some of these stories we wouldn't have this book today. *Merry-Go-Round and Other Words* is a classic collection and I really do hope people get behind this because great credit is due to Bryn Fortey, a man who has seen tragedy, but is getting through it, day by day, in the only way he knows how: writing. And what a writer!

Johnny Mains, March 2014

SHREWHAMPTON NORTH-EAST

"Do we change anywhere?" my mother asked the ticket collector as he punched little holes in our tickets.

He handed them back. "Five twenty-five for Lower Mallerton leaves from platform three. Change at Little Haslop and Shrewhampton North-East," he recited.

"Thank you," said my mother as she put the two tickets into her handbag. "Little Haslop and Shrewhampton North-East," she muttered while taking my hand and hurrying towards platform three.

It was already five twenty-two, and a train was standing at the platform. We approached a porter who was stacking parcels onto a barrow.

"Is this the Lower Mallerton train?" asked my mother.

"Five twenty-five for Lower Mallerton. Change at Little Haslop and Shrewhampton North-East," recited the porter.

"Thank you," said my mother. "Little Haslop and Shrewhampton North-East," she muttered.

"Is there a Shrewhampton North-West?" I asked the porter.

"If you don't hurry up, you'll miss your train," he said, ignoring my question.

"Yes!" exclaimed my mother. "Come along, come along. Don't bother people when we have so little time."

She pulled me past half the carriages, dipping and bobbing as she looked into each one, before we actually got on.

"I always like an empty compartment," she remarked. "Don't sit with your back to the engine."

I swopped to the opposite side.

"Settle down now," my mother told me, while fussing around herself.

She sat down. Then stood up, and took off her coat, and sat back down again. "Little Haslop and Shrewhampton North-East," she muttered. "I wonder how long before Little Haslop?" she mused.

I lowered the window and leant out. The porter who had previously been stacking parcels onto a barrow, the one my mother had asked whether this was the Lower Mallerton train, was no longer stacking parcels. Instead he had removed his cap and was scratching his head while staring in the direction of the compartment from whose window I was leaning. He saw I was looking at him and gazed expressionlessly into my eyes.

"Shut the window and sit down," ordered my mother as the guard's whistle sounded.

The porter had stopped scratching his head now, and was picking at his nose with an index finger instead. I poked out my tongue at him as I withdrew my head from the window. His only reaction was to smile knowingly.

"I said shut the window," my mother shouted.

As I did so the train started to move. It chugged past the porter who had been stacking parcels onto a barrow when my mother had asked whether this was the train for Lower Mallerton. The one who had stopped stacking parcels when I'd looked through the compartment window and had scratched his head instead. The one who had stopped scratching his head in favour of picking his nose. That one.

As the train chugged along and our compartment drew level with him, he stared straight at me through the glass and grinned broadly.

The grin could have been because he'd been amused by my poking out my tongue, or that he had accepted my cheekiness with good grace because he knew something I didn't. The evidence was too flimsy for a definite decision, so I pestered my mother for a sweet instead.

"All you ever think of is your belly," she exclaimed, her goitre bobbing frantically. She was very thin and scrawny, my mother, and her thyroid gland very prominent. "What do you think I'm made of, money?" she continued. "Give me, give me, give me! That's all I hear," she grumbled.

"I only want one," I wheedled.

"Here," she pulled the bag of sweets from a coat pocket, "have them all!"

I picked up the bag from where she'd thrown it and stuffed three into my mouth quickly.

"Oh you greedy, greedy child. Give them back to me at once."

Back into her coat pocket went the bag.

"Little Haslop," muttered my mother.

"And Shrewhampton North-East," I added for her.

"Little Haslop's first," she crowed triumphantly.

And it was.

"I hope there won't be a long wait for the connection," worried my mother.

"The five forty-four train is waiting at platform one," boomed a loudspeaker. "Passengers for Lower Mallerton to change at Shrewhampton North-East."

"Come along," said my mother.

I was disappointed at the required information being supplied by a loudspeaker. I had been hoping for another porter who stacked parcels, who scratched his head, who picked his nose, who grinned when I poked out my tongue. I had wanted to ask someone else whether or not there was a Shrewhampton North-West.

We reached platform one and my mother successfully found another empty compartment.

"I always like an empty compartment," she remarked. "Don't sit with your back to the engine."

I swapped to the opposite side.

The guard's whistle sounded, and as it did so our carriage door was pulled open and a breathless man clambered through, slamming it shut behind him.

He sat down with his back to the engine, but my mother did not tell him not to.

The train started to move.

"Phew," gasped the newcomer, mopping his forehead with a large white hanky. "I thought I was going to miss it."

He smiled at us both in turn. "Beg pardon, but this is the Lower Mallerton train isn't it?"

My mother nodded. "Change at Shrewhampton North-East," she told him.

"Ta," said the man.

"We had to change at Little Haslop as well," I informed him.

"Oh yes?" he said

"Don't bother the gentleman," scolded my mother.

"No bother, ma'am."

"Is there a Shrewhampton North-West?" I asked.

The man looked out through the window without replying.

I glanced towards my mother, but she only held a finger to her lips in a secret hush sign.

"Can I have a sweet please?"

"Your eyes are bigger than your belly."

"Please, mother," I pleaded winningly.

She took one from the bag and gave it to me. I sucked in silence, listening to the noises of the train.

My sweet finished, I turned my attention towards the man who had jumped into our compartment just as the train was about to start, and had failed to answer my question about the possible existence of a north-west Shrewhampton. He was still looking at the passing countryside, so I was able to study him quite openly.

He was a large man, not in height, but in girth. One of those plump people who are supposed to possess jocular tendencies. A round and ruddy face was topped with sparse sandy hair. Rimless spectacles rested on his nose in front of his eyes.

My mother tapped the nearest of my shoulders. "Have another sweet," she said loudly. Then, while giving me one, "Stop staring," she whispered.

This man, I decided while sucking my newly acquired sweet, was nothing like the porter encountered at our original station of departure. The one who had stacked, scratched, picked and grinned. He had been completely different in appearance, though both had failed to answer the same question.

Suddenly the man jerked away from the window. Turning, as if in panic, towards my mother and I. "What?" he said. "Eh!" he exclaimed. "What was that?" he continued. "Oh dear, dear, dear," he concluded.

"Pardon?" said my mother, somewhat taken aback.

I just sat and stared, once again quite openly.

"Oh dear, dear, dear," the man repeated.

"Did you want something?" my mother asked.

"Not again, not again," he moaned softly.

My mother's hands fluttered with birdlike bewilderment.

"I'm afraid I don't understand," she trilled nervously.

The plump man dabbed his face with the same white hanky he had used similarly at his time of entry into our compartment. "Profuse apologies, ma'am," he offered.

"Accepted I'm sure," said my mother.

"It's my ears," he stated by way of explanation.

"Your ears?" chorused my mother and me.

"For many months now I have suffered, oh how I've suffered; with them, through them. You'd never believe, but I'll try to explain if you wish. May I?"

My mother was all attention by now. "Please do," she agreed.

"Doctors have been baffled, specialists bemused. My case has proved beyond the medical community."

"Just fancy," murmured my mother.

"Yet what I suffer from is so simple it is almost non-existent," he continued. "It is just that every now and then, as happened a moment ago, I sense that someone immediately behind me is about to speak. I don't actually hear any words, but seem to be on the verge of doing so. It's most disquieting."

"It must be," agreed my mother. "Yes indeed."

"I've been examined for everything from a brain tumour to psychiatric disorders. All to no avail.

"Tcha, tcha, tcha," tutted my mother sympathetically.

"Tcha, tcha, tcha," I mimicked.

It all sounded vaguely symptomatic of a mental aberration to me. A more visual ailment, such as a third eye or missing toe, would have been much more interesting. My mother, however, appeared to be finding it all quite engrossing. "What it seems to me you are experiencing," she stated knowingly, "is a premonition of impending speech."

"Oh very aptly put," agreed the plump man.

"And there is never any basis to it?" she queried.

"No, never! There is either no one present at all, or only those who will swear they were not even considering speaking."

"Very strange."

"Indeed it is, ma'am."

They both nodded wisely.

"And it's not just imagination, I do assure you. When it happens I absolutely know that some form of message is on the verge of being communicated. A doctor once told me that I would know no peace until I actually hear the words."

"In that case, I hope you hear them soon," said my mother.

"No more than I," said the plump man.

"Is this Shrewhampton North-East?" I asked as the train pulled into a station.

"It is too," agreed my mother.

"Well done, lad," said the plump man.

The train ground to a halt and we all disembarked. "I hope there won't be a long wait for the connection," worried my mother.

No loudspeaker provided an answer, as had happened at Little Haslop. "Don't expect so," said the plump man hopefully. "Let's hope not, anyway," he added.

A porter approached where we stood, pulling a loaded barrow behind him. He was nothing like the porter who had stacked, scratched, picked and grinned two stations back. Not that I remembered what that porter had looked like now. But however he'd looked, it was nothing like this new one.

Neither was there any resemblance between him and the plump man who had jumped in to our compartment and experienced premonitions of impending speech, and who now spoke as the second porter drew level with where we stood at the platform's edge.

"Excuse me," he said politely, "could you tell me how long it will be before the train to Lower Mallerton, please?"

"Lower Mallerton?"

"Yes, Lower Mallerton."

"Ah, Lower Mallerton. Not for quite a bit yet. A two hour wait you've got."

"Oh dear," sighed my mother.

"You're sure?" asked the plump man.

"Two hours it is," confirmed the second porter.

"That's it then," decided the plump man.

"Is there a Shrewhampton North-West?" I asked.

"There's a waiting room on platform two," the second porter informed us, completely ignoring my question. So he had that much in common with the first porter and the plump man, even though he didn't look like either of them.

"Thank you," called the plump man as the second porter moved away, pulling his barrow behind him. He turned to my mother. "Too bad," he said.

"Better go to the waiting room," she decided.

"Can I have..." I started to say, but my mother absentmindedly handed me a sweet before I could even complete my request.

"Come along," she said, taking my hand in hers.

The three of us made our way to platform two and found the waiting room. There were already five men and three ladies sat in there, but since the room was by no means full that didn't bother us.

"Two hours is a fair old spell," said the plump man. "May I sit with you and the lad?" he asked my mother. "Be a bit of company for us both," he explained.

"Why certainly," agreed my mother.

We sat together in a corner of the waiting room, not far from the fireplace. There was no fire in the fireplace. "How often do you have these strange turns of yours?" asked my mother conversationally.

"An average of about three times per day I suppose," replied the plump man.

My mother and he continued to discuss his unusual affliction, but the topic still lacked interest for me. Instead of listening I took a good look at our waiting room companions.

None of the five men were in any way similar to the second porter or the plump man. One of them, however, did strike me as being something like the first porter. Naturally I could not be absolutely sure since I still couldn't remember what the first porter had really looked like, but I felt quite confident that it was something similar to the third of the five men I had just finished studying in the waiting room.

There were of course six, counting the plump man, but I wasn't counting him in this context since he had already been studied on the train.

Of the three ladies, one was as extremely thin as my mother, but features-wise there was no resemblance. Another was remarkably similar to the second porter, but none of them were in any way like the first porter or the plump man.

I was sorry there were no other children present.

The conversation between my mother and the plump man became spasmodic, then finally petered out. It seemed they had said all there was about his problem. The eight earlier arrivals had not said a word since we'd come in. We all sat in silence.

Then, "Hrrrmph," went one of the men as he cleared his

throat.

I thought for a moment that he was going to say something. But he didn't.

Another man blew his nose and a lady coughed daintily behind a lace hanky. Various shoes squeaked and shuffled as positions were changed and legs crossed. Finally one of the men, the one who had previously cleared his throat as if he were going to speak but hadn't, jumped to his feet, bowed in our direction, and actually did utter words.

"Pardon me," he started, "but might I enquire if you good folk too are Lower Mallerton bound?"

"Why yes, I am," agreed the plump man. "Also, this good lady and her son, I believe."

"Indeed so," confirmed my mother.

The man who was standing, who had cleared his throat as if to speak, but had not, who now had, fleetingly stroked his military looking moustache. "As I thought," he stated.

"I don't quite follow," said the plump man.

"We are all waiting for the Lower Mallerton train," the military-moustached man told him.

"Oh," said the plump man.

"Oh," said my mother.

"Can I have a sweet?" I asked.

"Sweets," exclaimed the man I thought resembled the first porter, who was not the man with the military moustache who had cleared his throat, but another.

"Easy, sir, I'll handle this," stated the moustachioed man on his feet who had said things were as he thought.

"But sweets," whimpered the man who had just joined the conversation. "They've got sweets."

The man on his feet turned from the man who had

interrupted the conversation and faced us again. "I take it that you have not long arrived here at Shrewhampton North-East?"

"That is correct. I caught the train at Little Haslop, and this lady and her son were already aboard."

"At what time, and this is important, do you expect to leave this station?"

"Well, the plump man thought a moment. "We got off at about six-twenty and a porter told us we had a two hour wait before the train to Lower Mallerton. So I assume the train is due around eight-twentyish."

"Eight-twenty!"

"Hear that?"

"What does it mean?"

"Quiet please," the military moustached man barked at the chattering people around him.

"Might I ask the reason for all these questions?" asked my mother, rather primly.

"Of course, madam, you have every right."

"Then I do."

"None of us here are Shrewhampton North-East residents. We all arrived via other trains, expecting to catch a connection to Lower Mallerton. We have all been given different times for the same train. Some of those times have long elapsed. We are beginning to doubt that the Lower Mallerton train will indeed ever run!"

"This is very strange," decided the plump man.

My mother looked towards the lady who was every bit as thin as herself. "What time were you told the Lower Mallerton train would leave?" she asked.

"At seven fifty-nine," replied the equally thin lady.

"Well it's not that yet," pointed out my mother.

"Seven fifty-nine, yesterday," the equally thin lady expanded.

"That's nothing," shouted the man who had reacted so strongly to my request for a sweet. "I've been here three whole days!"

"Three days!" exclaimed the plump man in horrified tones.

"What's going on?" asked my mother of no one in particular.

"What indeed," responded the military-moustached man.

"They've got sweets," said the man who had said the same thing before.

"I wonder if the station buffet is open yet?" asked the lady who looked at lot like the second porter.

"I'll go and see," yelled the man who had previously been obsessed with my sweets. He leapt to his feet and ran from the waiting room.

"It won't be open," stated the military-moustached man, "but after three days the poor chap has to cling to whatever hope he can."

"I had never even heard of Shrewhampton North-East before today," muttered the plump man.

"No more had any of us," said the equally thin lady.

"Nor I," added my mother.

"Then it's no good my asking if there's a Shrewhampton North-West?" I enquired, without much hope. Nobody answered, or even appeared to hear. This was something everybody had in common with everyone else.

"We are all hungry to varying degrees, with some bordering upon starvation," said the man with the military moustache. "I must ask you to let me share out whatever edibles any of you may have."

My mother handed him what was left of my bag of sweets.

"Thank you, madam."

The plump man gave an unopened packet of ham sandwiches.

"Thank you, sir."

The man who had gone to check on the station buffet returned with such a desolate air about him that we all knew the place to still be shut before he actually told us. He bucked up a bit when given one of my sweets, as was everyone else too.

"The ham sandwiches," declared the military-moustached man, "will be kept for later."

"What about the porter?" asked my mother. "Surely he should be able to do something."

I assumed she was speaking about the second porter. The first, being at a quite different station, would certainly not be in a position to act.

"No joy in that direction," said the lady who happened to look like the porter under discussion.

"Yet another link in the mystery," said the equally thin lady.

The military-moustached man took up the topic. "We all saw him, as you did yourselves, at the time we disembarked from our various trains," he said. "To each of us he told a time for the Lower Mallerton connection, and suggested we come here to the waiting room. None of us has seen him a second time, though some have searched high and low."

"This is ridiculous," insisted the plump man. "I can't wait here for a train that might never come!"

"But what else is there to do?" asked my mother.

"Catch a bus," answered the plump man. "Shrewhampton North-East can't be all that far from Lower Mallerton," he explained. "I shall go into town and catch a bus."

"It seems such a waste though," remarked my mother, "after having paid for a ticket all the way."

"Better than being stranded here," decided the plump man.

"You might be right," said my mother, "but what if there is no bus and the connection arrives while you are gone?"

"A chance I'll have to take. Tell you what I'll do though," he offered, "if there is a bus service between Shrewhampton North -East and Lower Mallerton I will telephone you here at the station and tell you about it."

"That would be very kind," said my mother.

The plump man stood up. "I'm off then," he said.

"Good luck," said my mother. Then, "Take care."

"Thank you, ma'am." He turned and strode out from the waiting room.

"He'll be back," said the man who had kept on about my sweets before he'd had one.

"Why should he?" asked my mother.

"He'll be back," repeated the same man.

"Isn't there a bus service then?" asked my mother, who was very good with questions, but not so hot with answers.

"We have no idea, madam," said the military-moustached man. "One thing we do know though, there is no way out of this station."

"No way out?" echoed my mother.

"No entrance, no exit, nothing. We're not so stupid that we haven't already considered the bus possibility, but there is no way of leaving the station!"

"Then why didn't you tell him?" asked my mother.

"The only way to believe such a strange fact is to find out for oneself."

"You're probably right," sighed my mother.

Fifteen minutes later the plump man returned. "There's no way out," he exclaimed.

"We know," said the man with the military moustache.

"I can't believe that this is really happening," said the plump man.

"But it is," said the equally thin lady.

"Where is this Shrewhampton North-East?" wondered the plump man. "Why haven't any of us heard of it before?"

"I don't think it really exists," said a man who didn't look like anyone else and had not spoken before saying that he didn't think Shrewhampton North-East existed.

"But it must exist," argued the lady who looked like the second porter. "We are here, aren't we?"

"Where are we?" responded the man who doubted Shrewhampton North-East's existence. "We are in the waiting room of a station that boasts no entrance, no exit, a closed buffet, a porter who disappears, and seems to lack trains. I for one have never seen this supposed town of Shrewhampton North-East!"

I knew without having to ask. If there wasn't a Shrewhampton North-East, there definitely wouldn't be a Shrewhampton North-West.

At that moment the missing porter appeared in the doorway. The second porter that is, not the first who wasn't missing but at a different station altogether.

Everyone stared in silent surprise as he placed a canteen of cutlery on the floor. "Mr Ash knows all," he said, then left.

The military-moustached man ran to the waiting room doorway and looked outside, both ways. "Dash it," he exclaimed angrily. "The fellow's disappeared again." He strode back to the centre of the room.

"What did he mean?" asked the man who'd kept on about my sweets.

"Exactly what I intend finding out," barked the man who again held the central position. "The porter said that Mr Ash knows all. Well the first thing I want to know, who is Mr Ash?"

The plump man looked around nervously. "Ash does happen to be my name," he admitted. "Alfred Robert Ash. But I can't be the Ash the porter meant because I don't know anything."

"That's what you say," called the lady who bore a marked resemblance to the second porter, who had disappeared once again.

"All right, madam," insisted the man with the military moustache. "I think it better if I conduct the interrogation."

"Now look here..." started the plump man.

"No, you look here," interrupted the self-appointed interrogator. "We know you know what's going on, so you may as well tell us first as last."

"But I don't know anything!"

"It will go hard on you if you maintain this stubborn attitude."

"I can't tell you what I don't know!"

"I warn you, sir, don't make me resort to force."

"Force?" echoed the plump man.

"A desperate situation demands desperate measures," explained the military-moustached interrogator.

"Torture him!" shouted the equally thin lady.

"Pull his finger nails off," screamed the lady who looked like the second porter.

"Gouge his eyeballs out," raged the third lady, who looked like nobody and had said nothing until then.

"Just give me five minutes alone with him," begged the man

who had mentioned my sweets before going to see whether the station buffet had opened.

"Shall I let them loose on you?" threatened the military-moustached man.

"Stop!" My mother leapt to her feet, hands held high. "Mr Ash is not a well man," she told them. "He suffers from premonitions of impending speech."

"Is that a National Health Service recognised illness?" asked the man who didn't believe in Shrewhampton North-East.

"What?" said the plump man. "Eh!" he exclaimed. "What was that?" he continued. "At last…" he concluded.

"There you are, his affliction has struck," announced my mother.

Everyone stared at the plump man as he dropped to his knees, head cocked as if listening to something being said. Only no-one else could hear anything.

I knew that this time was different for him. This time, the someone immediately behind him when he sensed words were about to be spoken, had spoken. He was hearing the words at last.

The plump man's eyes were closed and his lips turned up at the corners in a contented smile. His head was still cocked to one side in a listening attitude.

"His premonition has come to be!" cried my mother.

The lady who was equally as thin, the one who had not long before shouted for the plump man to be tortured, crossed herself and began to mutter a prayer.

"Mr Ash knows all, now," I told them, but nobody took any notice.

"What does it mean?" asked the lady who looked like the second porter.

"I believe in only what I can see and touch," stated the man who doubted Shrewhampton North-East.

"I'm a man of the world, not a man of the mind," said the military-moustached man whose interrogation seemed to have come to an end.

"I don't understand, but I'm glad for his sake," murmured my mother with a wistful smile.

I couldn't grasp why all these grownup people found what was happening so mysterious. It was all perfectly clear. I knew who the plump man had heard, and could hazard a good guess as to what had been said. Adults are not so clever really.

"Enough of this tomfoolery," snapped the man who wanted to continue his interrogation. He walked across to where the plump man knelt and prodded his shoulder with an extended finger.

The plump man, Mr Ash, gently toppled over onto his side and lay still.

The military moustached man examined him then looked up. "The blighter's dead," he announced.

"He heard the words and found peace," whispered my mother.

"As if we haven't got enough troubles," moaned the man who no longer carried on about my sweets. "Now we're lumbered with a corpse!" But even as he spoke, saliva dribbled from the corners of his mouth and his breathing became laboured.

"Yes indeed," agreed the ex-interrogator while tugging thoughtfully at his military moustache. "What to do with such a large cadaver might well pose problems."

He went across and picked up the canteen of cutlery from where the second porter had left it. Going from person to person, he gave everyone a knife and fork each.

"A desperate situation demands desperate measures," he said for the second time.

"Three whole days I've been trapped here," muttered the man with saliva dribbling.

"That train's never going to come, and we've got to live," said the man who only believed what he could see and touch.

"It's almost like manna from heaven," decided the equally thin lady.

"I don't think Mr Ash would mind," said my mother. "In fact I'm sure he would be only too pleased to help us."

"If we are going to be stuck here at Shrewhampton North-East forever, as seems likely," pondered the lady who resembled the second porter, "what are we going to do when he is gone?"

Nobody answered her. They were too busy forming a circle around the late Mr Ash.

"What?" said the man who doubted the existence of Shrewhampton North-East and only believed what he could see and touch. His head jerked round to glance over his shoulder. "Eh!" he exclaimed. "What was that?" he continued. "That was most strange," he concluded.

Nobody else noticed, only me. Everyone else had their eyes glued upon the plump form upon the floor. But I knew that the question posed by the lady who looked like the second porter had been answered.

And I knew, now, why the first porter had stopped stacking, scratching and picking so that he could grin so knowingly as my train carriage passed by.

"Shall I carve?" asked the man with the military moustache.

MERRY-GO-ROUND

The thing that had been Alexander Brand was now nothing but a bloodied lump of raw, lifeless flesh. Battered, bruised, torn and dead.

Very much dead indeed.

Still, now, his fury spent, David Morgan stood panting over his victim. "I hope you suffered," he gasped, gulping air into heaving lungs. "I hope it wasn't too quick."

Then reaction set in. He noticed the blood that stained the clothes he wore, none of it his, and stared hollowly at the body lying on the floor. Morgan turned his head away, feeling tired, empty, and not a little sickened as the full realization of his own violence struck home.

David Morgan, twenty-two years of age, six foot three and a well proportioned sixteen stone, was as fit as a professional rugby player on the brink of international honours. The body that lay at his feet, the man he had just killed, was nearly three times his age. Thin, frail and weak.

It had been almost too easy

With an effort he stopped the trembling which suddenly threatened to overwhelm him and forced away the horror that had started to fill his mind. Brand had asked for it, the way he had treated Jayne. The subtle cruelties and indignities, his refusal to agree to a divorce. Morgan clung to the reasoning that helped justify his brutal act.

The man had deserved all he'd got.

Good grief, he'd even tried to lie his way out of it. "I have no wife," he'd whimpered when told just why he was about to die. "She's been dead for fifteen years…"

But Morgan had been wise to him. Jayne Brand had shared his bed that very afternoon, and she been anything but a ghost.

Behind him a door opened. Turning quickly, he saw that she had entered the room.

"It's done," he said flatly.

"You're sure he's dead?" asked Jayne.

"Look for yourself. He's more suited to a meat hook than a coffin."

She leant against the wall just inside the doorway and closed her eyes for a moment. "You know, there were times when I doubted you would really do it."

"Well I have."

"Yes, and that makes me an extremely wealthy young lady."

Morgan glanced up sharply at that. "I didn't kill him for his money," he snapped. "To make you free of him, that's why I did it. Free for us to be together."

"Of course, David, you murdered for love."

He didn't like her choice of words, nor a certain edge to her tone, but this was not the time for petty bickering. The business at hand still had to be completed. "You had better show me what to take to make it look a genuinely interrupted burglary."

"Oh yes, it must all be done properly. We must all play our parts."

"What's got into you, Jayne?" All it needed was a touch of panic or hysteria, and all their carefully conceived plans would erupt into chaos. "Don't lose your nerve now."

"Stay where you are, David," she ordered as he started towards her. "There's been a change of plan," she continued when, surprised, he did indeed stop.

"Change of plan?"

"Oh we shall still play our roles, have no fear of that. We shall speak our lines with well acted sincerity."

Like a non-swimmer out of his depth, Morgan struggled against currents he was ill-equipped to deal with. "What are you talking about, Jayne?"

"Poor David, but you will soon understand." She smiled then, a cat-toying-with-a-mouse sort of smile. "This is where the script rewrite takes effect."

Morgan's mind was spinning in bewildered circles.

"Paul, darling," called Jayne in a voice emanating false surprise. "Come here quickly. Poor Uncle Alex has been murdered by a burglar!"

As if in the throes of a nightmare, Morgan watched as a man of about thirty came through the door in answer to the summons. In his hand was a gun, pointing straight at Morgan's heart.

"Why yes, so he has, my dear. What a tragedy!"

"Opportune though, Paul, considering that I am heir to Uncle's millions and your creditors are busy demanding their legal dues."

"Just a drop in the ocean compared to what you've got coming, but the timing is spot on."

Rage and bewilderment fought for supremacy over Morgan's swirling emotions. "What the hell's happening?" he demanded.

"Well, it speaks," said the man named Paul.

"Jayne!" exclaimed Morgan, his eyes unable to leave the gun. "I don't understand."

"Of course, you two haven't met. Let me introduce you. Paul, this is David Morgan, second row forward with the Birmingham Rugby Union Football Club. Was a member of last season's Welsh squad, an unused substitute against Scotland

and France and many expect him to win his first cap this year. Also, until very recently, my lover.

"David, this is Paul Radford unsuccessful financier. A loser on the stock exchange, the racetrack, and in casinos. Also, and rather importantly, my husband."

"I would offer to shake hands, but this revolver seems to be in the way," said Radford, obviously feeling in charge of the situation.

For Morgan, however, it was as if the house was crashing about his head, everything becoming a jumble of insane contradictions. "But he's your husband," he said, pointing at the body. "I've just killed him for you!"

"No, David, that's my uncle." She spoke as if explaining a very elementary problem to a backward child. "Thank you for getting rid of him, though. Paul has so many debts that must be paid, and we both have rather expensive tastes."

Morgan was frantic now. "You said he was your husband!"

"Stop being tiresome, David. This is my husband, with the gun. As for you, well you're a burglar who has panicked into killing an old man who disturbed you in the act. We have arrived too late to save my uncle, but in time to try and apprehend the culprit. Attempting to avoid capture, you will attack us, forcing Paul to shoot in self defence. It will be an open and shut case for the police. They should be quite grateful."

"You can't mean this Jayne?"

"Can't I? You idiot, David. Do you really think I have enjoyed your inexperienced slobbering these past few months? There were times you revolted me!"

"But I love you…" Morgan's voice tailed into silence, a commodity as ineffective and helpless as his total situation.

"Enough of this," snapped Radford, moving further into the room. Do you want to attack me before I squeeze the trigger? You should, if you want to play your part right."

"You can't just kill me!"

Radford laughed. "Let anyone else say that, but not you. Not with Uncle Alexander's body not yet cold. Honestly, Morgan, you really are a prize idiot. I can't imagine how Jayne managed to put up with you, apart from the fact that a gullible dimwit was necessary for our plan."

He stood there, the man with the gun, cruel amusement masking his features. "How did he compare with me in bed?" he asked sarcastically, glancing towards his wife. "I bet he was rubbish."

David Morgan had learnt his rugby in the toughest of schools, amongst the valley teams back in his Welsh homeland, where rugby was more a way of life than a sport. It was only recently that a lucrative professional contract had tempted him to Birmingham. Freely tipped to win his first international cap, he played hard, fast, and to hell with the rules.

Radford's sideway glance was the one small chance Morgan needed. He reacted with the unpremeditated response of a well-trained athlete going automatically into action. As his tormentor's eyes flickered away, Morgan launched himself forward into the type of bone-crunching tackle he had become renowned and feared for.

Jayne's belated cry of warning came screaming from her throat as his shoulder landed in the pit of Radford's stomach.

The revolver fell free to the floor as the two men went down in a heap. Jayne rushed forward, was just bending to pick it up when Morgan regained his feet. Striking quickly, he clipped her on the jaw. As she fell, he kicked the weapon under a table.

Turning swiftly, he caught Radford in the act of rising. Clenching his hands, Morgan brought down a tremendous double-fisted blow to the back of the other man's neck. Bone snapped under the jarring impact and, head twisted at an unnatural angle, Radford fell back to the floor.

This time Radford made no attempt to struggle back on to his feet. He didn't move at all.

The tables are turned, thought Morgan with a vicious elation. The stink of blood was fast in his nostrils. He was the hunter now, and what he caught he killed!

He watched as Jayne, sufficiently recovered from the blow she had received, crawled to her husband's body and cradled his rag-doll head in her arms. "Paul?" she cried brokenly. "Oh Paul, what went wrong?"

"You chose too damn well," Morgan answered in the dead man's stead. "When you picked me to do your killing, none of us realised just what an aptitude I would have for the job."

Her eyes were slits of hatred when she looked up at him. "You bastard," she hissed.

"I really did love you, Jayne," he told her, shaking his head as if he, too, now found such a concept totally unbelievable. A horrible mixture of desire and loathing filled him, causing his mind to scream out for this woman's destruction.

Morgan dropped to his knees beside her, hands seeking her throat. His rage filled fingers circled her neck, and then he was squeezing. Squeezing with all the hate that now filled him.

It was long after she had died before Morgan finally released the death grip from around her wrecked throat. Emotionally drained, he sat back on his haunches and looked down at his third victim.. Stone-like, he remained motionless for a long while before finally clambering to his feet.

Acting as if by automation, he searched for and retrieved the gun from where he had kicked it. No sensible alternatives presented themselves as answers to his shell-shocked condition. Indeed, only one outcome offered a clear-cut resolution.

Placing the barrel inside his mouth, Morgan pulled the trigger. With a destructive and explosive blast of noise, the back of his skull burst open.

***

Walking slowly, his mind in a daze, the man entered the Birmingham RUFC Social Club, not knowing why he was there. He was trying to remember, but everything remained a blank.

"Hail the conquering hero," called a voice.

Turning, he saw a smallish, curly-headed guy with the early discoloration of what promised to be a livid shiner surrounding his left eye. "Get away with you, Lloyd, it was a team effort." Even as he spoke, he wondered how it was he knew the other's name, and what he was talking about.

"Maybe, but you scored the try that mattered. Like a bloody bulldozer you were."

"Careful now, you'll be making me big-headed," he said with a smile, but his mind was asking questions he couldn't answer. Like, who was this person? Hell! He didn't even know himself.

Moving automatically, he passed by the one he'd called Lloyd. Another man waved at him and spoke. "I bet the London Irish won't forget you in a hurry, my boy."

He waved back and went on, before pausing in front of the men's room. Apparently making up his mind, though in reality he had no idea what was going on at all, he entered and started to comb his hair before the mirror.

While he appeared outwardly calm, inside he was all turmoil. The reflection that gazed back from the glass was the face of a complete stranger! Trying hard to control his racing thoughts, he strove to remember just who he was.

I am … his mind strained. *I am* ... *oh God!* Suddenly it snapped insanely into place.

I'm David Morgan and I have just blown out my own brains!

Then it all swept screamingly back to him. The old man; killing him. Breaking Radford's neck and strangling Jayne. Then finally his own suicide. Madness assailed him, yet he still stood there quietly combing his hair.

London Irish? Scoring the winning try? He knew it should all mean something, but what? Then the swirling fog lifted and light shone through. It all tied up. This was the evening he first met Jayne!

He had gone back, Morgan realised, four months into the past. The thought left him shattered, so completely beyond his powers of understanding.

But I'm dead, he told himself; *this just can't be happening*. Yet while he mentally knew the impossibility of the situation, his body insisted that all was normal.

Leaving the men's room, he made his way to the bar and ordered a pint of lager. He was, Morgan now knew, repeating everything he had done when it happened the first time. There was the curly-headed guy again, talking animatedly to a girl. He remembered him now: Lloyd Hooper, their scrum half. Another Welshman plying his trade in Birmingham. He played like a terrier, nipping at the heels of the opposition.

Damn it all, he told himself, *I have gone back in time*. And there could be only one possible explanation for such a miracle-like happening. He was being given a second chance.

His hand lifted the glass and, while he drank, his mind enthused over the solution. He knew everything that was going to happen. Forewarned, forearmed, he could change the original.

He felt exhilarated. Whoever had arranged this second chance for him would not be let down. He would finish his lager and leave. Go to the cinema, for a walk, anything but stay where he was. Straight away, his personal history would be altered. Jayne would remain unmet.

Morgan emptied his glass. Now was the time to act. His mind told his legs to walk to the door. To leave, get out, but his legs refused to obey.

"Another pint over here," he unwillingly called to the barman.

If he didn't go now, right at this moment, he knew that Jayne would enter his life. But he couldn't move. Instead, he drank from his second lager.

"Excuse me, Mr Morgan."

He turned to face Jayne.

"I hope you won't think me forward, but I was at the match this afternoon and, seeing you here, well, I simply had to tell you what a marvellous game I thought you played."

His mind screamed mental hate and abuse. He wanted to run, to get away from her, but his voice went smoothly into action. "Why thank you, Miss … er. I didn't catch your name?"

She smiled engagingly. "I didn't give it, but it's Jayne Brand."

"Well, Miss Brand." *Brand? Brand? Try Radford, you bitch!* "I'm glad you enjoyed the game. Do you watch us often?"

"I have done recently. I'm a new convert."

"Must look after newcomers to the code. Can I buy you a

drink? I really would like to."

"That's very kind of you. I'll have a vodka and lime, please."

In spite of everything, he had to admit she was stunningly beautiful. Now, seeing it all happen again, Morgan couldn't help but understand why he had fallen so completely under her spell the first time. Even now, a certain perverse desire was intermingled with the revulsion knowledge now provided. Indeed, he gradually stopped worrying about his present inability to alter the original chain of events. He knew, and that would be enough. He would make the break in time to avoid becoming a killer all over again.

So, confident he would be able to instigate future change, Morgan was content to let things drift. As she had previously used him, this time he would use her.

Time slipped by, and they soon embarked upon their fateful love affair. Though he had considered himself master of the situation, he found that in reality he was now disgusted by the physical aspects of their relationship. The knowledge he now possessed, that Jayne was merely using her body to ensnare him, and was, in fact, revolted by his touch, tended to overshadow his plan to use her in return. Desire withered and died, but still his physical side continued to respond to her sexual expertise.

Time and time again, Morgan became determined to break the pattern, but failed on each occasion. Whatever he was thinking at any particular moment, his words and actions were the exact duplicates of those used first time round. It was as if his body was independent of thought, leaving him with no control over it at all.

At times this helplessness brought on terrible bouts of fear, but he always managed to calm himself with promises of future action. Tomorrow's hoped for success became the only possible future his mind could salvage, so he clung to it with an embrace born of desperation.

Morgan, hating her, declared his passionate love. He listened to what he knew were lies, and fell in with the plot to kill the man she claimed to be her husband. He drifted along in a carbon copy of his previous existence until, finally, the fateful day arrived when he set out to meet his destiny. Again.

This was his last chance to walk the other way. Morgan knew it, willing himself not to go, but his feet would not obey. Then, he was there, ringing the doorbell.

The old man answered, peering short-sightedly through his spectacles. He was nearly three times Morgan's age, thin, frail and weak. "Yes?"

"Got to speak to you privately," muttered Morgan, pushing his way through the door.

The tremendous internal struggle was bringing him to the verge of madness. No longer could he fool himself into believing he could change course when it became imperative to do so. That time was long gone. The terrifying truth could be ignored no longer. Morgan had absolutely no control over his behaviour.

For all his wordless pleading, the continuity could not be broken. Neither he nor Brand could do anything other than play out their predestined roles.

"I'm here to kill you," he replied, when the old man demanded to know the reason for his ill-mannered intrusion. Mental tears drenched his mind, but nothing now could stop the macabre re-enactment.

And so the whole brutal killing was repeated. As he carried

it out, Morgan begged for the gift of total madness in the hope that it might blot out the horror of his bodily actions. But that too was denied him, and he remained fully aware of what he was doing – for a second time.

Then it was over and Alexander Brand was once again reduced to a bloodied piece of lifeless flesh. "I hope you suffered," gasped Morgan, gulping air into heaving lungs. "I hope it wasn't too quick."

He mouthed the words because he had no option, but inside he was anticipating the next stage with a vindictive pleasure. Whereas knowing the truth had made murdering Brand such a repugnant affair, it was going to make the killing of Paul and Jayne Radford enjoyable by comparison. His only regret was that he wouldn't be able to increase their suffering, but he knew that would prove impossible. Everything had to happen exactly as before.

And so it did.

Morgan expressed the same bewilderment as the truth was revealed. Radford pointed the same gun, for the same purpose, and made the same fateful glance towards his wife. Feeling an almost joyful anticipation at the havoc he was about to carry out, Morgan launched himself forward.

If only it could have been made to last longer. There was a lot more he would have liked to have done to both of them, but with the resigned acceptance of a puppet he knew that the strings directing his actions were not his to control.

Entering, again, the last phase, he retrieved the gun from under the table. Please, he begged whichever deity was master of his personal destiny, please make this second death permanent. Surely, he reasoned, what he had experienced was punishment enough, even for a murderer.

Placing the barrel inside his mouth, Morgan pulled the trigger. With a destructive, explosive blast of noise, the back of his skull burst open.

***

Walking slowly, his head in a daze, the man entered the Birmingham RUFC Social Club. Everything was a blank. He wanted to remember, but seemed somehow afraid to.

"Hail the conquering hero," called a voice.

"Get away with you, Lloyd, it was a team effort," he said automatically.

It was all rather blissful, this seeming lack of any need for thought. His body knew just what to do without any bidding whatsoever, and his mind was apparently left without reason to function. Indeed, something seemed to tell him it had every reason not to.

More words were exchanged, then he left the person he'd called Lloyd. Another man waved and spoke. "I bet the London Irish won't forget you in a hurry, my boy."

These words, too, were completely meaningless, but he waved back and moved on, pausing briefly outside the men's room before going in. Standing in front of the mirror he combed his hair.

The reflection gazing back at him from the glass was that of a stranger, but he didn't care. His mind was perfectly content to drift along, happy in its own lack of knowledge. It was sufficient that his body seemed to know what to do of its own accord.

But the dulled, zombie-like state was a passing phase that was doomed to end. As he stood there, combing his hair, so it struck. Total recall, unbidden and unwanted, flooded the vacant corners of his mind like a triggered time bomb.

He knew it all, and the terror was with him yet again.

Name: David Morgan. Second row forward with the Birmingham Rugby Union Football Club and a Welsh squad member. Also, treble murderer and suicide. Twice over!

And this was the beginning of the third time around.

Amid ravaging mental turmoil, one stark fact knife-edged through his mind. With a sudden and awful clarity he realised that this was his punishment, to relive the last four months of his life over and over again. This was him, David Morgan, for the rest of time.

For all eternity!

So much more abominable than all the manmade pictures of hellfire and brimstone, devils and demons. This was the real purgatory. No place of temporary suffering or expiation, but an area of recurring permanence.

For every sinner, his own private hell.

Leaving the men's room, he made his way to the bar and ordered a pint of lager. He would finish the drink, buy another, and then Jayne would enter his life. Morgan knew it, but could do nothing to alter the set sequence of events.

Over and over, never ending. His own personal merry-go-round.

"Another pint over here."

Round and round it would go, never stopping. Never giving him the chance to get off. His mind wept, but the merry-go-round kept spinning.

"Excuse me, Mr Morgan."

He turned to face Jayne.

POEMS #1

FIRST DATE

Odeon cinema
Bogart and Hepburn
African Queen
The date you would have refused
Had you realised it would be with me
Remember?
Sometimes your lack of English helped
But back to then:
Best seats
As I tried to impress
Front row balcony
With a box of Maltesers on your lap
Slipping an arm along the back of your seat
As was standard practise
I dropped a hand onto your shoulder
Up you jumped
Panic and mayhem
Showering those sat below with Maltesers
I thought this first date would be our last
Little did we both know then
That fifty-three years lay ahead

***

ONE ROOM AHEAD

You are always, now
One room ahead
Me, playing catch-up
Lounge, kitchen
Living room
Up the stairs

Bathroom, attic
Bedrooms 1 2 3
Back down, outside
Amongst pots
Flowers, plants
All tended with
Your love and care
Why is the garden
Looking so untidy?
Silence
I call your name
More silence
You're always in front
However fast I move
One room ahead
Now and evermore

One room ahead

***

SAYING GOODBYE

Saying goodbye
Is easy
It's loss that's hard
A number you no longer call
The phone that doesn't ring

Yes
Saying goodbye is easy
It's loss that's hard

***

WORDS FOR A SON

I say:
The time for your departure
Is long, long overdue

You laugh, ignore
Which is your way

You open your mouth
And I hear echoes of my past
And I feel guilt
At having influenced the person
You now are

You have the Italian family motif
Engraved upon your soul
And I do believe
You would cause damage
On behalf of your mother
On behalf of myself

You give me a lift
In your wreck of a van
And I watch you drive away
Hunched
Ponytailed
Total concentration
As you listen to a tape
Of your latest
Band-in-rehearsal

And I say to myself:
I love that boy

***

BOY IN A BOX

The church was packed
Standing room only
You didn't play many gigs like that

But the only guitar was a floral tribute
From your sister

Pink Floyd played you in
Led Zeppelin played you out

At the crematorium
Yes bounced off the walls
As a curtain closed around your coffin

Now your ashes are in a smart white box
In our front room
Where I talk to you

I know you can't hear
I know it's not the you I knew
I know you are dead

But that box represents what I have lost

Your mother knows that she will see you again
But I don't think so
I don't have her faith

I look at old photographs
I have memories

But that box has become a link
That I grab and cling to
I'm not the man I was
Not since you died

Miss you
Son

THE ART OF LETTING GO

Go
Grow
But not with my blessing

I made all the mistakes
Necessary for
Your education

But did you learn?
Did you take note?
Did you hell!

So go your own way
See if I care
(Oh yes, I care)
See if I bleed
(Oh yes, I bleed)

Go
Grow
But not with my blessing

Only my love

ITHICA OR BUST

So it came that Troy was obliterated, leaving only an empty orbit around the twin suns. A destruction that had finally ended the latest of the Great Galactic Wars. Such was the unleashed power necessary to reduce a whole world to nothing, that even the victorious battle fleet were scattered far and wide throughout space. A few managed to make straight forward journeys home, but many were forced into strange and tortuous complications.

The Fleet Commander, man-metal hybrid Space Admiral Agamemnon, was one of those able to overcome navigational problems. By allowing his robot half ascendancy he could plot a direct warp-route home. Unfortunately, during his long absence the planet Mycenae had banned all flesh, becoming the first world inhabited entirely by robot-evolved creations.

"Death awaits," intoned his Cassandra-box, but the conqueror of Troy was too used to his duality. So he landed as a Hero upon the purple plain, accepting the acclaim that was his due. Then roared old fashioned defiance as his flame was extinguished.

So died Agamemnon, joining those who had perished while the war had raged.

Palamedes was dead.

Protesilaus was dead.

Achilles was dead.

Ajax was dead.

Anticlus was dead.

And many, many more, but Odysseus, architect of the

victory, still lived.

***

Four-legged, four-armed, two-headed Odysseus: bravest of the brave, most cunning and clever of them all, now so far away from his home planet of Ithica. His warp drive still worked but the direction finder had ceased to function. His ship would plunge through the depths of non-space but there were no guarantees as to where it might emerge.

"Well, that's us finished," said the subservient second head.

The dominant first head frowned. "That's enough of that," he ordered.

"I told you the sub-particle intensifier would be too strong."

"It destroyed Troy didn't it?"

"But at what cost, tell me that?"

However smart, awkward or pettifogging the second head might be, the dominant partner always had the definitive option. He could direct enforced sleep cycles during which the subservient head would sink in its shoulder socket, leaving number one with a better all round view and the ability to act without interference.

Odysseus knew that a major failing with his species was a tendency to impulsive over-reaction, which had made the double-head system so important in their development from primitive to now. Number Two's function was to offer advice, suggest caution, to worry over fine detail. No Ithican would be without his second head, but it was good to be able to shut them up now and then.

If the direction finder no longer worked it might be best to engage the warp drive in short hop sequences only. He had tried one massive jump and had ended up where they were now, in an unrecognised corner of space with unknown star constellations so distant they were only faint glimmerings.

Number Two had, of course, warned against such a big jump. So, short hops only from now on. He entered the relevant instructions into the propulsion guidance network, then gave the order for the first of the shortened flights through non-space.

It wasn't long before Head Two woke and rose from its shoulder socket. "You're using the warp drive again," he stated.

"Only for short hops."

Number Two said no more, but smirked that know-it-all, I-was-right-all-along expression so disliked by all Number Ones.

Four hops later, a life bearing planet was found, according to all retrievable data.

"Maybe at a pre-radio stage," suggested Two when none of their available bands solicited any sort of response. Visuals were out too. Not being able to penetrate a fog-like blanket that circled the world,

"Guess I'll have to go down," decided Head One.

"I?" grumbled Two. "I? Shouldn't that be *we*?"

"By the Great Godheads of ancient times!" thundered One. "If I go, you go. It's a biological necessity. So no more nit-picking!"

After locking the battle cruiser into an unequivocal orbit, Odysseus summoned a ship to surface transporter and set off to investigate. Once through the vapour layer he could see what appeared to be a world of rich grasslands, dense forests and high mountain ranges. There were also strange triangular buildings dotted here and there, though not in any profusion.

Landing on flat grasses, he put on full battle gear and left the craft while nodding vigorous agreement to the subservient head's whispered entreaties for care to be taken. There being no immediate signs of life, he moved at a steady four-legged pace towards a nearby area of forest.

The people of Ithica stood an average five metres tall with a body sturdy enough to cope with their four legs, four arms and two heads. Indeed, of the sentient races making up the combined attacking force sent against Troy, none were bigger. Odysseus was used to standing tall, so when a large lizard-like creature over twice his height stepped out from the trees he adopted a speedy defence posture. Weapons primed and ready for use.

"Hang on, old chap," called the creature. "What is one supposed to say in these circumstances? I come in peace. Will that do? Or shouldn't you be the one saying it?"

"He's right," whispered Head Two. "We are the intruder."

"Shut up!" hissed number One.

"Pardon?" asked the lizard.

"No, not you."

"I should think not."

Odysseus had heard of such giant creatures, but not of them being intelligent. Some such wild breeds were said to have roamed the jungle regions of Troy. "I do come in peace," he called, "but how can I be sure of your intentions?"

"I am a Deinonychus. I am fast as the wind and have teeth that could pierce your puny armour as easy as cracking coconuts, which I find very easy. If I had meant you any harm, you would already have been seen to."

"I knew we should have sent an unmanned drone," whimpered the subservient head, but Odysseus was willing to let his dominant part meet force with force, if necessary. "I am Odysseus, Lord of the planet Ithica, Galactic Prince, destroyer of Troy," he shouted. "I have weapons to match your natural advantages. As you'll find out if you make one false move."

The Deinonychus laughed at that. A deep laugh which seemed to contain echoes of its ancestral past. "Let us not put it to the test, friend. My meat-eating days are long gone. My companions converted me to vegetarianism more years ago than I care to remember. I have shown myself merely to greet you. Visitors are very rare in this long forgotten corner of space."

"That I can well believe," muttered Number Two.

"Ignore my lesser head," said Odysseus quickly through his dominant side. While he would take this giant lizard at its word, he would also keep weapons primed, just in case. "There are many questions I would like to ask," he continued, "but tell me first, what world is this?"

"This is Machu Picchu, Cloud Planet of the Fourth Quadrant. The cloud bit is obvious, but don't ask me what the rest means. According to local legends, there are individuals here who are the last surviving members of what would otherwise be extinct species. Some even from other planets! Rather odd, don't you agree?"

"Odd indeed."

"And by the way, my friends call me Denny. So much easier than my full mouthful."

Denny the Deinonychus. A talking lizard. Big! Odysseus had never come across anything like it before.

"A four-legged, four-armed, two-headed intelligent being," said Denny with a rumble that passed for a chuckle. "I've never seen anything like you before."

"Nor I you, Denny. You must be the biggest creature in all the universe."

"Oh my. You definitely don't know dinosaurs. Just wait till you meet my friend, Sunny. He's a Supersaurus, all fifty tonne of him."

"Fifty tonnes?"

"That's what I said, and thirty metres long. Don't worry, he's always been a vegetarian. Let's go and find him. I'll walk slowly so you can keep up."

Odysseus would normally have challenged such a slight, but even his dominant head realised that though he could march for days on end, the big lizard would certainly be able to out speed him. So he adopted hike mode and trudged along without comment.

They saw Sunny long before they reached him. Or at least, as they followed the edge of the forest and approached a bend in the outline, they saw a head towering above the tallest trees.

"Sunny! Sunny!" shouted the Deinonychus, jumping up and down and waving. But the monster carried on eating the succulent tree-top leaves. "He's not the most clear-sighted being on the planet," explained the lizard.

"He is the biggest, though, isn't he?" asked a flabbergasted Odysseus, who was relieved to hear that he most certainly was. But nothing had really prepared him for his first sight of the creature's size when they finally turned the bend.

The huge body.

The pillar-like legs.

The long, long neck.

"Put me to sleep, please," begged Head Number Two.

"No way," replied One. "We need full input on this,"

The Supersaurus lowered his head to see them better. "Well, well, Denny. Who have we here? Not another near extinction?" The voice was not as loud as might have been expected from such a large being, but was loud enough.

"No, just a visitor," explained Denny. "Odysseus by name, from the planet Ithica."

"Welcome to Machu Picchu, Odysseus," said the Supersaurus, swinging his long neck to bring his head in line with the newcomer. "What brings you to our quiet little world?"

"To be honest, a faulty direction finder on my warp drive," said Odysseus. "I'm executing short hops through non-space until I emerge near a planet where I can get repairs carried out."

"No luck here then," said Sunny.

"We are not industrialised," added Denny.

Odysseus's two heads looked at each other, wide-eyed, hardly able to credit that he was in a conversation with two dinosaurs.

"I hope you will stay a while though," continued the Deinonychus. "I would value your opinion on my collection of moving pictures. And you must try our broccoli pie."

"Oh him and his broccoli pie," smiled Sunny indulgently. "He would live on it if he could."

"Scrumptious!" exclaimed Denny. "And here's the master chef."

Coming out from the trees was a thickset two-legged, two-armed, one-headed being, with that single head being flattish on top and with a sharply receding chin. Odysseus was relieved to see a being shorter than himself.

"Come and meet our guest," called Denny.

"Guest? Not staying for lunch I hope. Broccoli pie! Broccoli pie! That's all I do. All I cook. Enough broccoli pie to feed a dinosaur."

"Consider yourself lucky I prefer my tree-top leaves," said Sunny.

"This is Keb Moust, last of the Neanderthals," introduced Denny.

"I am Odysseus, Lord of Ithica," said head Number One.

"And we would quite fancy a slice of your broccoli pie," added Two.

"More mouths to feed," grumbled the Neanderthal. "And he's got two of them!" And off he stomped.

The Supersaurus returned to tree-top munching then, while the Deinonychus showed their visitor around. "I christened him Sunny because he gets nearer the sun than anyone else I've ever known," he confided.

The strange triangular shaped buildings turned out to be called pyramids and contained tunnels and chambers, so it had been reported; Sunny and Denny being far too large to explore themselves. Some had already been there before the dinosaur's arrival. Others had been built since, by beings who stayed only until their particular construction had been completed.

"That one is the King Minos Pyramid," pointed out Denny. "It's filled with what Keb refers to as treasure. Shiny. Yellowy. Pretty in its way but of no interest to Sunny and myself."

Another was called the Knights Templar Pyramid, but that only held a single artefact, according to Keb, in what he called the Star Chamber. In both cases the aliens had arrived in numbers and had deemed Machu Picchu a suitable place for the building and guardianship of what they left behind.

Odysseus also saw a number of other near extinct species, including a bad tempered and rather ugly bird called a Dodo.

"No wonder they fell away in numbers," suggested Head Two. "I wouldn't want to wake up next to a face like that every morning."

"Now you know how I feel," said One.

Then it was time to eat, and broccoli pie was the only thing on the menu. Head Number One saw food as merely a means to an end, as fuel for the body, so ate whatever was put before him. The lesser head though, had more in the way of taste buds, and actually did find the dish to be most enjoyable.

The entertainment that followed, however, was strange indeed for Odysseus. On Ithica, sporting achievement and physical power were held as ideals to strive for. The tiny minority who tried to write books other than instruction manuals, who wanted to recite something they called poetry, who wanted to stand on a platform and pretend to be someone they weren't, were not tolerated. They were condemned, sneered at, even physically abused. So for him to watch these images of different species indulging in what Denny described as acting, well, his reactions veered from revulsion to a guilty interest.

The Deinonychus sat transfixed throughout, even though he had obviously viewed it all many times before. "I don't suppose you have any of these entertainments in your space vehicle?" he asked. "Any you could spare?"

Odysseus assured him that such things were unknown on his home planet. "Otherwise I would have willingly let you have them."

"Well thank you for that at least," responded the lizard.

Denny and Sunny were both disappointed but gracious when Odysseus told them his search for a repair planet would have to continue. They walked to his transporter craft to see him off. Keb Moust even brought some broccoli pie as a farewell gift, for which he thanked the Neanderthal most sincerely.

Later, back on board the battle cruiser, Odysseus prepared for the next short hop. "I think there may be many strange places ahead, before getting back to Ithica," said the dominant head.

Number Two finished eating a piece of broccoli pie. "Tell

me, if they should ever make a – what did Denny call them? – flim, movings, flickers? One of those. If they should ever make one of our journey, who could pretend to be us?"

Number One considered for a moment. "Not that I was really taking notice, but there was a being in samples from a planet called Earth who caught my eye."

"Planet Earth?" Number Two was shocked. "But they were mere bipeds! How could one of those convince as a mighty Ithican?"

"I know, I know," muttered head Number One, feeling more than a little ashamed. "But that Kirk Douglas being did seem to have the right attitude."

With a shrug, Odysseus tried to dismiss the thought, giving the order for his next short hop into non-space.

DADDY

My name is Joseph Carpenter. Joe to those who know me. Just an ordinary Joe, I always thought, but not anymore. Not ordinary at all. Not now. Not since I assumed at least some degree of parental responsibility. Well, sort of...

My name is Joseph Carpenter. Joe to my friends. This is my story...

***

I married Julie, my first and only serious girlfriend, when we were both twenty-one. Three years later our son Jarvis was born, and we could not have been happier. He was a good kid, our boy, right from day one. Sweet-natured, good-humoured, well-mannered. So delightful a child that Julie and I would have liked a houseful. But, for all our efforts in that direction, it never happened for us again. Not that being an only child seemed to bother Jarvis. Indeed, each of us seemed to draw strength from our wonderful sense of togetherness.

"We're a gang of three," I would say with a smile.

"More like The Three Stooges," Julie would retort, laughing.

"Or The Three Degrees," Jarvis would suggest, naming one of his late grandmother's favourite vocal groups, and we would join together singing a couple of lines from "When Will I See You Again" before laughing too much to get the words out.

The only slightly oddball thing in what was really a perfect family set-up, was Jarvis's overriding interest in religion. Julie was a non-practising believer of sorts, while I considered myself an agnostic, so he didn't really get it from us. Nevertheless, from quite an early age our son considered himself a Christian and church services were not to be missed. Something his mother was more than happy to comply with, which got me off that particular hook.

The long and short of it coming as no surprise when, at the age of twelve, he told us that he wanted to make the Church both his calling and his career. It was so obviously right for him that, although I could not actually share his beliefs, I was overcome with happiness that he would be devoting himself to something of such immense personal importance. School-wise, he applied himself diligently, teachers expressing confidence in his ability to succeed.

Is it possible for everything in the garden to be too rosy?

At the age of sixteen, Jarvis was riding pillion on the back of a friend's motor bike. Swerving at speed to avoid trouble ahead, both boys died. Jarvis under the wheels of an articulated lorry. Just another motorway-pileup statistic.

Can you imagine what it's like to bury your child?

Your only child?

No, of course you can't. It's an exclusive club. One that no-one wants membership of, but only someone who has been there can truly understand that terrible grief. I knew what I was going through, but Julie, my wife, was beyond devastation. A mother carries her child for nine developing months, culminating in the pain and trauma of miraculous birth. It's bad enough for a man to lose his son. Ask me, I know, but I think it is maybe even worse for a woman.

There we were, both forty and suddenly childless. Marriage-wise, with our twentieth anniversary coming up, we had probably been drifting along quite steadily. Like a comfortable but slightly worn favourite pair of slippers. But nothing prepares you for what we were then experiencing. Julie was gripped by a grief eating away at every level of her existence and I soon came to realise that looking after her was going to be my prime consideration from then on.

I guess that by concentrating so totally on her, I was helping mask my own devastation. We each deal with such things in our own ways, and that was mine.

Other children might have helped. I don't know. You couldn't have a gang of two, three being the minimum requirement. A wider sharing of grief through a larger family could possibly have eased the burden, or might have spread the suffering just as thickly over many as over few. All supposition though, as you can only play the hand you're dealt.

In spite of my best efforts, Julie grew more and more diminished until, after five long years, she too died, leaving me totally on my own.

***

"Did you know, Mr Carpenter, that your wife was pregnant?"

***

Because Julie was not seeing her doctor at the time of her passing, a post-mortem examination was required to establish the cause of death. Which was straight forward in itself and turned out to have been a brain haemorrhage, but there were other ... issues.

"Pregnant? Impossible!"

I looked at the faces of people whose names I had already forgotten.

"Well, er, maybe not pregnant in your understanding of the word, Mr Carpenter, but a life source has been located in the womb area."

"Life source?" I repeated, turning it into a question. I was starting to feel angry.

"It's hard to explain because, quite frankly, none of us has come across anything remotely similar before."

"I understand your wife did once give birth," cut in another of the faces.

"Yes, twenty-one years ago. Our son, Jarvis. He died."

"Indeed. Very tragic. But it would almost seem that your son had a twin who has remained unborn and dormant all this time!"

I could only gape, foolishly. If this was a joke, it wasn't funny.

"It's a shock, I know," said someone. "Here, sit down."

I allowed myself to be guided to a chair and did sit, but quickly stood again. I was grieving, angry, bewildered, all at the same time. "I don't understand," I said loudly.

"No more do we, really, Mr Carpenter." An admission that drew much in the way of muttered support.

"The situation is medically impossible, on that we are all agreed," offered someone else. "Yet it cannot be impossible because it is there, housed within your late wife's body. Small and unformed, as yet, but with a life force all of its own pulsating like an SOS. Almost as if telling us it is there and wanting to finally emerge."

"But for twenty-one years?" It was more than I could take in. "Jarvis's twin?"

"Well that is only a theory at the moment. We cannot be sure of anything, apart from the fact that an undeveloped living entity does exist. But it can no longer draw sustenance from Mrs Carpenter, the host, so will not survive without help."

There was a long pause. Then: "The late Mrs Carpenter was your wife. Whatever she has been harbouring, for however long, might be your child. We need your permission to remove this living entity and try to keep it alive."

***

The prospect of being a father again, however fantastic the circumstances, was something my grieving mind could not turn down. Did I give permission? Of course I did.

***

No amount of description and explanation could properly prepare you for the reality of seeing the monstrosity for the first time. The hospital room set aside for the exclusive purpose of nurture and study seemed to my inexpert eye like a smaller version of a space flight control centre. Pumps, wires, tubes, screens galore. White smocked and masked staff scurried here and there. Reading, writing, studying, pressing buttons, and central to all this activity was IT.

"He has asked to see you," whispered the doctor who had brought me in.

***

The thing was like a grotesque Plasticine model. Seen only through a lace-like network and pierced with needles and tubes, it was a poorly formed caricature that I could not accept as being human. Nor that it could have come from Julie's body.

"My wife could not have carried *that* in her for all those years," I snapped coldly, feeling that some sort of trickery was going on.

"Oh but he's growing, Mr Carpenter. He was only a little egg shape when we removed him."

Growing it might be, but, seeing it lying there, I could not imagine normal human functions being either possible or desirable. "What did you mean?" I asked. "When you said it had asked to see me?"

"Just that." The doctor shrugged. "If I tried to explain you probably wouldn't believe me. Best to let you experience it for yourself."

"Experience what?" I demanded, but the doctor was lost to me. He stared, trance-like, silent, seemingly oblivious to my presence. Turning to follow the direction of his gaze, I knew a moment of real terror and mental pain as whatever this thing was locked eyes with mine.

"*Daddy!*" boomed a deep echoing voice in my head.

***

Eye contact was the basis for his ability to communicate, and once he had you, he had you good. It was as if he were able to build a library of individual contact data based upon a one-off visual link. And once he was there, fully inside your head, it was impossible to refuse any request, or order.

"You are Daddy," he decided. "I feel the need for someone with free will. To talk, discuss, even argue with. Someone not yet compelled to obey. Maybe one day, Daddy, I'll need to establish full control over you too, but not for now."

There were some things I really needed to know, and he was only too willing to boom the answers into my mind. "The entity you refer to as Jarvis had seniority in our initial development, which was why he achieved first birth. We were twins of opposites. Yin and yang, black and white, strong and weak. He was the milksop to my power. As for fatherhood, you were needed for the physical act of conception. So though we both owed allegiance to opposing paternal influences outside your participation, you were nevertheless the biological instigator. You're not Father to either, but Daddy to both."

***

At his instigation, and I was now referring to him as something more than a thing, I was given living accommodation at the hospital, and was treated with the respect due to my parental position. Everybody else had only slave status. None of which blinded me to the fact that however innocent I tried to consider myself, I had undoubtedly contributed to the making of a monster. When comparing himself with Jarvis, he'd left out one very important coupling; good and bad, and I knew which one fitted where. There was simply no corner of my mind left undisturbed by his invasive tentacles.

"Oh was it such a nice gang of three?" he threw at me one day. "Or Three Stooges?" He laughed. "Or Three Degrees?"

I tried to block his voice from my mind. Failing, as usual.

"D'ya wanna be in my gang, my gang, my gang?" he sang, evilly. "D'ya wanna be in my gang, *Dadddeeee*?"

He knew I hated him at such moments, but revelled in my discomfort.

***

I tried, sometimes, to ignore the implications of his very existence. To ignore the fact that, given time, he could probably enslave as much of the whole planet as he wanted, but then he would remind me.

"I am growing, Daddy. Getting stronger. Every day a little bigger."

And he was.

There were less needles and tubes. Less panic amongst those tending to his welfare. His survival was no longer in doubt.

I looked into his eyes and shuddered.

Then somehow it was leaked to the press and all hell broke loose.

***

The so-called quality papers tried to maintain an even-handed stance while the red tops had a field day, each trying to outdo the others with sensationalist headlines. TV cameras were soon parked outside and what started as a trickle of sightseers grew alarmingly.

The local Police and Crime Commissioner was summoned, looked into his eyes, and gave orders to surround the hospital with as many policemen as necessary, irrespective of all other duties. Next to come was the Minister of Health, deciding to see for himself what was happening at a NHS hospital. He was soon ordering the transfer of all other patients and unwanted staff. Everything here had to be devoted to the sole care of ... well, what should I call him?

Son?

Master?

He still hadn't enslaved me the way he had everybody else. It still amused him to have at least one person not totally subservient to his every wish. But the time would come. That much was certain.

***

The next step was quite predictable. The rubber-necked sightseers were replaced by placard waving protestors. Some for, some against, with about a fifty-fifty split. SECOND COMING, PRAISE THE LORD and THE MESSIAH IS REBORN were typical messages waved by one faction. While DEVIL'S SPAWN, KILL THE MONSTER, and GO HOME HELL CHILD typified the other side. The two groups were kept apart by a line of tired-looking policemen, which at least gave the television crews something to film.

It also prompted the Minister of Health, helped along by whispered messages weaving in and out of his consciousness, to suggest that it would be a wonderful photo opportunity for the Prime Minister, who was badly in need of some positive publicity. So down he came in a hastily arranged visit.

First he met with leaders from the two banner-waving groups. Smiling, shaking hands, looking serious. Promising each that their points of view would be taken on board by the Government. Then he entered the hospital.

Next day the police were replaced by tanks and armed military personnel.

***

"What are you going to do now you've got the Prime Minister?" I asked. "Are you going to run the country by proxy?"

"Oh Daddy, you think in such petty terms. No ambition, and no understanding. You looked no further than your cosy little threesome. My gang, though, my gang will take in millions, billions, trillions, numbers without end."

His eyes glowed.

"And in spite of that I am merely a pawn, paving the way for what will follow. I'll have my fun, bringing pain and suffering to the whole world. But after that, when my True Father finally walks the planet, taking his place as King of Kings, that will be when horrors beyond imagining will rain down on this benighted place."

His eyes burned.

"Your poor Jarvis thought he could offer love and redemption, but I sowed the seeds of his future destruction at the very moment of conception. Which is why he failed and why I'll succeed. Why I am succeeding. Oh, Daddy, you have no idea!"

His eyes shot flames.

***

They had taken him from my dead Julie when nothing but an

egg. I had later likened him to poorly formed Plasticine, incomplete except for his eyes. Then he'd become more dough-like, an unhealthy dirty white. Larger, but still rough at the edges. Two poked holes for nostrils, mouth a slit, web-like fingers and toes, but all the time with those hatefully mesmeric eyes.

He was much larger now, though still not fully man-size. His pasty skin was pierced by only three needles. Potentially, he would soon be mobile, at which stage his ravings could become reality.

***

Am I still an agnostic? Should I embrace total atheism? Should I fall to my knees and pray? All certainties have been drained like blood from a severed artery.

Heaven help me!

Mankind forgive me!

Like it or not, I had some sort of responsibility for this abomination. He had been ripped from the dead womb of my darling wife. Because of that, and because for some reason it amused him, I alone in this secured place still had free will. I alone could act against him.

But for how long?

I had a nasty feeling that Daddy would soon be surplus to requirements.

***

Was it exaggeration to think the future of mankind rested on my poor and ill-equipped shoulders? Jarvis, who should have lived for the benefit of all, had died. Now his twin lived. The other side of the coin, promising darkness and destruction, and I was the only one who could stop him.

***

It was easy enough to cast myself in the role of planetary saviour, and if it had only been the latest big-screen blockbuster I could just have kicked down the door and gone in with all guns blazing. But he was never fully alone and every one of his aides would willingly die in his defence. And I wasn't really sure that it was in me to kill people who were basically innocent. Nobody could help being enslaved. Even the Prime Minister had succumbed, and that in itself led to another major concern.

Could I dodge those glowing eyes?

I had tried not to look directly at them, but it could not be done. His eyes were large and protruding. Alive with fire and swirling colour. They drew you into an orb to orb confrontation that was totally unavoidable. If he suspected danger, that would be that.

Enslaved!

So those were my problems. To get past those protecting him without arousing suspicions, so no obvious weapons. Then to resist the irresistible. His eyes.

Then again, was it even in me to kill him, if it got that far? To end the life of someone to whom I had been named the biological father? Someone who called me Daddy?

I am not a natural killer. I could never have harmed Julie. I would willingly have taken Jarvis's place under the wheels of that articulated lorry and would never have hurt him. I was kind to animals. I had always thought that everyone had a right to their own opinions, even when they didn't tally with mine.

So did I think I could kill him?

Yes!

However difficult, and even though my blood did flow in his veins. Yes, I did think I could.

The plan, when it finally came to me, was barbaric in its simplicity. Not easy. These things never are. But as long as I could hold my nerve, it could be done. I think.

I suppose, taking the long view, I am making this attempt on behalf of the whole human race, but at the forefront of my mind are much more personal reasons. I'm doing it for Julie, in whose body he hid all those years. Skulking, lurking, controlling. And I'm doing it for Jarvis. The good twin. The plus to his minus.

I'm doing it for everyone, but especially for them.

***

My name is Joseph Carpenter. Joe to those who knew me. Just an ordinary Joe, thrust into extraordinary circumstances…

***

The man known as Daddy stood before the door, frantically going over and over the layout of the room he was about to enter. Hanging from his belt were three axes with hooks screwed into the ends. Hidden under a loose fitting coat so that those aides present wouldn't realise his intentions until too late. There were three so that if he dropped one there were others he could quickly reach, and use

One final run through the layout: eight paces in, three to the left, fourteen forward and five to the right.

Then, lifting a pointed stick in each hand, with a high pitched whine that grew into a gargling scream, he plunged the pointed ends into both his eyes.

Blinded, barely able to control his actions as he fought the hideous and mind numbing pain, the man called Daddy pushed open the door and entered the room…

Daddy entered the room.

POEMS #2

DEFINING MOMENT OF IMPROVISATION

At mike
Accept spotlight
Tenor sax
Music to die for

Hot daddy	jazz daddy
Whispering	bellowing

Sweat droplets spraying
Tenor man playing

Notes like fountains
Falling   falling
Each savoured gem
A rich delight

Half the Devil
Half sweet Jesus

Power of darkness
Power of light

Thank you bad
Thank you good
Thanks for the music
In the night

Honey dripper
Teasing   tempting

Riding roughshod
Stamping   stomping
High wire walking

Ice man   hit man
Drawing bead on
Sweat drenched temple

Trigger finger
Starts   slow   squeeze

***

THE GLENN MILLER STORIES

Screenplay One:

Good guy Glenn
All American Hero
   at a time
   when heroes
   were needed
Pipe
Slippers
A hot milk drink
   served in
   a *Little*
   Brown Jug
Concerts
Records
Films
US Army Captain
Trendy rimless specs
   I never knew
   Jimmy Stewart
   played trombone

Supposition:

But what if he'd not stayed with
the single-engine Norseman D-64
that took off from Twinwoods on
the 15th of December, 1944

What if he'd switched to a Dakota
at Bovingdon, Hertfordshire, with
his own personal agenda for a
more secretive visit to Paris

Screenplay Two:

When this *American*
went on *Patrol* in
the red-light Pigalle
districts with a *String*
of Pearls on offer
In the Mood for
something more than
just a *Moonlight*
Serenade

Shag-happy Miller
    dead, murdered
    skull caved in
    amongst the pimps
    and prostitutes
That nice June Allyson
would not have liked
this version

***

JAZZ-NOIR

Quirky runs, muffled growls
Black and white, unlit alleys

Unorthodox arpeggios

Funky blast, bop era
Double crossed, hard boiled

Rhythmic unpredictability

Blues jam, roaring horns
Dark spot, lonely place

Melodic continuum

Chorus patterns, cool riffs
Tough guy, classy dame

Solo horn heard in the night

***

HONKY TONK

The radio was playing the
Meade Lux Lewis 1936 version
Of *Honky Tonk Train Blues*
When I came across your
Long lost photograph

My heart skipped a beat then
Latched on to that pounding
Honky Tonk rhythm and I was
Ready to jump a ride on
Meade's train and set out to
Find the girl you once were

But the mood soon crumbled
When common-sense kicked in
More years have passed than
I like to count and I don't know
Where you are or even if
You're still alive

Instead I allowed a tear to

Trickle down my old-man face
And returned the photograph
To what seemed to be an
Excellent hiding place

Then I went to the kitchen
And made my wife a cup of tea

***

BLUES FOR BESSIE

Gone down sister
Know what I mean
Hard drinking woman
Crossed Jordan
Lift your head
To the throne
Sing like a Queen
Gone girl
Down girl
Hey Bessie Bessie
Did they do you bad
From birth to grave
Did you have any soul
Left to save
Injured woman
Arm hanging off
Hey there
Pray there
Blues unfold
Oh Lordy Lordy
Have mercy

***

MARCHING INTO GLORY

New Orleans
Funeral jazz
Pump slow blues
Into memories
Of waxen discoloration

Full toned
Resonant
Sadness and tears

Beautifully played
In unwanted circumstance

THE OSCAR PROJECT

Christian (kris'tyan) a & n (person) believing in, professing or belonging to, the religion of Christ ... showing character consistent with Christ's teaching, of genuine piety ... civilized, decent (person)

(1)
A WORLD DIVIDED

Yesterday a shaft of light cut into the darkness... For the first time, an agreement has been reached on bringing the forces of nuclear destruction under international control... It offers to all the world a welcome sign of hope ... but the achievement of this goal is not a victory for one side; it is a victory for mankind.

— John Fitzgerald Kennedy (July 1963)

Christopher Nihill coded his apartment door with an undisguised sigh of relief. Reaching home successfully was getting more difficult with each succeeding day. He'd have to give serious consideration to the offer of a staff-dorm cubicle. It made sense, yet he continued to hesitate. This apt wasn't much, little more than fold-down bed with kitchen, but it was his. He luxuriated in the privacy it provided for non-working hours. Facts had to be faced though. London streets were increasingly hazardous, with violence and death an everyday occurrence. He'd be compelled to move to the dorm sooner or later.

"Bloody world," he muttered with feeling, peering into his eye-level freezer. Wider issues suspended as he debated the more immediate problem of whether or not to prepare a meal.

Finally slamming the frig shut and retreating to the living space. The unexplained absence of his black market contact compounded the strictly enforced food rationing. Foodwise, Nihill knew he was in for a rather frugal period. "Bloody world" he repeated. It was fast becoming his favourite phrase.

Even his stash of genuine Acapulco Gold cigarettes was exhausted. He lit up a synthocig and drew hard upon the tasteless tube. His thin, pale face adequately expressing his dissatisfaction. Too many consumers. Rapidly decreasing natural resources. Result: universal shortages. He was all too familiar with the equation. Yet as an acknowledged expert in holography, he was better-off than most. Worse still for the masses, he supposed. For them, surely, if it wasn't for Krill-Kubes they'd be at starvation level.

He shook his head and ran worried fingers through untidy black hair. If only the fools in charge could get together and deal with the important stuff, instead of yelling abuse at each other from behind rows of nuclear ramparts. Draping his lanky form untidily along the comfee-couch, Nihill activated his tridi. If the contrast was still playing up, back it would have to go … but no, colour-clarity was perfect as newscaster Mark St John's face filled the screen. Nihill switched his attention to the man's words.

"…said the French President at today's Moscow meeting of Communist heads of states." He continued by condemning the new Amero-China defence pact as the biggest single threat to world peace of the decade. "In no way comparable to the peaceful Soviet-French friendship treaty of last year, as has been falsely claimed," he is quoted as saying. No pictures of the meeting have yet been released…"

After a decade of Right-Wing Fundamentalist isolationism,

dedicated to re-consecrating the US as the shining City Upon a Hill, why should President Rev. Followill choose to align with China? To encircle the heretical Soviets, that's why. Because there was only one thing worse than an atheist for him, and that was a Papist heretic. The Reverend Followill had even amended the constitution to allow himself a three-term presidency because the "great work" of building his New Jerusalem was not yet done. Nihill half-watched a sidebars scroll of extreme weather events battering the US west coast. A tsunami submerging what was left of Bangladesh. The spread of skin cancers in the sub-Saharan dustbowls.

"Here at home, the continuing violent anti-Draft clashes are forcing more and more citizens to take up residence within the safe confines of their work places. Today's heaviest fighting occurred when a Draft Enforcement Unit clashed with Draft Ignorers in Trafalgar Square. An eye-witness reported that..."

What a state of affairs, thought Nihill, rapidly losing interest. He relit the synthocig. The damn things need continual stimulation just to stay alight. And we've been here before, he thought moodily. It was all very reminiscent of American's draft-dodging call-up for 1960's Vietnam. But that had been an actual shooting war, and they protested their opposition by torching draft cards in what amounted to ceremonial pyres. Looking back, it seemed somehow more dignified than today. Now, though the dark spectre of war might be threatening, there was no actual big-time conflict. The Free European Community had reintroduced conscription merely because the global situation was worsening. Of course, military service usefully mitigated unemployment figures too. But it struck him as pointless, and the masses agreed. There were no demonstrations. No draft-card burning. Those targeted just ignored it. To counter such mass indifference special Draft Enforcement Units had been set up, latter-day press-gangs to place overdue draftees within reach of military jurisdiction. Their methods were their own business. Strong-arm tactics or otherwise.

Nihill shuddered. Glad his nimble intellect marked him out for social elevation. He shook his head, as if to dispel a bad dream. And tuned back into the tridi drone.

"…it will be Ms Marco's fourth marriage, and the second time she's got together with the 'Pop Scene's Mr Rave'. Our next bulletin, in an hour, will be devoted to the Japanese Hitachi Jupiter probe, on course to arrive in four weeks time. Until then, this is Mark St John signing off. Remember, for the latest it's News Desk, Studio Five. 'Bye now."

Damn. Rationing or not, he needed a drink. Where have we gone wrong? He poured a small whiskey … then topped it up. We have Lunar bases, the Chinese are on Mars genetically-engineering Tibetan extremophiles to live there, and we've got the Hitachi probe checking out Europa, Ganymede and Callisto. Yet the eco-system is unpredictably shot, and the biggest war of all is looming fast. France brimming-over with idealistic visions of the Great Catholic Orthodox Destiny, prompting the New Soviet Block's increasingly antagonistic posturing towards the West. Now the Sino-US link nudging it all ever-closer towards a final showdown. Somewhere on the long traipse up from Cro-Magnon, mankind had taken a wrong turning.

"This isn't the Dark Ages," he muttered to himself. "It's the year of the New Barbarism." Having returned the now empty glass to recyc, he watched the last of the blipverts as his next prog-selection cued in. *"The Crime of the Century Show"* bellowed a deep baritone as various murder-methods scrolled across the screen. Had he *really* selected this…?

At that moment, the doorbell rang. Nihill didn't move for a long moment. Nobody made casual visits these days. An innocent ped could too easily become involved in random street violence. The bell chimed again. He crossed to the door and peered cautiously through the spy-eye. Two men. Neither wore uniform, but somehow officialdom was as obvious as if they had.

"What it is?" he called through the speaker.

"Government business, concerning Mr Nihill."

"Credentials?"

One of them thrust a Courier's pass and then a document addressed to Nihill up against the spy-hole. "Hold on." He unlocked the door to admit them

"Sleeverton always raped and tortured his victims before killing them" a "distinguished" expert was saying as Nihill zapped the tridi. He turned to face his visitors. One had followed him to the centre of the room, while the other remained by the door, as if on guard.

"Christopher Janos Nihill?"

"Yes." He passed over his ID, which was carefully scrutinised. "Just what is this?" he asked, replacing the card.

"Mr Nihill, I am a Government Courier attached to Draft Enforcement…"

"I'm a registered employed," interrupted Nihill. "What have I to do with drafting?"

"With the military, nothing," agreed the Courier. "However, I must inform you that under the terms of an unannounced Government Bill covered by the Official Secrets Act, selected employed persons are eligible for call-up to industrial or research service at stipulated Government establishments. Such persons, being selected for specific functions, are dealt with individually."

Nihill felt it was a bad dream. "I've never heard a whisper of such a thing," he muttered.

"Nevertheless, sir, this is your official notification. We will escort you to the stated establishment."

Though shocked, Nihill was hardly surprised that such exigencies existed. It seemed in keeping with these troubled times. "When do I have to leave?" he asked quietly.

"Now, I'm afraid."

"Now? But what about my present situation? My employer? I have affairs to settle."

The Courier shrugged. "Sorry. I'm authorised to allow you time to pack a few personal items. Everything else you need will be provided. Your employer will receive official notification. Your belongings here will be placed in storage until the completion of your service. And *before* you ask, no, I've no idea how long that will be."

"You've got it all figured," grumbled Nihill, tense and pale-faced.

"Think of it like this: the Government values you for a specific task. That makes you important. You can't be allowed to ignore the draft the way the rest do. It's got to be this way."

Nihill tried hard to assimilate what was happening, tugging nervously at his hair. "What if I simply refuse to go?"

The man at the door took a pace forward, the other quickly motioning him to remain where he was. "I sincerely hope it won't come to that."

"But you'll use force if you have to?"

"Look Nihill," snapped the Courier tersely. "The world's literally going to Dante's vision of Hell. Me, personally, I'm hoping and praying our side is working on an agenda, and until I learn otherwise I'm going to continue believing that. As I see it, these establishments, whatever they are, are vital. Maybe one of them will develop a workable defence system, or a weapon lethal enough to hold to the Big Guy's heads. I don't know. All I know is that I'm holding out for some sort of answer, and you're one of those fortunate enough to be selected to find it. So you're damn right I'll use force if I have to."

Nihill's shoulder's slumped. The man made a kind of sense. Even if that didn't make Police State methods any more palatable. He would go. He had no option. But also because there might be a vague chance that this was also an opportunity, *and there is an answer*. He quickly stuffed a few personal effects into a grip and was ready to leave. After coding the door he passed the swipe to the Courier. Waiting in the street was an electric runaround. Nothing fancy. Just a standard urban bug. Nihill slumped in the back beside the Courier, while his companion – the silent one – did the driving.

"Do you always travel incognito?"

"Mostly. Our business is shunting people like you; we can do without involvement with security."

Nihill gazed glumly at the empty streets as the car hummed along, as if he was seeing it for the last time. "I neglected to ask, where am I being taken?"

"Government Research No. 5. It's in Gwent. We'll take the heli from Hyde Park."

They travelled in silence for some ten minutes. Then the driver slowed a little. "Trouble ahead," he stated flatly. "Hear it?"

"Not 'til you mentioned it, but I do now," replied the Courier.

Nihill listened intently. Sure enough he too could hear the shouts and noises of a street brawl. "Your press-gang colleagues," he muttered without thinking.

"A Draft Enforcement Unit" cut in the Courier sharply.

Nihill didn't argue the point.

"Well…?" queried the driver.

The Courier shrugged. "Keep going," he decided. "There are no reports of large gatherings this evening. We should be able to drive through whatever it is."

Although he'd seen plenty on the tridi, Nihill never actually witnessed more than two or three very minor skirmishes – and those at a distance. He'd been luckier than most, but was now approaching what sounded to be a fair-sized riot. The noise grew louder. Then they hung a curve from the overpass and were suddenly plunged into the midst of a battle-crazed mob.

"Hell!" grunted Nihill.

"Don't stop," instructed the Courier, "just get through fast."

Nihill watched in a daze as faces and bodies swirled by in a blur. An arm swung, a voice screamed, a face contorted with pain. Then he saw the car, and everything else faded into the background. A runaround, similar to the one he was in. It was lying on its side. The bodywork shattered, belching fire and smoke, but the manufacturer's claim fully vindicated in that its plexiglas dome, resting on the road, was intact and completely undamaged. Though they approached, drew level, then passed – all in a flash, the image registered each horrible detail.

"Maureen!" There was a girl in the autowreck. A girl he knew. Her eyes bulging, her mouth strained in a silent scream. Blood from a gaping head-wound seeped onto the internal curve of the dome where it congealed in the heat. Her hair was on fire! Nihill turned to wrench at the car door nearest him.

"Stupid bastard!" The Courier dragged him back and forced him down into the seat.

"That girl, she's hurt," protested Nihill.

"I saw, but there's nothing we can do."

"She was burning." He struggled towards the door again, but the other was too strong, and held him firmly until they were well clear of the disturbance.

"Molotov by the look of it," noted the Courier, shaking his head. "Hell of a thing, but we couldn't risk stopping."

Nihill, his shoulders shaking, leant forward and buried his face in his hands. "What a bloody, bloody world," he sobbed.

(2)
THE PROJECT
The Almighty has his own purposes.
— Abraham Lincoln (March 1865)

The helijet, which had been waiting beyond the Hyde Park blast -apron, docked in darkness. Touching down within the Research Establishment's grounds where a thorough security check processed the Couriers before they handed Nihill over and left. It was well into the night. He was tired. Needed coffee, and a shower. But instead was escorted into an empty conference room and told to wait. So he waited, his attention drawn to a sound-down screen replaying an events-loop. First up was the Pilgrim Crusade Armada embarking for Hawaii, the last US Democrat state to resist the purges that had cleansed continental America of blasphemers and non-believers. Then the completion of the Greater Israel fortress wall, to the north along the Turkish border, and to the south-west where the loose affiliation of Libyan statelets began. He watched it over and over for at least fifteen minutes, before the door opened to admit two newcomers.

"Mr Christopher Nihill?" boomed the first, striding forward with hand outstretched.

Nihill nodded, appraising the man. He was big, a good two metres, with iron-grey hair and a strong prominent chin. He exuded physical and mental strength. "My name is Falk" he said. "I'm the Director of No. 5. We've been looking forward to your arrival."

"Am I allowed to ask why?"

"All will be explained. But first I'd like to introduce Professor Jocelyn Proysen," said Falk, indicating his companion.

Proysen was a slightly-built woman in a moss-green trouser suit. Her small pinched mouth giving her an expression of permanent exasperation. "Glad to have you on the team, Nihill," she said, offering a limp hand that contrasted noticeably with Falk's strong grip.

"I'd be better positioned to say how glad I am to be on the team, Professor, if I knew anything about it."

"Ah yes. Explanations are in order, I think…" agreed Proysen.

"Which I shall now deliver," interrupted Falk.

Proysen shrugged. "Of course, Director."

Falk crossed to a cabinet, unlocked it, and retrieved a case which he hefted across and laid on the table. "Understand, Nihill, ours is an official centre. As such this, your personal security-case, is on the secret-list. The documents in here will tell you everything, in detail. It's pretty damn impressive too. I appreciate your reservations now, but you won't regret coming here." He shoved the case across the table towards Nihill. "This contains the most vital reading of your life. Believe me."

He uncoded the case and gingerly raised the lid. Nestling alongside the self-destruct mech was a bulky *Most Secret* file. The first he'd ever seen. This was all happening so fast. Nihill was aware of mounting tension as he stared at the case and its contents, but before he could examine it, Falk reached over and placed a forbidding hand firmly across the dark-blue folder. "Welcome to the Oscar Project." The big man smiled expansively, closing the case with a faint click. "Oscillating and Cepheid Amplification Research."

"I'm still no wiser." Nihill gazed at him intently.

"Let me explain." Falk straddled a chair, making himself comfortable. "Four months ago, while on Lunar taking routine stellar sightings, Professor Proysen noticed something unusual. So strange, in fact, that initially she was reluctant to share her findings."

"As I'm sure you know," broke in Proysen, "Cepheid variables are stars which display a luminosity-cycle. Which makes them particularly convenient in determining interstellar distances. Now, quite suddenly, those variations have become more frequent, and the degree of brilliance increasing. But even more remarkable, as I learned, this phenomenon has become consistent with all Cepheid's. Cross-references across an array, both here and the Lunar Observatory, confirm this…"

"Quite." Falk silenced Proysen with one word. He placed both hands flat on the table and pushed his face close to Nihill's. "And the velocity of light from these stars far exceeds 186,000 miles a second."

"Impossible," said Nihill.

Falk ignored his outburst. "You'll find the theoretical science for this even more weird. The only explanation that fits is that the universe has entered a new cycle … something Einstein never anticipated. You see, Nihill, we no longer merely exist in an expanding universe, but an oscillating one. Big Bang to Big Crunch, and back again. And after completing its expansionary phase, it's now transgressed over the cosmic tipping-point."

"Dark Matter and Dark Energies not withstanding, the universe is reversing into a state of contraction…" added Proysen.

Nihill slumped down onto a chair, his mind spinning.

"But that's by the by. A single oscillation takes fourteen-billion years," continued Falk, "so there's no cause for alarm. No reason to get planning permission for that deep-impact shelter. Much of this needs long-term confirmation. However, in view of the extremely unstable global situation, rampant Creationism across the Atlantic and all that, it's been decided the data should remain classified."

"And that's how the Oscar Project began. Routine spectroscopic tests revealed further bizarre results. Every Cepheid star now shows an identical spectra – that of our own sun." Falk paused, as if for effect. But Nihill's alert mind was reeling ahead far too fast for him to make any coherent comment. The implications, if true, were fantastic.

"I see it's hitting you," continued Falk more quietly. "Just as it did us. You realise what it all means…? That we are seeing the reflected light from our own solar system. We are seeing light that was emitted hundreds, thousands of years ago … light that contains images of people, places, events."

"It's beyond incredible," whispered Nihill.

"Give yourself time. You'll get used to the idea." Falk turned towards Proysen, who'd been fidgeting in the background. "Professor, perhaps you'd care to give our new colleague a speed update?"

"Certainly, Director." Proysen turned to Nihill and waved fussily in the direction of the security-case. "You'll find it all there, in detail. But briefly, what we've been doing is devising an advanced type of collimating-lens that succeeds in splitting the reflected light into parallel bands. By selection, a coherent beam can be amplified by electron microscopes. A sensitive tridi camera then picks up the image, which is built up by the received-signal altering intensity as it scans. Although we can modify the contrast to an extent, there is, unfortunately, a resulting degradation of detail…"

Falk stabbed a finger at Nihill. "You know holography. You're the best we have. That's why you're here. We intend overcoming these techno-glitches by introducing a hologram to obtain three-dimensional images. Mr Nihill," he added with a thin smile, "we propose going back in time…!"

(3)
A GIFT OF WINGS

I am Alpha & Omega, the beginning and the ending, saith the Lord, which is, and which was, and which is to come, the Almighty

— Revelations 1:8

The underground lab was silent now, almost deserted – only Nihill remained, sprawled wearily at a terminal. Dim lights were glowing. He yawned and fumbled for another cig. Being a virtual prisoner of No. 5 has its compensations, in both food *and* genuine cigarettes. "Damn, I'm cold," he groaned, glancing around at the confusion of hastily-assembled equipment –

instrument racks, digital recorder arrays and, dwarfing everything, the dark bulk of the *holo*-projector.

He was in a room within a room. A claustrophobic chamber of impenetrable blackness in which Nihill had spent more hours than he cared to recall. Fine-tuning cameras and responding to instructions, until he was white-faced and trembling. But the Oscar Project was on-target. After weeks of frustrating failure it was finally yielding results. This night he'd witnessed history. And history in the making. He'd taken a glorious spatial glimpse into the past.

Falk received their congratulations dispassionately, before excusing himself to make his official report. Jocelyn Proysen was in uncharacteristically high spirits, and left with several others to celebrate. Only Nihill had stayed, slowly resurfacing into normalcy, like a deep-sea diver rising from the ocean bed. He shivered slightly. Stubbing his cig, he rose and picked his way across the lab towards the computer array, sidestepping the cable-snakes that coiled everywhere.

He slid open the glass door of the temperature-controlled chamber. "'S better," he grunted, as warmer air enveloped him. He tried to relax, but his tense body refused, his mind still racing at the scenes he'd witnessed only a space of moments ago. He'd seen Louis Bleriot fly the English Channel … on 25th July, 1909!

Variations in depth-of-field, distance and camera-angle had been achieved in much the same manner as a standard tridi, and after a full shot of the chill grey dawn, Nihill had panned in for a close-up as the tiny monoplane winged its way towards the coast. And there he was: Bleriot, his face reddened by slipstream, yet sweating as he struggled to maintain control. He peered ahead, through goggles, into the half-light as the grey cliffs loomed into view, his lips mouthing a silent prayer.

Nihill tracked for a long-shot, followed the plane as it approached Dover Castle, recording every detail, the pale sun gleaming on the fragile wings, and the inflated airbag intended to keep the plane afloat should it plummet into the sea. The Frenchman was frantically working the warp-controls. The plane swung round, slowly dipping one wing, rapidly losing height as it approached Northfall Meadow. And then, suddenly, it was down. Its wire-wheels skidding across dew-damp grass, fuselage slewing violently, slamming the aviator from side to side. The undercarriage splintered and collapsed. The propeller snapped, a blade spinning high into the air as the plane slid to a halt, one wingtip gouged into the soft earth.

It was over. The world's first overseas flight in a heavier-than-air craft. The whole thing had taken just 37-minutes, and Bleriot was richer by £1,000 – the sum offered by Lord Northcliffe for achieving the feat. A small crowd ran forward as Bleriot heaved himself up from the crude cockpit – a policeman in a knee-length blue tunic with silver buttons, a leather belt around his gut, two farmers with heavy side-whiskers, wearing breeches of coarse brown worsted…

The partition door slid open, jolting Nihill from his reverie. It was Proysen. Vague, charming, impossibly erudite from the off, now she looked pale and dejected, all signs of exhilaration gone.

"The overflowing bowl run dry already?" grinned Nihill.

"I've just come from talking with Falk," she blurted out. "The project is to be shelved."

Nihill jerked upright. "Shelved…? But why … for what reason?"

"The Government has determined the project has 'no

strategic benefit', and demands No. 5 kindly conform to more 'serious' research."

"But how could this be any less serious? The past is there, ours for the taking. It's a great historical lucky dip. Just think of the implications!"

"That's precisely their reasoning," Proysen answered. "The world situation is far too volatile for them to start disturbing the dust of ages. Think how current treaties would withstand an action-replay of the Alaskan incursions, or last-century's Korean campaign. How about a replay with freeze and rewind on who triggered the drone that reduced Iran to a rad-wasteland, extinguishing Islam as completely as Hiroshima extinguished Imperial Japan? Would they really want that? No. The Oscar Project is dead and buried … like the past it was meant to resurrect. It's not as though we can reach back and change the past, edit history."

He thought of Maureen. Her hair a nest of flames. No way to alter her destiny. No way to retrospectively reach out and save her. Although it was now possible to replay the last moments of her life, over and over again. Nihill was suddenly uneasy. Work at No. 5 was exhausting, of course it was, but he'd grown accustomed to eating well, to sleeping undisturbed as armed security patrolled the grounds. The meagre food-quotas, the swarming mobs, the brutal violence of the outside world had all receded from his memory like a bad dream. Now the nightmare would resume.

"What shall I do, Jocelyn?" he whispered, his voice edged with fear. "You, you're lucky … you've got a permanent position here. Me, I was only requisitioned for this project."

"Perhaps Falk can help. Maybe he'll keep you on. If not, I guess you'll be sent back home, to your previous life. I'm sorry,

Chris."

Nihill nodded dully. "Bloody world. Things never get better. Only worse. Remember all that guff when the American Great Revival began … when? Must have been ten years back. All the disgusting hypocrisy of 'if a man says I love God, and hateth his brother, he is a liar: for he that loveth not his brother, whom he can see, how can he love God whom he hath not seen?' You know what, Jocelyn, if humans hadn't saddled themselves with so much religion we might have turned out better. Only people can save the world. Resurgent Christianity is a 2,000-year-old comic-book." He laughed harshly. "I mean, I like a good comic-book as much as the next person. But, 'I believe, O Lord; help thou mine unbelief.'"

Proysen gave a thin smile. "Yet religions advocate brotherhood."

"While they blithely stab each other in the back."

"But that's the fault of individuals. You can't blame the doctrines."

"Of course you can. The Church sustains the idea of God. Those 'mysterious ways' that can never be questioned. People have been fooled into accepting the unacceptable."

Proysen frowned. "The world would be a poorer place without some of the truly good people motivated by Christian principles."

"And a lot of good it did them. Good people would still be good, without the mantle of myths." Nihill shrugged. "It's not the principles I'm opposed to. It's the add-ons, supernatural gimmicks and ambiguous interpretations that always exert a social retarding effect. The Nazarene was a political rabble-rouser who got nailed to a tree, right? If he'd been stoned or beheaded the symbolism would be all wrong. No cross, no

Christian cult."

"He supposedly arose from the dead too. Do you deny that?" Proysen looked thoughtful. "You pose a conundrum. We have a bunch of imponderables. We have the means of resolving them too. We could find out, once and for all. So why don't we?"

Nihill regarded her with new respect. "Like I said, this project is a great historical lucky dip. We can check out the veracity of all the great enigmas of time. The Kennedy shootings. Area 51 UFOs. How the Gorbachev accommodation with the Orthodox and Catholic forces reconfigured the Warsaw Pact. Hitler's final bunker-hours … or the Messiah. We could do it. But Falk would never allow it. Not now."

'Falk would never know. And this might be our only opportunity."

Without waiting for agreement, Proysen commenced setting up operations. Nihill, pleased at the results of his subtle manipulation, joined her. They worked with feverish haste, knowing that at any moment someone – maybe Falk himself – would stop them. The recalibrations took less than an hour. He found himself becoming increasingly apprehensive as Proysen locked onto the beam and made final calculations. He sat at the camera, sweating despite the lab's chill air. "I need a drink," he muttered into the darkness, trying to suppress a rising panic.

Proysen's voice came through audio, as Nihill crouched expectantly over the controls. A spot of pure, dazzling radiance shimmered. It grew brighter, expanding to fill the tridi projection, and then, just as Nihill thought it would blind him, it separated out into a swirling riot of moving colour. Shifting images and disjointed shapes swam as a three-dimensional tableau slowly materialised.

A grim-faced man, bearded and wearing a loosely-fitting

coat of woollen material strode into a milling crowd. He was slightly taller than most, and the mob fell back as he moved through them – except one man, dark, with a prominent nose and wild eyes, who stepped squarely in front of him. He seized the other about the shoulders and kissed him full on the lips. Two cuirass-clad soldiers, swords drawn, shoved through the mob and seized the taller of the two. More men rushed forward and a scuffle began, men pushing and lashing out with fists or clubs. One soldier lost his sword in the melee; another reeled from the crowd grimacing with pain, blood pouring down his face, his ear almost severed.

And then, unaccountably, the scene began to change – gradually at first, almost imperceptibly, movement became sluggish and spasmodic, the colours indistinct, fading and reappearing.

"Something's wrong, Jocelyn," Nihill yelled urgently, "hold the beam … it's drifting..."

The screen was now a writhing, spiralling vortex. Nihill was unable to turn away. A pulsing, vibrating drone drove mercilessly through his body. A surging void opened up before him, a vivid emptiness. The air became unbreathable. Nihill screamed – a shrill hysterical scream – and pitched forward into darkness...

(4)
A TWO-THOUSAND-YEAR-OLD COMIC-BOOK

It is time for a new generation of leadership, to cope with new problems and new opportunities. For there is a new world to be won

— John Fitzgerald Kennedy (July 1960)

However close we sometimes seem to that dark and final abyss,
let no man of peace and freedom despair.

— John Fitzgerald Kennedy (March 1962)

Nihill staggered on rubbery legs. The ground beneath his feet was solid. He was no longer falling, but he was naked. His eyes tightly shut, and it seemed he was still screaming, until he realised the sound was made up of many voices echoing inside his head.

He ventured his eyes open, first one eye, a cautious crack, then the other. Blinking in the harsh sunlight of a scene that filled him with terror. All around him men were fighting and yelling. Once – a lifetime ago it seemed – he'd been caught up in a riot while travelling across London in an electric bug with two Couriers. This provoked the same panicky fear. The same hatred and animal-violence disfigured the faces of rioters. But these men were wearing the same garments he'd observed on the tridi projection. Before he could even wonder at what was happening, a heavy blow struck his shoulder, knocking him to the ground. Nihill grovelled on the stony soil, sobbing deliriously and covering his face with his hands. The noise, the oppressive heat, even the dust that choked him, all were secondary to the single fact that seared across his uncomprehending mind. However impossible it was, he was there – physically!

Christopher Nihill lay on the ground in the Garden of Gethsemane, by the brook of Kidron, while around him the followers of the betrayed Nazarene struggled with those who'd come to arrest him. He lay there, certain his mind had finally cracked under the strain of recent weeks. Abandoning the project must have provided the final nudge into this nightmare.

Surely, it must all dissolve, and he would open his eyes to see nothing more startling than Proysen's worried face looking down at him? But the dust still choked him. Someone trod heavily on his ankle. And it hurt. Still not really believing what his eyes told him, Nihill scrambled to his knees. He could see the fighting becoming more spasmodic, the losers breaking away and fleeing. Those who remained shouting their triumph in a language he couldn't understand. The nightmare showed no signs of fading.

The tall, bearded man, the one he'd previously seen in the tridi projection, was being led through a sneering crowd, now firmly held captive by guards at either side. Their path led directly towards where Nihill knelt. The man paused, and looked down at Nihill. His captors glanced at each other, relaxing their grip on his arms. His followers had fled. He could not escape them now.

"Kam yedid," said Jesus, for surely that's who it was. "Ata ger ba'aretz. Omed ve'osey et hamakom haseh."

Although Nihill heard, the words mean nothing. He tried to call out. His lips twisted, but no sound would come. He could not speak. And as Nihill stared up into those deep, compassionate eyes, realisation finally dawned on him. This is no fantasy. Proysen once said, "It's not as though we can reach back and change the past, edit history." She *had* said that. Yet in some way, he was the living proof of that statement's contradiction. He'd been hurled back in time.

Right. Until a more rational explanation presented itself, he would accept that this was happening. Acceptance at least cleared doubts of his own sanity. But what he wanted more was to be alone so he could attempt to think straight. To seek some thread of reason. Instead he was kneeling in the dust before the man Christians would call the Son of God, surrounded by the High Priest's men, unable to understand what was being said, or even speak for himself.

"Enchs lo oneh," Jesus murmured. "Ulai ata domen?" He stretched his hand towards Nihill's upturned face. "Ani mitstaer, elah…" He touched Nihill's ear, His fingers gently stroking, "…accept from me the gift of understanding."

And Nihill understood. The gentle hands moved around to brush his lips. "And that of speech."

"Master!" exclaimed Nihill, almost despite himself.

The guards, growing impatient, once more gripped the tall man by the arms. "Come on, to the Palace with Him."

"This place is not for you," said the Nazarene as He was led away. "Go home, friend, go home."

Nihill watched as the strange prisoner was led away. He stayed on his knees until the Garden was empty. "But where is home for me?" he asked no-one in particular.

For a long while he remained in the now-deserted Garden, lost in thought. A gaunt yellow dog snuffled hungrily around him, but apart from some passing mule-drivers who gazed curiously in his direction, he aroused scant attention. Meanwhile, Proysen must still be there, in the subterranean laboratory. What was she seeing? Could she still see Nihill? What exactly was occurring? Was he in two places simultaneously, in the lab, and here, in ancient Judea? When Proysen turns off the beam will he be released? Will he re-awake in the lab? Or be stranded here?

What was it Falk had said? Why hadn't he paid more attention when he had the chance? *An expanding universe, yes, in which gravitational attractions became more tenuous, forever drifting apart.* That was the prevailing idea. But now, against the odds, that was no longer true. They'd reached the tipping point. The universe had done with exhaling, and had gone into a great inhaling contracting phase. It was reversing its physical laws. And the space-time linkage was as old as Einstein. So was time also reversing, and by tapping into retrieved Cepheid light they'd also encountered an advance wrinkle of decaying time? That was absurd. But if so, then time was really there to be experienced, and edited. It might even be possible to correct recent events. Maureen might yet be saved. If he could only get back. Go home.

The cause of his predicament would likely remain unknown. But the result was clear. He was no longer in the lab. He was here. There was no going back. In spite of it all, Nihill couldn't prevent a smile as he imagined Proysen's reaction to his abrupt disappearance. He could imagine her trying to explain to the big bawling Falk, her small pinched mouth giving her an even more stressed expression of exasperation. They'd likely be organising a fingertip search of the hermitically-closed No. 5. There'd be an official enquiry. What its findings might be, Nihill couldn't begin to guess. Heads would roll. Poor Jocelyn would certainly be indicted for her part. Falk himself fortunate to emerge without serious discredit.

Wait! The *now* that Nihill was considering was two-thousand years into the future. The thought jolted him. Why me? Is this some kind of absurd cosmic accident? Or part of a vast divine Plan? Has this always been my fate? Has it already happened? Is this a ghost déjà vu echo? If so, to what purpose? It posed more unanswerable questions than he could deal with. It seemed at times that madness must surely overcome him. What of the way Jesus gifted him complete understanding of ancient Hebrew? Is that madness too, or does it constitute a minor miracle? Doesn't it imply the possibility that the Nazarene was what Christians had always claimed Him to be, man … and God? Nihill found himself having to reconsider. What if he'd been wrong all along?

Christopher Nihill felt supremely and utterly lost…

(5)
THE END OF DAYS

This conflict of conscience is now behind us. The Christian citizen and statesman can in future do nothing but pray for peace and work for peace – in his own interest and in the interest of his children and his country.

— Dr Fritz Baade, *The Race to The Year 2,000* (1963)

Daybreak was near. Jagged edges of night's black clouds stubbornly fought the sun, but the stars had begun to fade as a pale tide of crimson washed across the sky. Nihill woke shivering. He was still here. Proysen hadn't cut the beam. If she had, it hadn't had the effect he'd hoped for. He was still here. He'd slept in a grove of fig trees, wrapped in a coat torn from someone's back during the brawl, hugging the hard ground for warmth, until it turned as chill as the night air. Now his whole body ached. His mouth was parched. His stomach knotted with hunger. At the moment he'd even settle for a mess of Krill-Kubes. Instead he pulled a handful of green figs from a low-hanging branch. And spat them out. They were bitterly unripe.

Already weakened by shock and exposure, he was near collapse – another night spent in the bitter cold would surely kill him. He stared around helplessly. A narrow track wound through the grove into a valley quilted with crops, across which he could see the stone walls of Jerusalem, softened by the dawn rays of the sun. With sinking heart, he decided there was no alternative but to enter the city, to beg or steal food. Shuddering inwardly he recalled the ancient penalty for theft, the offending hand lopped off and thrown to wild dogs. Hugging the coat even more tightly around him, he began trudging disconsolately down the steep path.

The guard – indifferent to everything but perhaps for thoughts of the servant girl he'd see tonight – waved him sleepily through the massive gates. Now he stood just inside the city walls, uncertain, not knowing which way to turn. Ahead ran a maze of twisting alleyways, littered with refuse and human sewage. He near-retched at the foul stench hanging in the still air.

An unkempt figure stumbled towards him, face cowled and hidden within the folds of a tattered robe. Nihill started forward, barring the way. But the man, sensing his approach, hunched his body and shoved Nihill roughly aside. Infuriated, Nihill twisted and caught at the man's hood. "I only want..." he began, then drew a sharp breath, recoiling in horror. The face that stared back at him was a mosaic of white rotting patches – cankerous patterns of leprosy. Nihill shrank back as the leper pathetically covered his ruined face with handless stumps and fled along the alley.

Shaken and trembling, almost without conscious volition, Nihill turned in the opposite direction. As he walked the sleeping city came alive around him – the streets now a dispute of confused din, of jostling markets, and the spicy smell of cooking. At last he could go no further. He'd emerged into a central square, paved with stone slabs, and faced by an obviously important building, constructed of rough quarried blocks. Steps led upwards to a portico of monolithic columns, which framed massive bronze doors, their panels and architrave embellished with friezes of alabaster and porphyry, surmounted by an impressive dome.

Several hundred people were gathered at the base of the steps. There was a low, incessant murmur, like the buzzing of angry insects. Nihill joined the crowd's outer fringe, craning forward. He turned to a richly-dressed merchant beside him. "What place is this?"

The man stared hard at Nihill, disdainfully eyeing his dirt-caked clothing. "The Palace of Caiaphas," he muttered warily, edging away, clutching his money-belt.

Then, without warning, the doors swung ponderously aside, and a man swaggered into view – Caiaphas, High Priest of the Temple of Jerusalem. He was squat, with a broad flat face, and small cold eyes. His beard hung in thick greasy locks over grimy vestments. Elders, scribes and chief priests of the Sanhedrim spilled out behind him. Then the Nazarene Himself was dragged into the sunlight, and shoved roughly forward to the top of the steps. He was haggard now, and He stood swaying slightly, His wrists shackled, His head slumped forward.

Caiaphas raised his arms, imperiously demanding silence. "This man," he sneered, "this Jesus of Nazareth, claims to be the Son of God ... the Messiah!" He minced forward, lisping the final word. The crowd roared its delight; Nihill couldn't guess at their reasons. He gazed at the faces surrounding him – these people were in a dangerous mood, almost beyond control. Caiaphas stood directly behind Jesus. He reached out, grabbing the prisoner's hair with stubby fingers, viciously jerking His head upright.

"He has blasphemed against the Torah..." The mob began

shouting and shaking their fists, and Caiaphas raised his voice in order to be heard. "The council find him guilty of sedition and blasphemy," he shrieked.

The mob surged up the steps, spitting at the accused and striking him with their fists. They were demanding His death. Some tried to drag Him down, but a squad of temple guards charged forward, beating them back with staves and the flat of their swords. Caiaphas waited silently as the guards brought the crowd under control, a faint smile on his face. He's got them, thought Nihill. He's got them where he wants them. The High Priest was a theatrical showman, expertly manipulating the mob. Whichever way he directed them, they would go, and the reason became suddenly clear. These people lived the year round on what the Temple provided – the cattle-dealers who made profit by raising beasts for sacrifice, the moneylenders who were glad to deposit their treasure in the Temple vaults, the poor who lived on their crumbs and leavings. Even the priests, who claimed the best of flock at harvest-time.

As the tumult died away, Caiaphas stepped forward. "You, the people of Jerusalem, have demanded death," he cried. "The High Priest is but the servant of the people. As you have decreed, so I will do, according to the law." The crowd roared its approval. "So be it," continued Caiaphas. "Tomorrow we take this false Messiah to Pilate. Tomorrow we will let the Roman put his hand to the wishes of the people."

Caiaphas signalled to the guard commander, and the entourage – with the dishevelled prisoner at its centre, turned and filed back into the Palace, the doors echoing shut behind them. The crowd gradually dispersed, fragmenting into many smaller groups. Some left the square, others remained to discuss what they'd seen.

Nihill stood alone, mind numb with the weight of foreknowledge. It was all to come. Crucifixion. Spreading the world. The complete falsification of the Nazarene's message into inflexible dogmatisms, the schisms that would shatter it into so many denominations. Clear down to the disgusting hypocrisy of the Great Revival of his own time. This 2,000-year old comic-book had already happened, now it was about to happen all over again. Must it all unravel again? Did it have to? The implications were staggering. He was here. He knew the story. He'd never been what one would call a Biblical scholar, but it's impossible not to pick up these bits and pieces. Even from those "Bible-in-Pictures" apps briefly popular during the Great Revival's first wave. He knew the script. But could he change it? Whether you called it fate, or accident, was something beyond knowing. But once planted, there's no way the seed of the idea could not grow. Hadn't he always argued the world would be a better place without religion? This was his opportunity to test that theory to destruction.

The square was almost empty now. Nihill looked around him, drinking in the scene with new eyes. Thoughtful. The future could be changed. The new future would be better than his familiar time-line. But temporal-meddling's tricky. He'd read enough science fiction to realise just how tricky it could be. Wasn't there a story – "A Sound of Thunder" – about a time-traveller who accidentally crushes a Jurassic butterfly, and skews the course of evolution? He might be writing himself out of existence. A risk worth taking. What kind of "bloody world" did he have to lose…? Making the decision was easy. Formulating a viable plan was something else.

A loud sobbing interrupted his internal dialogue. Turning, Nihill saw a man staggering up the steps towards the Palace gates. A face that, though distraught with grief, looked somehow familiar. Where had he seen that face before? It came rushing back. He was the dark deliverer of the traitorous kiss. The betrayer, Judas Iscariot, now into his remorse phase, ready to fling his miserable pieces of silver at the High Priest's feet. Maybe he'd not anticipated the result of his treachery would go so far? Just intended the Nazarene's increasingly inflammatory pronouncement to be chastened, a little? This was the solution. The key to open the portal to a better tomorrow. A man who regretted his actions enough to commit suicide. After all, the violent remorse that would drive him so relentlessly to seek death is there, in the gospels. If that torment could be correctly channelled, this man would make a useful accomplice.

Impulsively, almost without thinking, Nihill found himself mounting the steps. He caught the other just as he reached the gates. "No, Judas," he gasped, seizing him by the arm, "that isn't the way." Nihill swung Iscariot around the face him. "Listen, you led them to Jesus. Because of you he was arrested. Because of you they will nail him to the cross."

"Let me alone," protested Iscariot, struggling to free himself.

"Why did you betray him? Did you hate him enough to want him crucified?"

"Hate him? I don't hate him. I love him." He stopped struggling, weeping pitifully. "I love him too much."

"If you love Jesus, then help me save him. Hanging yourself won't undo what you've done."

Supporting the weeping man, Nihill led him back down the steps, away from the square. Here was the proof he needed. The future *could* be changed. It already *had* been changed. Judas Iscariot was no longer following his preordained path. They wandered the winding streets until they came upon an inn, a short distance from the palace courtyard. It was little more than an enclosed square surrounded by a rough wall, with a wooden loggia providing a sheltered space for animals. To the rear were a few small rooms.

Nihill directed his new companion past the few customers to an empty corner and sat him at the low trestle, seating himself opposite. So far so good, but what came next? He tried to concentrate, but the aromas of food made it difficult. God, he was hungry – forgive the blasphemy, but he hadn't eaten for twenty-four hours, or maybe two-thousand years, depending on perspective. Iscariot, though morose, was somewhat recovered following his earlier outburst. He sat, eyes downcast, gazing at the chipped coarse-grained table surface.

A serving girl approached, wiping her hands on a soiled apron. Iscariot demanded wine, but before she could turn away Nihill grasped his sleeve. "Food, get food," he hissed fiercely. Iscariot raised his eyes and stared at Nihill as if to question his right to give him orders.

"Together, we can save Jesus," Nihill broke in quickly. "Or do you still want to hang yourself?"

Iscariot flinched, then nodded to the girl, who stood to one side, waiting. He turned back to Nihill, a hint of fear in his voice. "How do you know the unspoken secrets of my soul? How do you know I meant to kill myself…?"

Nihill hesitated. Judas would find the truth beyond understanding. He scarce understood it himself. And yet the entire plan hinged on his next words, on gaining this man's trust. "I am Yahweh's messenger," he declared slowly and as impressively as he could contrive. "Jesus must be spared the cross. You must aid me. In that way you serve God … and atone for your sin."

"What do men call you?"

"A name familiar, and yet strange to you. Christopher Nihill."

"And you've been sent by God?"

Nihill nodded.

Iscariot bowed his head. "I'll do anything. I would help you even if you were not Yahweh's servant."

Nihill grinned wryly. "Your first task will be to put those thirty pieces of silver to use, and pay for my meal. Yahweh's beneficence did not extend to sending me here with a full purse."

"Would that my purse were empty," cried Iscariot bitterly.

"What's done is done. Now we must rescue the Messiah from the tomb." Iscariot favoured him with a quizzical look, then lapsed into a moody silence. After a while the girl returned, carrying a well-laden platter, which she placed before them. Iscariot poured wine into an earthenware mug, a look of distaste on his face as he watched Nihill ravenously cramming food into his mouth. The richness of taste was startling. Despite the unvarying diet and strict rationing of the twenty-first century at least he'd eaten regularly. He couldn't recall ever having gone so long without food. Now, this lush freshness more than compensated.

Once his initial hunger was sated, Nihill paid more attention to what he was eating. One delicacy was particularly pleasing, a sweet crunchy walnut-size covering, filled with a fleshy meat-like substance. He had no idea what it was, but the taste was so succulent he ate with obvious relish.

"You're certainly enjoying those," remarked Iscariot dryly.

"What are they?" he said around a mouthful, while simultaneously reaching for another.

"Ox brains, fried in a ground locust batter."

Nihill felt his gut twist violently. Grabbing a mug he drank deeply to take away the sickeningly-rich taste. The wine was bitter. Little more than vinegar. But it did the trick. Fighting nausea he pushed the dish aside, wiping his mouth with the back of his hand. As he did so, the girl sidled towards them, staring boldly with languid eyes. He could see her nipples outlined through the thin material of her gown. Obviously there was more on offer than just food and drink.

Nihill offered a wan smile. "I have no money. But…" he shrugged his shoulders and glanced towards Iscariot.

"Him?" she hooted derisively. "He has no use for a woman. He calls men 'brother' yet embraces them like dogs."

Iscariot ignored the outburst, looking away, but his face was dark with rage.

"Then it seems there's nothing more we need," conceded Nihill quietly.

"Except to pay for your food and wine," she retorted. Iscariot threw down the required coins, and the girl sauntered away to try her luck with other customers.

Nihill regarded history's great betrayer thoughtfully. "Why *did* you betray the Nazarene?" he asked suddenly. "Is that all it was? A lover's spat…?"

"If only that had been all. I loved him, yes, but he rejected me. Spurned me." He reached across and gripped Nihill's hand. "Oh, he was sympathetic. 'I love all men' he said, 'but a love of the spirit, not the flesh.' His words came as a knife in my heart. My only thought was to hurt him back. But now it is too late for remorse, for Caiaphas has condemned him."

Nihill shook his head. "People are fickle. They are capricious. Their opinions can be changed." He leaned forward, confident. "I have a plan…"

(6)
BEHOLD THE MAN

Every man's work shall be made manifest, for the day shall declare it, because it shall be revealed by fire; and the fire shall try every man's work of what sort it is.

— *1 Corinthians* 3:13

Christopher Nihill stood before the Praetorium, centre of Roman rule in Jerusalem. Though the hour was early, a large crowd waited with impatient expectation in a constant haze of noise and movement. It was the morning following his encounter with Iscariot, and it had been a busy night. Although, in truth, Nihill had done little more than issue instructions, he now fretted about the outcome of his scheme. There were so many ways it could fail. The atmosphere was oppressive, he was uncomfortable and ill-tempered.

Gathered closely around him was a ragged mob of trouble-makers and outcasts, dregs hired by Iscariot, who was also close by with a similarly disreputable group. Still more were scattered throughout the crowd. They'd been hired with the blood-money. Their loyalty made certain by promises of more should the plan succeed.

He knew that, at this very moment, inside the Praetorium, Jesus was being closely questioned by Pilate. By a man resented by the locals as the symbol of Roman domination, and equally detested by the priests as the enemy of their religion. Yet they were grudgingly compelled to defer to him for support. The Sanhedrin could condemn, but sentence of death could not be carried out without sanction from Caesar's representative.

There was a sudden scuffle at the edge of the crowd. One of Nihill's men had been caught attempting to rob a street-seller. Others joined in to help the hawker, and the thief fell to the ground under a rain of blows and kicks, where he lay unmoving.

"No more of that," hissed Nihill to the others, beside himself with anger. They were few enough as it was. A sharp, strident fanfare rang out, stilling the crowd. Six legionaries marched from the Judicature and stood immobile, like images of bronze. A serious-looking Pontius Pilate strode onto a raised dais, flanked by his personal bodyguard. A tall sparse man, yawning sleepily, displeased at being forced from his bed at such an unusual hour, he did little to disguise the bitter contempt he felt for his subjects. The crowd surged forward, but were checked by the soldiers. Inside the guard, Caiaphas waited. One word from Pilate and he'd be rid of the meddlesome Nazarene forever.

Although Pilate spoke softly, his voice carried to all who listened. "You have brought to me this Jesus of Nazareth," he said, "and ask that I pass sentence upon Him. I have listened to Him, and considered His case carefully. I find in Him no fault at all."

At this, not the answer they'd been expecting, the crowd erupted. Caiaphas, his face contorted with rage, shook his fists at the Governor, mouthing words that none could hear above the uproar.

"What then shall I do with this Jesus?" Pilate asked, as soon as he could make himself heard.

"Crucify Him, let Him be crucified," they howled.

"But what evil has He done?" Pilate insisted, almost to himself.

"Get ready," Nihill urged. The moment was approaching. Everything depends on getting in loud and early, shouting before the High Priest's followers did, and so swaying enough of the waverers in the crowd.

"You have a custom," shouted Pilate, "that one prisoner shall be released at Passover. How say you, shall I release this 'King of the Jews', or the murderer, Bar-Abbas?" Taken by surprise at this new turn of events, the crowd was momentarily stilled to complete silence. They wanted only Jesus, but now the Roman was confusing the issue with another name.

It was time. "Now!" bellowed Nihill, before the uncertain crowd could recover. "Jesus! Jesus! Jesus!" he yelled, over and over again. The men he'd bribed obeyed their instructions to the letter, surpassing even Nihill's wildest hopes. "Jesus!" they screamed. "Release Jesus." Easily swayed, many of the crowd joined in.

The High Priest spun around, almost on the verge of epilepsy. "No, not this man," he screeched. "Give us Bar-Abbas." His followers took up the cry, but it was too late, the call for Jesus had swept through the mass of people and drowned the counter-cry. Nihill kept shouting. It was working, a rough and ready plan that could so easily have failed, but seemed that it was to succeed. I've done it, he thought triumphantly. Without the symbolic cross Christianity didn't stand a chance. He glanced at Caiaphas, who had so nearly unintentionally ignited a world-wide movement of fantastic proportions. The High Priest who now stood staring at the normally-compliant crowd with utter disbelief.

A second flourish silenced the crowd. "The choice has been yours," said Pilate, with seeming indifference, yet honestly pleased at the outcome. "Jesus of Nazareth shall be freed for the

Passover." Nihill felt suddenly drained. I've changed the future, he thought with a sense of a giddy intoxication. One man lives, another dies. On such small changes hinge the destiny of worlds. The divided world he'd known no longer existed. No more "Great Revival". No more President Rev. Followill. No more Great Catholic Orthodox Destiny. It was a staggering realisation, tinged with regret that he'd never see for himself the results of what he'd achieved today.

"He comes," a voice shouted excitedly, as the Nazarene appeared at the head of the steps, a look of bewilderment on His face. He was free, yet hardly conscious of the fact, so convinced that His fate was sealed. Denied His anticipated martyrdom. The rank of legionaries parted as Judas Iscariot raced up the steps, throwing himself at Jesus' feet. A Centurion strode forward. After him, surrounded by armed soldiers, came Bar-Abbas and the two thieves to be crucified with him, each bearing his own cross.

One of the hired men grew impatient. "We've more money due to us," he looked around, cursing. "He's gone. The paymaster has fled without giving us our due."

"But he was here a moment ago, right next to me," gasped another.

Yet though they searched, Nihill was nowhere to be found. It was as if he'd been wiped from the face of the Earth. As if he'd never existed.

(7)
TO BE CONTINUED...

Odysseus: "Curse you, Atreides. I wish you had some other army to command, some contemptible army instead of us. Zeus it seems has given us from youth to old age a nice ball of wool to wind – nothing but wars upon wars until we shall perish every one."

— *The Illiad*, Book XIV

If the growth of Christianity had been arrested by some mortal malady, the world would have been Mithraic.

— Ernest Renan (1882)

The April sun shone brightly, its rays streaming through the window. A good, good omen thought Christine Nihill, as she gazed at the wakening Cymric countryside. There was a light, deferential tap. Turning, she crossed the room and opened the door.

"Good morning, Christine," said Jerrold Proysen. "May the Sun shine upon you, this day of all days."

"And on you, Jerrold," she replied automatically.

"Are you ready?" he asked.

She shook her head. "Not quite, but there's plenty of time. You're rather early you know."

"Excitement, I guess."

She stood to one side. "Come on in and wait for me, then we can go down together."

Proysen nodded and entered. He looked around. "Our rooms are exactly the same size and lay-out, but mine is merely functional accommodation. You've made yours into a home."

"That's a woman's touch for you," she laughed lightly, moving towards the bedroom. "There's coffee in the pot. Help yourself while I finish up." Christine sat at her cramped dressing-table. "Are you still bitter at Heiffe's choice for the test run?" she called through the open door.

"No, not really," replied Proysen, "but I certainly don't agree with it. The occasion demands something much more, you know … significant."

"I disagree, Jerrold. This is Heiffe's one chance to observe an event of special importance to him personally. Surely all that matters is to determine if the technique works or not. If it does, fine, then a planned study-programme can be initiated."

"I'm not about to argue today, but this would never have arisen at all if we hadn't had a dedicated minority-cultist as Project Leader."

"I'm inclined to agree. I bet you've done your homework though, for all your reservations."

"Naturally. However insignificant it might be, we must still check out the accuracy of our historical records."

"I found it all rather intriguing," she said, studying her face carefully in the mirror.

"Intriguing? Christianity has fewer than a quarter-million followers in the world. How can that be remotely intriguing?"

She quickly brushed her short straight hair and joined Proysen, pouring herself some coffee and refilling his cup. "It's the fanatical fervour of that quarter-million, I suppose. What if their Jesus – their Messiah figure, really was the son of a god, sent to save the world? What if…?"

"You have a vivid imagination. Mithras, long shine the Sun, is the one truth," he intoned heavily. "You've never made the pilgrimage to the Persian Shrines, have you?"

"You know I haven't."

"I went, two years ago. It was a most moving experience. You really should make the effort."

"One thing at a time, Jerrold. Let's get the project up and running first." She finished her coffee. "Shall we go?"

They left the apartment block and rode the elevator down to

the project-hub. "What exactly does Heiffe hope to view?" she asked as they followed the gleaming white corridor towards the Lab.

"Initially, the trial, much of which is still pretty obscure. And then, if all goes well, through to Jesus being stoned to death outside the city gates."

"Alongside Judas."

"That's right. Although Heiffe seems mainly preoccupied with this interlocutor, the rabble-rousing messenger, Christopher."

"The one who mysteriously disappeared?"

"Correct. Saint Christopher the Modest."

They turned a corner. "Whatever, I'll soon be operating that damn camera again. That's enough for me to be getting on with."

"Wait." Proysen seized her arm, turning her to face him. "Were you serious? What you said back there in your apt, about Christianity being the true religion. You weren't serious, were you?"

"Not really. But just consider, Jerrold, another major war seems almost certain. The Caliphate is massing Moslem troops along the Polish border as we speak, and already fighting has been reported in Spain..."

"I don't really see what that's got to do with anything."

"It's got everything to do with it. You know as well as me that Mithraism has a history of warlike endeavour, cruelty and violence. No point in denying it. And it just struck me that ... while reading up on Christianity, that it seems a religion of peace. Perhaps, just maybe, the world might be a better place if we'd all been Christians?"

"Christine. May the good Aurelian forgive you. I fear this

project is warping your judgment. The gift of science allows us to go back and observe time. The way you're talking, it's just as well we can't reach back and change the past, edit history." He was only half joking.

"No Jerrold." She shook his hand from her arm angrily. "I'm right. I know I'm right. What the Christ-cult lacks is a strong symbol. Their smooth stone lacks resonance. They need something to match the Mithraic sign of the Sun."

"There can be no more powerful symbol than Sol Invictus, the Sun."

"If Christopher hadn't saved Jesus and he'd died a crucified martyr, nailed to a cross, what a symbol that would have made," she insisted defiantly. "The resulting cult might have won a worldwide following, who can tell? But think of it, Jerrold. Peace. No more wars. Could such a thing ever be…?"

POEMS #3

A TAXI DRIVER ON MARS

Not much call for taxis on Mars
But there has to be a couple
Ever on standby
Ready for the occasionally needed journey

Good job for a dreamer
Someone with a hobby
Able to occupy time spent
Both hanging around the domes
Or travelling the corroded planetary surface

Too much concentration
On the intersecting planes
Of the unchanging landscape
Could lead to a boredom induced stupor

Me?
I do courses
Take exams
Keep the old grey matter ticking over

My taxi
For example
Bears a passing resemblance to a World War II tank

(Mother Earth, World Wars 1–4, University of New Moscow)

Tucked into cocoon-like protection
During between dome taxi rides
Some passengers complain about the silence

Tough!
I think
But don't say
I'm a driver not an entertainer

They should provide their own simulations

There was a time silence was in such short supply
People could buy some on a jukebox

(Mother Earth, The Rock & Roll Years,
New Liverpool College of Musical History)

I bet you don't even know what a jukebox is
Do you?

A pity about Earth though
Old Mother Earth
I think it's only right we keep her in our
Martian education syllabus

What was that?
A jukebox?

Take the course youself
That's what I did
Between fares

***

PLANETARY OBSERVATION

Watching from concealment
I followed her long trek
Along the purple beach
As she lingered over
Half-noticed specifics
Hoping to match
Existing contours
With those of her mind
While far away
A blood-red sea bubbled
And individual dust pockets
Rose and fell

With a sudden burst
She spun on winged heels
Turning in my direction
And though I was hidden
I felt uncovered
As if she were
Watching me watching her

***

SAFARI

Bruised and battered
A life beyond control
I holidayed alone on Safari
The reservation planet

Preferring a personal hover
To the organised trips
It was on my third day
I came across a herd of macronauts
Gigantic beasts now extinct
On their planet of origin
I settled to watch
At an appropriate distance
Soon spotting a sick old bull
His black skin turning a dull grey
Who stood apart
Proud head lowered
Scarlet ruff in bedraggled strands
Around his neck
He sat suddenly
Hind legs seeming to collapse
And the whole herd bellowed thunder
Galloping over to form
An open ended square
Allowing an ancient cow to enter
Placing her head against his rear

Trying to lever him upright
Instead he toppled forward
Onto all six knees
And the whole herd gave voice
To this new anxiety
While the cow tried to force grass
Into his slack-jawed mouth
But the bulls head sank
Gigantic body rolling onto its side
The cow roared her frustration
But there was no response
All else having failed
There was one final card to play
She threw back her head
Uttering the plaintive mating call
Of her species
At this signal the gathered macronauts
Performed an abrupt about-face
Guaranteeing privacy as the desperate cow
Thrust her head between his hind legs
Nuzzling against him in a forlorn attempt
To stir an erection
But the bull was barely breathing
Beside herself with grief
Yet still refusing to believe that death
Could match her sexual attraction
She tried to straddle
To lower herself onto him
But the old bull shuddered his final agony
And died
I lowered my gaze at this
In a moment of reflection and respect
When I looked again
A younger bull was gently moving the cow
He then sniffed the corpse and bellowed once
Turning again the macronaut herd faced in
"The King is dead, long live the King"
I whispered as I watched the new leader
Pierce the body with his frightful battle horn
In time honoured custom

The one I would have wished
Will not be there to pierce my dead corpse
But someone would
Between birth and death
There is life and living
I left Safari the very next day

***

SIREN WOMEN OF TREMULAN III

A decadence of jewellery glittered in their hair
Multi-coloured halos promising false piety
But their teeth were set for slashing
And it was time again for the ritual slaughter of the males

***

SATELLITE L'AMOUR

You should be mine
One day you will
Somewhere you are
But not in this reality

The space-time equation is not of our calculation
Liken it to a book with a trillion pages
And I have already turned more than I can count

I have seen alternatives where we:
Do not meet
Pass unknowingly by
Actively dislike
Too early
Too late
Come within 'that much' of making it really happen

So I continue
Seeking the world where nothing is denied me
But each page I turn finds me becoming
More and more
As one with the fabric of space itself

Cut me and I would bleed
Not blood
But the flowing patterns of unborn galaxies

One day
I will emerge at the very moment of creation
To explode and expand
A turbulent mass spinning around a brand new sun

While you
Your essence
Torn free yet held
Circling me for eternity
My ever attentive lover and companion

DENTON'S DELIGHT

The sixties chart explosion by jazzmen such as Acker Bilk, Kenny Ball and lesser luminaries as represented by Bob Wallis and Terry Lightfoot, is usually credited to the surprise 1959 hit 'Petite Fleur' by Chris Barber's Jazz Band. The seed, however, had already been sown when the Humphrey Lyttelton Band had charted in 1956 with 'Bad Penny Blues' and again the following year when the Hal Denton Heptet made it big with the teenage tenor player's self-penned "Denton's Delight".

— Toby Harrington-Smythe
The British Trad Boom of the Sixties

From schoolboy clarinettist in traditional jazz bands it had been but a short hop to a big-toned tenor sax and fronting his own seven piece swing outfit. A smooth and easy transition accompanied by the dropping of Harold in favour of Hal. A name much more in keeping with dark glasses, zoot suits and a crew cut hair style. Confident, even precocious. The music press had soon tagged him a jazz prodigy. It had not taken him long to follow the Lyttelton lead of leaving traditional jazz behind and embracing the more mainstream areas of the music.

University gigs. Top London clubs. European festivals. And all while still in his teens. Then came "Denton's Delight", an unexpected hit parade success, and even the USA beckoned

Top American impresario Norman Granz wanted him for both a Jam Session recording and a Jazz at the Philharmonic tour. Contractual difficulties prevented the former but he had joined the European leg of that year's JATP. Guesting with the

Roy Eldridge Band and sharing tenor sax duties with Flip Phillips.

It was all there. The whole bag, and his for the taking.

Too much too soon, said the early whispers. Too young to know what to do with it. But he had known, or thought he did. And there were plenty of willing helpers with anything he wasn't sure about.

At first it had been The Thing To Do. Readily available. Common amongst his peers. Everybody smoked a joint or two in those days. It sucked him in and blew him out. In no time at all he was being called The Opiate Kid. Heroin became his drug of choice but he was more than willing to try whatever was in the syringe.

He could, of course, have stopped whenever he wanted to. But why should he when it was such a welcome aid to his artistic development? Yeah, yeah. Old news. The standard excuse trotted out by the self-deluded.

It was a sickness. And it had him by the balls. Hal Denton was an addict. End of the news.

He smoked it. Injected it. Give him something to sniff and he sniffed it. They could have potted it up his arse with a snooker cue. Just as long as he scored. And as he became ever more trapped within the downward spiral of all-out addiction, so his behaviour became more and more unreliable. From missing an occasional booking he was soon absent from as many gigs as he played. The septet would become a sextet and the big tenor feature became an embarrassment when the Boy Wonder himself was not in attendance.

Sidemen came and went until finally the outfit was disbanded. Not that there wasn't other work available. He was too good a musician not to have offers, and he was in constant need of money to feed the blank reality of his total dependency. But his unreliability followed. Losing him job after job.

The addiction had always mattered, from day one. Demands that had to be heeded. But whenever he did make it to the bandstand the music had mattered too. That big warm and booting tenor sax sound he was known for. Swinging out one moment, flowing and lyrical the next. It made him worth taking a chance on, until the day the final ember died and the last light went out.

Zilch! Zero! This was what his years of sickness had been preparing him for. He spent his life taking shit, and now he was playing it. This was creativity down the plughole.

***

The man stood at the station entrance. Recognisable by the instrument case at his feet. Tall and gaunt, with the parchment-like skin hereditary to many who have managed to exit from the fast eroding maze of a drug induced nightmare. A man in his fifties, going on five hundred.

"Mr Denton? Hal Denton? Hi, I'm Arthur Jenkins."

Denton shook the offered hand.

"I used to call myself Art years ago," said the other. "Back when the ability to knock out a few chords made me picture myself as the next Art Tatum. Marriage. Kids. I'm even a grandfather now. It's been back to Arthur for a long, long time."

"I'm still Hal. I never did get back to being Harold again."

"No ... I guess not. My car is over this way. Fancy the train being on time. Wonders will never cease!"

Arthur Jenkins helped run the local jazz club. One night a week in the upstairs room of a pub. Local musicians sat in with a more-or-less resident trio and once a month they tried to book a guest soloist. These were the true enthusiasts. People with their record collections, memories of bygone concerts and a willingness to get off their butts and do something.

"I saw you on a Jazz at the Phil tour," said Arthur Jenkins, starting the car and pulling away from the kerb. "Back in … when was it? '58? '59?"

"A lifetime ago."

"Maybe, but I remember it like yesterday. You played with the Roy Eldridge Band, sharing tenor sax duties with Flip Phillips. The Oscar Peterson Trio and Ella were both on the bill."

"Spot on," confirmed Denton with a nod. He was operating on auto-pilot now. He'd made this car ride, had this conversation, played this sort of gig so many times he could float through it with a minimum of effort.

Dundee had been last week. Plymouth was in a fortnight's time. Which meant that he was in … Newport. That was it. Newport in South Wales. A pub called The King William Arms. Jazz at the King Billy.

Numerous treatments had been attempted during his twenty-odd year delirium. Most arranged by friends and family who had continued to care, in spite of it all. There had been cold turkey. Gradual reduction. Sleeping cures. Hypnotism. This wonder drug. That wonder drug. Drugs to get you off drugs!

None had worked. Bar one. The last. The one he had finally got around to arranging himself when his personal need equation had hit terminal disaster level. Most sunk without a trace while just a few managed to kick arse and scramble. Denton had kicked. And if he had known why, and could have bottled it, he would have made enough of the folding stuff to have been able to relapse in both comfort and style.

"What a concert," reminisced Arthur Jenkins. "You and Flip Phillips were billed as being an Anglo-American Tenor Showdown. A Jazz at the Phil gig was never less than lively."

Denton nodded, and even managed a smile. "That was Norman Granz for you. He loved the music, but he was a showman too."

Norman had been a great promoter and a good guy. And so was this Arthur Jenkins of the Newport Jazz Club who was at this moment performing chauffeuring duties and would soon feed him. Then later they'd let him blow a few numbers, pay him, and maybe give him a return booking if the evening went well. And why wouldn't it? Just as long as it was remembered he was an aging ex-addict. A shell. Someone within whom the spark had long been extinguished.

He could still play his instrument of course. Could still play the notes. But no longer did he break away from the general structure of an original melody. Even his most booting solo was planned and executed note for note, with not one moment of real improvisation in any of it. What he played might well be a good facsimile, but it wasn't deep down genuine jazz. And often there would be an ache in the place where his heart should have been. At such times he would give anything to be able to play, just one more time, with the verve and passion and originality that had once been his.

At gigs like these, he wondered. Maybe tonight.

***

Jazz at the King Billy was having a good evening. The resident trio had played a successful opening set and were now backing their guest with a much higher degree of musicianship and understanding than he usually met up with at these backwater gigs. A good turn out too, filling the upstairs bar. Which would please both the club organisers and the pub landlord alike.

The applause died down for the old jazz standard "Perdido". "Thank you, Wales," said Denton. If they'd done nothing else, bookings like this had taught him how to milk an audience. "When they told me I was playing Newport I said: Hey! Back in the big time. No, said my agent, not the Newport Festival in Rhode Island. This is the King William Arms in Newport, South Wales. That's where I meant, said I. Newport, home of the mole-wrench. The real big time."

Happy good-natured cheers came from the crowd, most of whom were perfectly content to bask in a mellow haze of pleasurable nostalgia. They were a good audience and the whole evening had a buzz to it. Denton wished he could have given them a flash of the young Hal. Hell! He wished he could give himself a flash of the young Hal!

"And next up is another number I'm sure many of you will know. The famous Lionel Hampton signature tune 'Flying Home'."

It was during the next number, an original blues from those far off teenage years, that he first spotted her. Tallish. Slim to thin. Short black hair capping a pale face that could only be described as lean. Standing right at the back of the room, there was really nothing about her to make him take any special notice. Except for the fact that he had.

Denton, you old fool! Just what the hell do you think you are doing, he asked himself. It had been years since he'd last checked out an audience for whatever women might be on offer. Not that he had really been looking. Not like that.

Feeling more than a little bit embarrassed with himself, he dragged his gaze away from her and played out the blues to a nice warm response. It was a better-than-average evening deserving more than the note-for-note-by-rote which was all he had on offer.

"Now we are going to slow the tempo down with our version of Errol Garner's 'Misty'." It was a lovely tune, once given a superb vocal treatment by Sarah Vaughan. Denton played a gentle melody line before giving way for the pianist to come in with a solo.

From the back, the woman was now half way into the room, and as he looked at her again their eyes locked. She held his gaze. Unblinking. Tantalising. With a hint of something strange.

Then she looked down. Breaking the link and drawing his eyes down to her mouth. Down to thin scarlet lips that stood out in such a pale background. Parted sufficiently to show small even teeth. It struck him as a nasty mouth set at threatening angles and promoting an aura of cruelty.

The piano player's solo having ended, Denton's tenor slid effortlessly to the forefront with an unhurried stream of tasteful ideas. Startled, then bewildered, he missed a few notes before picking up the melody line again. For one brief moment a lost spark had flickered. The treble clef had been forgotten and he had been more than merely coasting.

Hey! What shit did they put in this Welsh beer?

But he knew it had nothing to do with what he was drinking.

"Misty" limped to a ragged conclusion before a, yes he was willing to admit it, a scared Hal Denton looked out into the crowd again. The girl had moved once again and now stood directly before the slightly raised bandstand. Short black hair. An unhealthily pale face seemingly without any makeup. Dark unfathomable eyes and the most unfriendly mouth he had ever seen.

There was something strangely manic about her. The way she held herself. Her whole bearing. A hunger. A yearning. Something so intense it hurt. Suddenly, at such close proximity, he felt trapped.

It being his one flirtation with commercial success, and the number most associated with him, Hal normally saved it for the end of a gig. But now, only halfway through the set, he found himself saying: "And now we are going to play my one top twenty entry, for those with long memories, 'Denton's Delight'."

She tilted back her head so he could see less of her face but more of her mouth. Lips wet and shiny. Glistening. It held him hypnotically. A rabbit caught in a ferret's terrifying hold. Then the scarlet slash became a gash as it slowly opened. Sharp little teeth appearing and saliva dribbling from both corners. And while this happened the pockets of emptiness within him started to slowly fill.

And then he was playing...

Denton ripped out some short booting momentum gathering phrases. Manipulated a number of chord changes that had the backing trio struggling to follow. Then moved to longer swinging lines, played with a warmth he had not known for a lifetime. This was jazz improvisation at its best. The young Hal blowing through the old Hal's mouthpiece. It was what he had yearned for. But not the way he wanted it.

The music was burning. Scorching. But not from his heart. Nor his soul. The way it should have been. Good as it was, it was being torn from him purely to satisfy this woman's monster greed.

He had been playing "Denton's Delight" for more than thirty years but suddenly he was shaping the well-known tune into new musical concoctions. A twist here. A turn there. Tracing unexpected highways and byways. It was formidable, but it wasn't really his.

***

Without the woman providing the spark and swallowing the results it would not be happening. He knew. She gorged on creativity. Feasted on talent. Other's creativity and talent. His! And it was tearing him apart.

The jazz club crowd cheered and clapped and stamped their feet as the number climaxed. But it wasn't allowed to finally end until the woman closed her mouth and slowly swallowed. Denton's head drooped then. Arms encircling his saxophone as they might once have held a lover. And when he finally looked up, she was gone.

Denton was crying by then. Tears running down the face of an old and broken man. He had no proper idea of what had happened. Nor of the woman's part in it. He was no longer entirely sure that she had been there at all. Indeed, there was only one certainty filling his shaking and dilapidated mind and body. He knew he was finished.

Hal Denton would never play his tenor saxophone again.

WORDSMITH

Nobody wrote. Not anymore. A subject, rendered unconscious and with induced mental irritation, was crowned with a net of micronic impulse absorbers. Deep-down, root-level brain activity was picked up, driven along plastic coated wires and punched onto coded reels of tape. These were automatically transcribed into both computerised attachments and sheets of printed words.

That's the modern publishing game.

That's why only insane subjects provide best sellers.

Piller Presavorrat knew this but dodged all obvious conclusions with dogged determination. He produced words, all dragged with blood and sweat from his own mind – through his own effort. Piller was a writer, and that was the end of the news.

Piller Presavorrat: Writer (unpublished).

He submitted manuscripts by both post and e-mail, pestered publishers, wrote bitchy letters to the press, and achieved nothing but sweet zero. Most publishers hated him and very few would even read his submissions before rejecting. He was a throwback, fifty years out of date and seemingly unaware of modern trends.

The dinosaur is best extinct.

It hurt, this constant failure, of course it did. All that creativity down the pan and flushed away with only a gurgle in the pipework to show it had ever existed at all. But wasn't that the way of things, and hadn't it always been, in spite of early hope and ambition?

The party had been a wasted effort as far as furthering his

non-existent career was concerned; but the free booze had been one consolation, and a surplus of available women had been another. Especially with one who had found this strange wordsmith an attractive proposition.

"I write of love and hate," Piller had told her. One hand cupped her breast, thumb flicking the nipple. "I paint word pictures of stark truth and beauty. The printed page is my canvas." He had blown into her ear, nipping the lobe between his teeth and nuzzling gently against her hair. "One day my talent will reinstate the creative art of the written word."

"I'm sure it will," she had agreed, not understanding any of it, but fascinated by his fanaticism.

Presavorrat yearned to write in an age when the art had become redundant. No publisher was without a highly paid consultant psychiatrist, and readers wanted only to bask in the deep dredged thought processes of the mad.

Slopping drink over himself and the floor, Piller had staggered across to where a High Priest had held court. "Art is dead!" he'd cried, nailed to the cross of his own futility. "You have killed it, and are killing me!"

The publisher had raised a nonchalant eyebrow.

"You are dirty, obnoxious, philistine bums. No, I retract that. Some of you are, or might be, but not all. I mustn't generalise, but you do all sacrifice your everything upon the alter of fame and gain. Surely you could take one single chance for the sake of genuine human endeavour?"

Bored, the publisher had turned away.

Heavy time tonight, thought the girl who intended going home with him. This guy seemed the sort who got randy when drunk.

And she had been right!

"I will be published one day," he muttered between grunts.

"No, Piller, please. Don't talk about writing when we're making love."

He had wanted to tell her about how he hated all publishers, but held back. She was right, of course, and he knew it. Real love and genuine hate, opposite ends of the same spectrum, were areas that deserved total concentration. Neither warranted mindless intrusion, and were too close for one to overlap the other. His love for her should be kept separate from all other considerations. Free from the frustrations of his lifestyle. Untouched by all other relationships. A pocket of safety. A sanctuary from a world that misunderstood and misused him.

"I love only you," he grated, harshly, their sweat drenched bodies slipping and sliding in a riot of movement. *And I hate all the others*, he thought with a stark simplicity that turned his act of love into a moment of pure lust, and left him feeling dirty.

In that moment he knew sin and blanked his mind with a death rattle whisper like the tearing of ancient silk. His head seemed to explode, gushing globules of brain and gore along unclean gutters.

Why was it that childhood hopes had to grow into adult reality? he wondered; but sleep claimed him before an answer could even be considered. A sleep that brought no peace, just scenes that jumped and jerked before bloodshot eyes as the wordsmith grovelled in his own excreta. An idea lay dead, crushed by thoughts wrenched hard from lunatic fantasies.

***

Blank, loveless eyes proclaim yet another victim of the self destructive process. There is something here that causes fear.

Presavorrat stood upon a dusty plain. Beyond him a mountain grew up to the sky. Somewhere, up high, a wise man waited, but the terrain was too difficult for him to master.

Presavorrat wept, his hot tears irrigating the arid landscape. He stood in an area of disembodied failure, denying the sense of belonging that tried to fit so snugly around his drooping shoulders.

"The system can be broken," he muttered through clenched teeth, and a flower emerged from the tear-stained dusty soil.

The treadmills keep turning, but Piller still dreams of the time when written words will once again replace extracted thoughts.

Presavorrat awoke, retinas hurting in the pale morning light. Her arm lay across his bare chest. Today I will start a new novel, he decided, and this woman will be my inspiration.

"Jay Morast," he murmured aloud, bringing to mind the twelve month old affair of the man with no face. Yesterday's headlines now, but what a story could be made of the case.

The old excitement ran through him.

It was a gallop that cleansed. A glorious jaunt across fields of heather to a land of sparkling waterfalls. Hope was the means of transport and belief the power that drove.

Golden highways popped in his minds-eye.

The woman having been versed in the silent, non-stop supply of coffee, Piller prepared himself for a new onslaught on greatness. A virginal white page presented itself on the screen facing him. Daring, inviting, offering itself.

THE MAN WITH NO FACE, he typed, *by Piller Presavorrat.* Fingers poised above the keyboard, he concentrated his total self towards the act of creation upon which he was about to embark. At the appointed moment, his fingers flashed downwards. He was writing. A wordsmith, concocting letters to his own patterns and designs. An archaic pastime, but one that nevertheless provided the only substance that could keep the threads of his life from fraying completely.

***

Presavorrat typed on:

"No right to survive such an operation."

"He had no business surviving an explosion like that in the first place."

"It's always a miracle when someone lives through an accident in space."

"Accident? I wonder…"

Nearing the surface at fleeting moments, the patient in the private ward picked up vaguely heard phrases and blurred impressions before lapsing back into the state of complete unknowing the hospital tried to keep him in.

"It might have been kinder if we'd let him die!"

Jay Morast was a man without a face. Instead of it, the medical staff had provided a blank frame upon which he could fit features, as in a jigsaw.

"Not many people who can genuinely change their face to fit their moods," joked the pretty little night nurse.

Morast selected a look of love, and welcomed her into his bed.

What a sucker he had been! Universal fall guy number one. Smuggling, they'd told him. Looks a clapped out wreck, but that was just a cover to fool the law. Goes like a bomb really. Sure enough, it did too. Blew up just like a bomb

Out there in space, halfway between Earth and Mars. An ask -no-questions, out-of-work, spaceline pilot conned into a non-existent smuggling job which turned out to be an insurance caper.

And the bastards had meant him to die!

It was this thought alone that made him welcome his survival during the long recuperation period that followed the surgeries. Jay Morast was a man without a face, and someone was going to have to pay for it.

"It's like being made love to by a different man each time," said the pretty little night nurse. "As you change your face, so your performance varies to match the newly selected features."

She hoped his recuperation would last for years.

"What can I expect tonight?" she asked, then screamed as he revealed his face of death.

The doctors were worried in case seeing someone die from a heart attack might affect his recovery. The new night nurse was worried in case she might share her predecessor's misfortune.

Both sets of fears were soon calmed. Much to the hospital's surprise, he showed an even keener rate of improvement than before. As for the new nurse, well her concerns soon disappeared, along with her inhibitions and uniform. In Morast's bed, seemingly in the arms of a different man each night, she came alive for the first time in her life. A short life that stretched from death to death. From the heart attack of the previous nurse until the time when she herself leapt from the window of the tenth floor private ward. Before anyone could reach his room, Jay Morast had replaced his look of terror with one of repose.

He was ready now, and knew it. Ready to revenge himself upon those who had sent him into space to die. Not even Black Art, who came in dreams and sneeringly offered his own face to replace the one Morast had left in space, could spoil the gleeful anticipation of his planned vendetta.

Black Art, an intended character in a novel left unwritten. Denied even the fictional reality of his original conception, he *roamed the dark alleys of night. A stealer of dreams, with abuse and hate his only weapons.*

"Where's your face then, Morast? We both know it. A facial cripple is all, man. You dig? A facial cripple.

"I should have organised the bang that got you. Dead then, and better off for being so.

"Want to borrow a face, Morast? My face? A big black face? A big black real face? I'd rather wander dreams than have your blank frame and false features."

**

Presavorrat stopped typing, fingers twitching to a halt as his mind caught up with what he had written. It had all been flowing so well, as planned, until the unbidden appearance of Black Art.

What the hell had made him bring in that character?

Getting up from his chair, Presavorrat paced the room. It had been years since he invented Black Art, a Negro PI who smashed crime syndicates throughout known space. It had been, he remembered, after the National Film Library had run a series of illustrated lectures on the social significance of the age-old Shaft movies. He had shelved the idea before processing a single word, realizing that he was doing no more than update the old Shaft character into the modern world. And he had not brought Black Art to mind from that day to this.

It was strange, yet the idea had merit. An unwritten character whose only recourse was to invade dreams in a forlorn search for the reality forever denied him. A pseudo-being, held fast by the suction of night.

An excitement shook him to the very root of his ego. This could be his breakthrough. This could be the concept with which he could rival the extracted gibberish of the insane. This would be the novel to herald back the redundant art of the wordsmith!

The woman entered then, with coffee that was soon forgotten as Presavorrat danced her round the room. He babbled words which left her bemused, but his joy was infectious and she was happy because he was. She understood little of the motivating factors that drove him so remorselessly, but knew well the personal contribution that was demanded of her.

"Dream trips go no way towards providing true form and reality," said Presavorrat as he broke into a tango that headed them both straight for the bedroom door.

"I believe you, Piller," she replied with a laugh. Life with a wordsmith was anything but dull.

Later, as train whistles screeched and screamed, and all tracks led to a tunnel in the rock-face, Presavorrat slept. A restless slumber of twisted sheets and lumpy pillows. Full of dark alley whimpers and whispered obscenities.

"Poor Piller," murmured the woman as he tossed and turned, little realising that out of the formless night patterns Black Art was making his dream presence felt.

**

Big and strong, dark as the night that claimed him, Black Art came to Presavorrat while he slept. "Look at me, man," he ordered. "Powerful, cruel, a winner all the way. A creation destined for fictional greatness, but you shelved the idea and booked me passage on the oblivion express. Hell, baby, I would have had it made!"

Sleeping, Presavorrat suffered the blast of raw power until it seemed he would drown in his own mattress. Art towered over him, ferocious in his anger. "I would have been great!" he thundered.

"But publishers don't want written words," Presavorrat managed to whisper through his fear. "They'll accept nothing but extracted thoughts."

"If you were good enough you'd make it. Just a hack. No talent, no courage, no nothing. You'll never break the stranglehold of the extractors, not without a character like me to make life leap and tingle on your pages."

Denied even the fictional reality of his original conception, Black Art loomed malignantly over his dream-trapped creator. "Write me, you bastard!" he demanded. "Give me that much or by all that's unholy I swear to sever the chains that bind me and unfold your existence to replace the one you dangled so tantalisingly then withdrew."

Presavorrat could only scream as big black hands reached out towards him. Red tinged screams that seemed to pour from a gash, a second mouth in the throat of humanity.

Black blood spurted like demented rain, producing a rancid cancer that would melt in daylight. Green sparks fusing brains that plunged towards the pit of despair..

Presavorrat wept, and the hands that reached out balled into fists that shook with threatened violence. "You owe me!" shrieked Black Art with impotent rage as he faded into nocturnal mists.

The woman held him tightly, cradling him to her breasts. "There, there," she cooed gently, "everything will be all right."

But two hours later Piller still wept and muttered. "Black as the abyss," he said between tears. "After my life."

This was not what she had expected, and could make no sense of any of it. Not from his non-stop crying nor his insane ramblings. "Hell spawned, from the depths of my mind," he muttered as he sobbed. The realisation finally came home to her that she was in a situation way over her head.

The doctor she sent for decided he was also unable to help, apart from arranging for hospitalisation and expert opinion.

Poor Piller, thought the woman, closing the door on yet another episode in her life. Insane, they said. Completely, utterly, and with little hope of any sort of recovery. For her, he was now relegated to the past, but for others he was very much of the present.

The psychiatrist in charge of his case soon telephoned the publisher who paid him an annual retainer. "Got a sure-fire smash for you this time," he claimed with supreme confidence. "A real whacko, as you'll agree after reading the case notes I'm sending."

The publisher did indeed agree, and wasted no time in setting up a thought extraction session. This one certainly did have best selling potential.

SKULLS

There was a time I was pretty much addicted to horror fiction. Earlier, in my teens, I read the Beat Generation and always meant to revisit them sometime, but a new Ramsey Campbell would come along and horror would win out yet again. When I was a kid I read comics.

Batman, for all the fact that I enjoyed him, was not a true super hero. Bruce Wayne used his wealth, allied with invention, to enable him to give the impression of capabilities beyond being merely human.

Superman, Spiderman, Captain Marvel, Plastic Man, X-Men, etc, etc. Heroic figures possessing powers either born with, God-given or accidentally acquired. They were the true super heroes I admired so much in the comic books of my childhood.

We all dreamt of possessing super powers. I know I did, with X-ray vision being my particular favourite, the potential for naughty fun being endless. But we mostly knew that it was just make believe. Things found in comics, on television, in the cinema. People couldn't really swing on spider webs, fly unaided, or stretch their arms all the way around a building.

Could they?

We also thought that having super powers would be cool. Would make us special. In our games and day dreams our abilities were always used on the side of good against the bad guys. We did not understand, back then, that some powers could be neither helpful nor wanted.

My name is not Kal-El and I am not from the planet

Krypton. I do not dive into phone boxes to change into a one piece costume and fly off to save the world. I do not have a girl like Lois Lane chasing after me.

My name is Eric Brown. Mister Average, or so I thought for most of my life. I used to read horror fiction, but not anymore. Now I live it.

My name is Eric Brown.

I have a super power.

And I wish I didn't…

***

My parents both died young. My father when I was still an infant and my mother four years ago when only forty-eight. So I live alone, aged thirty, having severed the few meaningful ties that remained.

One that I had to end was my only long-term relationship. I liked Jean well enough. Probably loved her in my own quiet way and the complete ordinariness we shared did dovetail in a comfortable manner. We had been engaged for a number of years, drifting towards an inevitable marriage. So yes, I did have feelings for her.

I thought enough of her to break off our engagement, and to stop seeing her.

My only living relative is an elderly aunt, the sister of my unremembered father. I used to see her on an irregular basis, but have let those visits drop away now. I can't see her any more than I can Jean. Neither of them. Not for their sakes I suppose but for mine. I'm not strong enough.

So here I am, thirty years old and leading a very singular existence. I'm employed at a call centre where my fellow workers are colleagues rather than friends. I keep to myself and don't encourage familiarity. I can't afford to let anyone become too close.

***

I know now that I have always possessed my specific power, though not recognising it as such at first. On an as-and-when basis, the flesh would dissolve from an individual's face and head, revealing that person's skull. I assume that this so-called ability was with me from the moment of my birth. It was definitely part of my being as I became aware and memory kicked in, so I saw it as nothing strange or unusual. I thought, in my childish innocence, that everyone saw the occasional head become a peeled-back thing of bone.

It was only later, as the child became a boy, that I found out others did not share this particular trait. A learning curve that also suggested I should never admit to being in any way different to my peers.

"Bonehead Brown sees bone heads. Don't you, Brown?"

Words accompanied by pushes, digs, punches.

"Seen any of your skeletons lately, Bonehead?"

As the boy became a youth, I'd learnt the lesson well and kept my mouth shut. I still witnessed it happening, as I always had, but mentioned it to no-one. In every other way I was completely unexceptional, and worked hard to make it so. Sometimes I even tried to convince myself that what I saw was just a trick of the light. But it wasn't, and I knew it.

I would often go days without seeing a single skull, counterbalanced by seeing two or more in a matter of minutes. No pattern. No motive. It simply happened. And the person concerned simply carried on as if nothing had changed. Which it hadn't, for them, since I alone could see what had taken place.

***

For a while after I'd broken off our engagement, Jean kept

sending me text messages and left sobbing entreaties on my answerphone. I'd given no reason when ending things and she kept asking me: "Why? Why? Why?"

My Aunt sent me a single postcard, pointing out how long it had been since my last visit and asking me to fit her into what was obviously a busy schedule.

Busy?

Ha!

But how could I tell them that now I had discovered the full implications of my unwanted super power, I was afraid to see the only two people I still cared about. I just did not have the strength of character to deal with such potential for heart breaking knowledge.

Jean's attempts at communication gradually decreased over time and finally stopped altogether. My Aunt Eunice sent just the one single postcard, then left it up to me. She probably put it down to a bored nephew having other things to do. Jean, on the other hand, was most certainly hurt at being so unexpectedly and coldly dumped. I could only hope that neither, at least after time had elapsed, would think too ill of me.

***

It was because of my mother that I first began to suspect there to be more to my seeing skulls than just a visual occurrence. Always an early riser, she would have tea and toast ready for me before I left for work at the call centre. "Never start the day on an empty stomach," was a favourite saying of hers.

When I came downstairs on this particular morning my mother greeted me with a smiling skull. Though I was used to seeing this in other people, it was nevertheless a shock in it being her.

"Are you okay, mum?" I asked.

"Of course I am," she replied, her false teeth remaining firmly in place. I had wondered if they would fall without their usual support. "Why do you ask? I look alright, don't I?"

Not really, mum, I thought, but didn't say. "Of course you do," I lied. "Just being a concerned son."

She laughed at that, smiling a big toothy grin, and still not losing her dentures.

I hoped she would be back to normal by the time I got home from work. There was something disconcerting about it happening to my mother. It was too up-close and personal. Definitely not something I could pretend was a trick of the light or any other visual accident. But when I returned that evening it was still a hairless bone head resting on her neck. Jean, when she called round later, saw nothing different, as I had known would be the case. This was my special power, not hers.

Did she have one? Jean? A secret ability, however pointless, that nobody else knew about.

Did everyone?

Or was it only a few unlucky individuals like me?

Whatever the answers, it was a strange evening. I sat, ignoring the television, watching my mother's skull as she enjoyed her regular diet of TV Soaps.

"What's up with you tonight?" asked Jean, noticing I was even more preoccupied than usual.

"He's been like it all day," butted in my mother's skull. "He was even concerned about his poor old mum this morning," she added, laughing indulgently at the recollection.

I doubted that she still remembered but when still a youngster I had mentioned the way some people lost all their head flesh. Mum's reaction had been to threaten to deprive me of all future comics, obviously blaming their influence for what she saw as an overactive imagination. I, still at that time believing others saw the same, nevertheless gauged that mother was not well disposed towards the subject, and I didn't want to be banned from my comics. Then my later school experiences showed that nobody shared my oddball ability, so it was never mentioned again to anyone, mother included.

Seeing a stranger transformed was one thing. Somebody noticed only in passing, whom I was unlikely to ever see again. Or someone who maybe lived near but I would only come across infrequently. But my own mother, whom I still lived with. Whom I saw every day. That really was different.

She would sometimes say to me: "Come and give your old mum a kiss and a cuddle." And I always obliged, willingly.

But could I now?

Could I still kiss her?

Could I go cheek to cheek with a skull?

I dreaded her asking, but she never did. Not in the short time left.

A policeman came to the call centre the next day and broke the news. My mother, out shopping, had suffered a heart attack. The ambulance had arrived without delay and everything that could be done had been, but the heart attack had been massive. She had been declared dead on arrival at the local hospital.

It was with a terrible sense of dread that I approached the moment of seeing her body. It had to be done, but how would I react to looking at her lying there, skull staring sightlessly into space? But my worries turned out to be groundless. In death my mother's flesh and hair had returned. It was with tearful relief that I saw she had been fully restored.

The days between her dying and the funeral passed in a blur of form filling and decision making, as it does. It is only after that the full realisation of loss sets in. But I did notice that an elderly neighbour attending the church service had dissolved into a skull; then heard that he too had died a few days later.

Coincidence?

I didn't know, but did recall something from years before. Someone at the call centre had transformed into a skull only days before dying in a drunken road accident. These parallel occurrences did set me wondering: was there a link that I had not previously noticed?

I made up my mind to investigate further.

***

Sherlock Holmes I wasn't. Not even Sam Spade. But I did become something of a stalker, trying to identify anyone I spotted with a bony head on show. Some eluded me, my shadowing technique not being one of my strengths, but others I did manage to pin down. Each and every one died within days.

And so it was that I discovered the full scope of my super power. It was not just the visual thing I had always thought it being. Everyone spotted by me, whose head became a skull, was about to die. From being somewhat pointless, it now took on a darker element.

That was when I decided I would have to break up with Jean and stop seeing Aunt Eunice. With my mother gone, they were the only two who meant anything to me. So what would happen if, or when, either of them changed from flesh to bone? Could I cope with the knowledge that their dying was inevitable? And within days?

I didn't think so.

A cowardly reaction maybe, but I'd never pretended to be a hero, super or otherwise. I was Mr Average. Joe Bloggs, the bloke next door. I had spent years hiding the one thing that made me different under a blanket of ordinariness, and now it was threatening to flare up into something different. Something worse.

Little wonder then, that I saw retreat as my only option.

***

So there I was, left with acquaintances but no friends. With nobody close. Which was how I'd wanted it, but I still found I missed the limited, emotional connection I had shared with Jean and Aunt Eunice. Now lacking the outlet they had provided, prompted the sort of inward looking I had studiously avoided in the past.

I was Eric Brown and I knew when people were going to die. I knew because their heads became a skull, something only I could see. It was a special power, and it had ruined my life. During my darker moments I sometimes wished I had suffered the massive heart attack and not my mother. Which in turn led to another morbid thought.

Would my head, too, become a skull, prior to death?

I had to assume it would. Which meant I would have advance warning of my dying.

***

From sometimes wishing I was already dead, I switched completely, becoming quite paranoid when contemplating the possibility. I took to carrying a small pocket size mirror so that I could check my reflection, worrying constantly that I was going to see a skull staring back at me. I would set it up on my desk at the call centre so that I could view my face at all times, much to the amusement of the office joker. But I was already used to ignoring him so took little notice of his juvenile patter. His stand-up routine left a lot to be desired, and I had much more important things to worry about.

The next stage in my evolving attitude was to wonder whether or not this special power might turn out to be a blessing in disguise. When somebody converted to a skull, they died within days, and I knew it was coming. So if I looked in the mirror and saw a skull, I would be pre-warned that my demise was around the corner. Was it possible I could then do something about it?

I wouldn't know how I was going to die, but I could take precautions. So I stocked up with pills, lotions, remedies; medical paraphernalia of every description. I vowed that if, or when, I saw my own skull I would lock myself away for longer than the three day fatality limit I had seen in others. No traffic accident for this guy.

I checked my sugar levels, even though I wasn't diabetic, and my blood pressure. I could have written an expert article on the slightest deviations of my pulse rate. I ate healthily and dieted carefully, leaving as little to chance as possible.

During this period of self-absorbed paranoia I still saw other skulls. Either rarely or often, as chance dictated, but noted them only in passing. Only one skull had any meaningful importance now: my own!

**

The more time that went by, the calmer I became. My thirty-first birthday was coming up. I was the healthiest I had ever been, physically at least. Chances were that I would live to a ripe old age. I would continue to look after myself, which was only sensible, but the panic-stricken intensity of my concern could be allowed to fade.

It was with this brighter attitude that I approached a new week. Monday found me relatively optimistic when I sat at my desk and began working my way through the list of telephone numbers allotted to me. I had never taken the insults often shouted down the line on a personal level. You couldn't survive in a call centre if you did. But now I accepted them with a wry amusement. It could, after all, be a skull shouting the abuse. The thought was vaguely comforting.

Come break-time, when most were gathered around the drinks trolley, I made for the toilet for a pee before having my healthy Lucozade. No tea or coffee for me. Zipping myself up and swilling my hands, I checked the mirror before leaving. Flesh smiled back. Everything was fine.

I didn't exactly feel like tap dancing along the corridor. Keeping a low profile was too well engrained in my psyche. But I did feel a corner had been turned in coming to terms with my situation. Then I breezed into the office, and skidded to a sudden halt.

Wherever I looked, skulls stared back. Those still around the trolley. Those back at their desks. Even our manager, looking down from his lofty perch on high. All of them, skulls!

With a gasp of horror, I took an involuntary step backwards. But as I did I saw that those nearest me did the same, throwing up their arms in a defensive gesture and cowering away from me. I quickly reached for my face, expecting to feel bone. But no, it was still flesh.

They were all skulls, everyone that I could see, and they were scrambling to get away. They were seeing me as the monster. *They* were afraid of *me*.

***

I turned and ran from the office, along the corridor and down the stairs. Those I passed, and the people I could see in other offices, were all skulls. I exited the building, out into the busy street, and all passing pedestrians turned to look at me with blank eye sockets set in their bony heads. And all reacted as my erstwhile colleagues had, with fear.

Mothers shielded their children from me. Teenage girls and old ladies screamed. Men shook their fists, but backed away. Cars either screeched to a halt or drove off at speed.

It was mayhem. It was panic. And I was the cause.

It would have been pointless trying to board a bus so I just ran, trying to ignore what was happening. It was like a Mexican wave following me, arms being thrown aloft as I neared and then dropping as I passed. And everyone, everywhere: *skulls!*

It seemed that the whole world had been transformed.

Everyone except me.

I finally made it home, leaning breathlessly against the inside of my front door, wishing it had bolts as well as a single lock to secure it. I stood there for some minutes, my mind racing, before staggering to the kitchen where I gulped down a couple of glasses of cold water.

The world was mad. Either that or I was.

I kept checking my head, but it remained as always: flesh and hair.

***

It began as a murmur, a background drone, but soon the sound of voices drifted in from outside. Looking through my front bedroom window I saw that crowds of people were congregating around my house. Standing there, talking amongst themselves and pointing.

I checked from the back bedroom and they were in neighbouring gardens too, acting in the same way.

For one insane moment I felt as if I were Robert Neville, the character from Richard Matheson's 1954 novel *I am Legend*. The last human amongst the New Order of Vampires. But this wasn't a book and they weren't vampires standing around outside, just ordinary people whose heads had peeled to the bone. But I was different, that much fitted. Those outside were not after my life, though. At least, I didn't think so. Surely they were just drawn by the car crash mentality that attracts some people to the scene of an accident.

The problem, as I saw it, was that I had been cast as the accident.

I was back peeping through my bedroom window when someone detached herself from the crowd to step forward and call out to me. Her general appearance had suggested it might be Jean and her voice confirmed it.

"Come out, Eric," she called. "We mean you no harm."

I took an involuntary step backwards as she spoke, causing the curtain to sway.

"Up there," shouted someone. "He's in the bedroom!"

"Please, Eric," called Jean, lifting her skull to face the upstairs window. "We only want what's best for you. To help assimilate you into the new normality."

Assimilate? Me? Into the new normality?

Was this really worldwide, I wondered crazily. Was I the only non-skull left?

"Eric?" shouted Jean, more loudly this time. "Please come and join us."

It was then that my landline telephone started to ring and I staggered on unsteady legs from the bedroom and down the stairs. Not sure whether or not I should actually answer it, I stood and stared while it continued to ring. Reaching out tentatively, I lifted the receiver to my ear.

"Hello, Eric," said a disembodied voice. "It's mum."

I had spoken to my mother on the telephone often enough to

know her voice, and this was it. She had died following a massive heart attack. I had identified her and made all the funeral arrangements. I had seen her coffin lowered into the ground.

But it was her voice on the telephone.

"Speak to me, son."

"Mum?" I gasped.

"I'm coming home, Eric, to the house. You must let us in. I'm bringing your father with me. He is so looking forward to seeing you."

My mother, whom I'd buried, was bringing my father, who had died when I was still a baby? I dropped the receiver as if it had burnt my fingers.

It was a moment or two before I realised that I was screaming.

There was a knock on the front door.

I'm screaming still...

FIRST WORDS

The William Burroughs round trip grubfest. Miss it and let the Yage Experience remain untried. The Beat Hotel unlived in. The Methadone Programme unsigned. Miss it and be forever square.

Texas for breakfast.

Mexico for lunch.

Tangiers for high tea.

Paris for dinner.

London for supper.

New York for a midnight snack.

Call him William S or Old Bull Lee. But don't deny the truth of his warning that tomorrow's catastrophe is embedded within the causation of both yesterday and today. Remember that truth is not fiction. But not all offered as true will be real.

Call him a saint. Call him a sinner. Call him dogshit on the sole of a well-heeled size ten. But don't call him late for medication. Soon Old Bull Lee will tickle the ivories with "The William Tell Overture" and then you'll really know the Blues.

You get my meaning, muchacho?

Jazz. Rock. Soul. Funk. None of it would be worth a donkey's fart without that all important blues beginning. The chemistry from which it all evolved. Read the words. Hear the chords. Feel the power.

You get my meaning, brother?

Meanwhile Jack Kerouac's ghost sat in an upstairs room leafing through a Satori mail-order catalogue. "There are more fucking books about me than I actually wrote!" he said.

"The world caught up, Jack," explained Bobby Kent. "You might have died a forty-seven year old drunk who most publishers wouldn't pass the time of day with. But you are an all time literary great now."

The ghost lifted phantom eyes to heaven. "Bastards!" he muttered with feeling. "If they'd taken me that seriously when I was still alive maybe I would not have poured so much booze down my throat."

"Tough, Jack."

"Tough indeed."

It seemed to Kent that this should be when the ghostly figure started to fade. But Kerouac was looking past him into a far corner of the room, asking: "And who might you be?"

Jack's ghost was looking at *me*. Which was not in the storyline.

"Don't pretend you're not there," he continued. "I can see you."

"I'm the writer," I finally admitted.

"The *writer! You* are the writer?"

Bobby Kent, unsure of his role in this new situation, backed slowly out from the room. "Guess I'd better get back to the party," he said, and was gone.

"I'm not *The Writer,* Jack," I said, alone now with the ghost, "but I am responsible for this particular piece of..." I paused and shrugged, "well ... whatever."

"So what's your name, Mr Responsible Author?"

"Bryn Fortey."

"And are you one of my belatedly acquired fans?"

"Absolutely," I said quickly. "I'm even utilising your spontaneous writing technique in this very story. Not that my work could even be mentioned in the same breath as yours."

"A writer should never undersell himself. There are plenty of others who'll do that."

"Maybe. But facts have to be faced."

Kerouac's ghost was starting to fade. "Just keep writing," he said, his voice getting fainter.

Wow!

It was time to get my story back on track.

***

Bobby Kent, downstairs now, sighed deeply, realising he had missed an opportunity to get Kerouac to sign his copy of *On The Road*. Though maybe the ink would have proved no more substantial than the ghost itself.

The party, typically enough, was full of noise. Laughing and dancing, Miranda tried to catch his eye but he turned away and crossed to where Piano Boy was hammering sharp edged jazz chords into a frosty permutation of splintered glass. The kid was so cold he was hot.

Kent stood there letting the notes pierce his flesh and mind. Letting the random intervals blur whatever stood outside the manic dot-dot-dashing of the tonal summary on offer.

The kid was cold, like ice.

The kid was hot, like fire.

The piano sparked with an electric surge at every finger contact. What was he doing here playing at Miranda's boozy druggy parties? He would turn up and play some. Maybe drink a little or even chat. Then wander off as quietly as he'd arrived.

All themes explored, the number climaxed and ended. The kid got up from the piano to be immediately replaced by someone who stomped off on a boogie beat. "Your articulation at speed is phenomenal," said Kent. "You should be doing it for a living."

Piano Boy just smiled.

"No, I mean it," Kent continued. "Though for all I know maybe you are a professional. But if you are, then why are you playing in a dump like this?"

"Oh I don't know. It's not so bad."

"It's not the Ritz. Come on, let's get a drink."

Piano Boy opened a can of lager while Kent poured himself a brandy. "Did you know," said the kid while watching the dancers, "that gorillas often sing in the wild?"

"No. I didn't know that."

"But not in captivity."

"Maybe they don't know any sad songs."

The boogie beat blazed on while Miranda spun and twisted from partner to partner. "She sure can move," said the kid.

Kent nodded. "Our hostess," he said a little bitterly. "Miranda the Morphine Lady."

"That's an odd sounding nickname."

"It's said she can magic away your pain and hurt."

"But is she as addictive as the name suggests?"

Kent smiled ruefully. "There's always a downside," he said. But the upside had been worth it. Theirs had been a turbulent and riotous relationship at every level. They could have written a manual. But Kent had issues. Being merely terrific was not good enough for him. Not when perfection beckoned.

Miranda was a girl of many faults and one of them was being too honest. "Oh you are good, Bobby Kent," she had told him. "But you are not quite Superman and I'm not Lois Lane."

"I'm not a professional musician," said Piano Boy, interrupting Kent's private musings. "I play for my own need and enjoyment."

"So what do you do?"

"I'm a Music Therapist."

Kent considered that for a moment. But when he turned to ask just what the job entailed the kid was nowhere to be seen. Gone and disappeared. Just like Kerouac's ghost.

***

How Monkeys See The World: Inside The Mind Of Another Species by Dorothy L. Cheyney and Robert Seyforth.

Bonobo: The Forgotten Ape by F.M. de Waal.

The Mind Of An Ape by David and Ann Premack.

The Singing Gorilla by George Page.

Kanzi, The Ape At The Brink Of The Human Mind by Sue Savage-Rumbaugh and Roger Lewin.

Apes, Language, And The Human Mind by Sue Savage-Rumbough, Stuart Shanker and Talbot Taylor.

Peter Angelo had read all the books he could find that seemed in any way applicable. But had felt none the wiser at the end. He was young, inexperienced, and in over his head. And Professor Fielding was not much help either.

"We've tried a This-apist and a That-apist and got nowhere. So I suppose a Music Therapist might as well throw his hat into the ring," the Project Director had said on Angelico's first day.

The site was still officially called The National Primate Research Centre but the internal grassland and wooded areas were now encircled by high concrete walls and there was only a single investigation being currently undertaken. The Gorilla Vocalisation Project.

"Back in the nineteen fifties a chimpanzee named Vicki managed to learn a few vocal words in English. But that was all," explained Professor Fielding. "An ape's phonetic apparatus is poorly adapted for what we refer to as speech. When this was realised attention shifted to the teaching of sign language. Then the manipulation of symbolic plastic chips. Next came training based on a keyboard system. All had some successes. But not to the level wanted."

Fielding paused a moment, probably for effect thought Angelico, before continuing. "We know our anthropoid brothers have the potential for advancement. The brain is a fantastically sophisticated carbon based computer, and theirs can be upgraded. Accepting this moves the question out of the category of mysteries and into one of problems. The answer is speech."

"But I thought you said…" started Angelico, but Fielding waved him into silence.

"We have three pairs of mountain gorillas in the compound," he continued. "All have had their vocal chords surgically engineered to enable them to cope with human language. All have been given every opportunity to learn sufficient English for basic communication. Yet none of the six will utter a single word."

It was little wonder that Peter Angelico sometimes felt the need for a break from the Centre. Felt the need to just be Piano Boy for a few brief hours.

As far as he could tell, music had not featured much in primate studies up till now. There had been the case of Michael at the California Gorilla Foundation. He had listened to recordings of Pavarotti for hour after hour. Tapping in time and completely mesmerised. But little else. Gorillas were said to sing in the wild. Usually after a heavy thunderstorm when the rainforest air smelt crisp and sweet. But never in captivity.

Professor Fielding looked down his hawk-like nose and spoke in his best tutorial manner. "After seeing an ape in London, Samuel Pepys wrote in his diary entry on 24th August

1661: *I do believe it already understands much English, and I am of the mind it might be taught to speak or make signs.*

"Well the six gorillas we have here attend their daily lessons most willingly and offer rapt attention throughout. I am of the mind that they have indeed been taught to speak. And we know they are physically able to. But they won't say a single word!

"I think they are laughing at us and talk when alone. We have tried bugging the woods and their quarters. But they have found every one and destroyed them."

Fielding closed his eyes, took a deep couple of breaths, then looked again at Angelico. "Do your best Mr Therapist. Play your music and see if you can get any discussions going on crotchet and quaver issues."

"But you don't think I'll succeed do you?"

The Professor shook his head slowly. "Frankly, no," he said. "Your expertise is to use music as a curative aid. As part of a treatment. But these gorillas are not sick. The behaviourist branch of psychology argue that animals have no minds and to think otherwise is mere anthropomorphism. Not only are they wrong anyway, but in the case of our six animals they are doubly wrong. If there is thought, there is emotion. If there is pain, there is suffering.

"Look into their deep far-seeing eyes when you meet them. What we have done has already placed them beyond their rainforest cousins. They know what is happening but are playing by their own rules. For their own ends."

***

The gaunt spectral presence of the strange Doctor Benway helped enhance the odd party-of-the-doomed atmosphere.

The deals.

The cut-ups.

The fold-ins.

The ovens.

The deaths.

Miranda knew that Bobby Kent's manic need for perfection had oblivion written all over it. And it worried her that she was worried about him.

***

Jack Kerouac's ghost, meanwhile, knocked back booze like it was going out of fashion.

"Where's that Fortey guy," he muttered, gently slurring the words. "Putting me in a talking monkey story. I'll sue him for every last dime." Then: "Hey, that piano player sure is fractured."

Peter Angelico, Piano Boy, played cut-ups with the keyboard, ripping up what was left of the rule book and shredding the pieces. Professor Fielding had been right. Those ani— No, he couldn't even think of them as animals anymore. Those gorilla-people knew exactly what was going on. They still would not speak. But they sure knew how to respond on a non-vocal level.

Bobby Kent wilted under the relentless pressure of the kid's attack. The density. The speed. The underlying nagging worry. He should be on a concert stage, he thought. Somewhere with a proper audience. Not here. The jangling notes drew him into a face-to-face confrontation with himself. Making him see anew the cracked-mirror-image deep within his psyche. Kent felt both uplifted and downgraded at the same time.

Angelico first pounded the keys, then stroked them. He had played the gorillas popular music, but their interest had been only superficial.

"I have been put under considerable Departmental pressure,"

the Professor had complained. "Don't ask me which Department. There are covert Government groups involved and I can say no more. Except that the question of future funding is being looked at."

Angelico played them classical music, which did seem to interest them more. Though only on an intellectual level.

"If we don't start showing practical results soon our funding is going to end and the project will be closed down. They are not going to keep pouring millions down the drain without an end product in sight."

Angelico tried jazz and suddenly the response seemed emotional. The gorillas tapped fingers to the rhythms. They closed their eyes and rocked to and fro. He played them extracts and samples from New Orleans to avant-garde. Armstrong, Basie, Parker, Coltrane all seemed to hit the spot. Cecil Taylor held their attention. Bessie Smith rocked their souls. Angelico knew the music was getting through. But still they would not speak.

"I can understand interest from the scientific community," he said to Fielding, "but why is the Government pouring millions into this?"

"Don't ask."

"But I am."

Fielding waved his sticklike arms in jerky movements. "Can't you imagine it? Talking chimpanzees, talking bonobos, talking orang-utans. A new underclass there for the taking. Carrying out all the low and dirty tasks beneath our human dignity. Can't you imagine units of talking gorillas and baboons as part of our armed forces?"

Angelico could imagine it.

He had been going to take in a keyboard and play them some

of his own music. But was here instead, at Miranda's place. Pouring all his mixed-up feelings into his Piano Boy persona.

Maybe they knew what was being planned.

Maybe that was why they would not speak.

Later, drinking again with Bobby Kent, he became more and more agitated. "Of course they have the power and strength," he said, "but there is a gentility and wisdom that shines through their eyes. There is an age-old perfection in their bearing. They are so much more than just infantry fodder."

"If they have perfection then go for it," offered Kent with brandy fuelled yearning. "Seek it out."

Seek it out as I sought the Ultimate Experience, advised the conglomerated Burroughs-Lee-Benway spirit.

"Seek out the truth that waits at the end of the road," suggested Kerouac's ghost.

"Don't miss out!" shouted Kent over his shoulder as Miranda led him away. The Morphine Lady would cure his ills. And she'd learn to lie a little if necessary.

"I won't," whispered Piano Boy. He had always searched for truth in his music. Now he would do the same with life.

***

It was the first time Angelico had gone to the Centre at night but his clearance status got him through all of the checks and into the compound. There were a number of wooded areas dotted in the grassland, but he knew the one to make for. The one with the large central clearing containing the timbered dormitory building where they slept.

It seemed almost as if he were being summoned. Either there was something momentous about to burst free, or it was the drink doing silly things with his head. Too late to worry either way now. All he could do was stagger and crash his way through the trees and darkness in a desperate search for answers. Even though he didn't fully understand the questions.

Then suddenly he was there at the clearing's edge. The large dormitory building was silent, unlit, and Angelico started to worry that maybe there was nothing here for him after all. He crouched, waiting, for what seemed an eternity.

Then, without warning, it began.

First came the gentle rhythmic tapping of large but sensitive fingers. These were soon joined by irregular wood on wood patterns until the whole thing evolved into a throbbing, crashing, brilliant percussive ensemble. Noise that drove itself through every fibre and sinew. Pulling him upright. Drawing him to the source.

Angelico started to walk on unsteady legs towards the building. But stopped moving when the singing started. A thundering vocal that caught his heart in a vice.

"I woke up this morning," sang a voice full of pain and hurt, "and heard what the boss man said."

The tom-tom beats raged behind the singer.

"I woke up this morning, and thought I might be better dead."

Then Angelico was running. Hands over ears. Trying to blot it out. It was a New Blues. Still with elements of suffering and injustice. But with new dimensions added. And it filled him with guilt and shame.

Peter Angelico, Piano Boy, staggered through the trees. He had heard the future, and it filled him with dread.

POEMS #4

A SOLITARY DREAM

Some dreams draw mansions in the sun
And rivers on the moon
Short dreams have only just begun
And others end too soon

Some dreams are pennies made of tin
And whistle a sweet song
Fat men can think of being thin
Good men can dream of knowing sin
And others last too long

> But mine have only one strict theme
> And that is based on you and I
> And the way we said goodbye
> A solitary dream

Some dreams show monsters in the rain
And pictures on a glass
Tarzan can swing his way to Jane
A dream can make a madman sane
All things can come to pass

> But mine have only one strict theme
> And that is based on you and I
> And the way we said goodbye
> A solitary dream

***

THESE AUTUMN DAYS

I've been looking back
Remembering the joys and pains of yesterday
Looking down the track
And marvelling at all the things I used to say

The time was when
I knew it all
And yet again
How I would fall

These autumn days seem right for me to reminisce
These autumn days remind me of the things I miss
Rich tapestry of ups and downs along the way
Come sweeping back to haunt me in these autumn days

I've been spending time
Remembering the loves and hates of bygone years
Looking down the line
Remembering the chill of age-old ghosts and fears

The truths I learned
And then forgot
The fingers burned
When life got hot

These autumn days seem right for me to reminisce
These autumn days remind me of the things I miss
Rich tapestry of ups and downs along the way
Come sweeping back to haunt me in these autumn days

***

LET ME JOURNEY

The pitfalls of the mind
The desert wasteland of a squeezed out soul
The blind still lead the blind
The shallow acting of a played out role

Oh let me journey
Let me journey to a distant shore
Let me wander where the sun shines more
Let me journey far away

Cry now a frozen tear
The barren tundra of a cold cold land

The fearful rule by fear
So making certain that we all stay damned

　　Oh let me journey
　　Let me journey to a far flung world
　　Let me wander where no flag's unfurled
　　Let me journey far away
　　If only for a day

When darkness hides what's real
The stifled screaming of a smothered brain
Do eyes see what we feel
The stricken terror of a mind still sane

　　Oh let me journey
　　Let me journey to a promised place
　　Let me wander with no need to race
　　Let me go with no delay
　　If only for a day
　　Let me journey far away

***

NIGHTFALL

When the streets are bare and stark
I step out to make my mark
Only sinners trust the dark

Come nightfall

　　I hear the children of the moon
　　The padded paws
　　The jagged claws
　　They think that daylight comes too soon
　　The time that drives them back indoors

　　They live for nightfall

When the time is good and late
And there is no need to wait

I stride out to meet my fate

Come nightfall

> I sense corruption in the air
> A graveyard smell
> The signs that tell
> Join me amongst it if you dare
> Meet the inhabitants of hell

> They live for nightfall

When of day there is no trace
I look night-time in the face
And accept its dark embrace

Come nightfall

THE TELEPORTED
WOMAN'S HUSBAND

"Because I want to go shopping in America," Donna joked when I asked why it had to be her. That was six years ago. Six long years since the … well they called it an accident, but it seemed somehow larger than that to me.

We didn't need the money. I was big in insurance and doing okay. She was a tiny cog in the Teleportation Project at a lowly technician level. Donna worked because she wanted to. Finding it stimulated a need in her makeup. So stimulating that when a guinea-pig was called for she went and volunteered. Bad enough in itself, but then they accepted her and my objections counted for nothing.

The Sending Unit was in London. The Receiving Unit in New York. It had been very hush-hush up until then. Various insects and small rodents had helped iron out initial problems and then over one hundred successful animal trials had been carried out.

Time to try it on a human, the big boys had said. I wanted another thousand animals to go before her. But I was only Donna's husband. Not somebody to be listened to.

"She wouldn't have suffered," they told me when the realisation dawned that the cock-up was total. As if anyone could really know. Everything had gone right at the London end, they said. She had disintegrated as planned.

Disintegrated? Hell and high water, man! That was my wife they were talking about.

Problems were at the Receiving Unit, they continued. Something went wrong in New York. Or between London and New York. Donna had disintegrated but failed to reassemble. Her broken up atoms were gone. Nobody knew where.

I should probably have left it at that, but I was grieving in a way that no-one had ever had to grieve before. So I took the sack loads of money they kept throwing at me, but I kept digging too.

"What about her essence?" I demanded. Her soul? Her spirit? What about her thoughts? The accumulated personal knowledge that makes individuals of us all?

Finally one of them slipped up enough to admit that whereas her physical being had obviously been destroyed, there was no way they could be sure what had happened to her *awareness*, or even if such a thing could still exist.

But it might.

Donna's essence might well have turned up in New York, ready to be reunited with all those swirling atoms, only for them to fail to make it. Though since we were talking about pure mental energy, it might just as easily have zipped up through the solar system on its way to the stars. Or not.

Who could possibly know?

Not the so-called experts.

Nor me.

But six years have gone by. Donna has been declared legally dead. I am rich beyond my wildest dreams. But how can I come to terms with the possibility that her invisible essence might be floating nearby?

I can't even bring myself to enjoy the company of other women. Not with the prospect of my lost wife being there. Watching. Checking. Disapproving.

Six years.

It's driving me crazy!

I've told them, the big-shots at the Teleportation Project. When they are ready to try again, just knock on my door. I've told them to look no further. I'll be their next volunteer, and with any luck it will all fail again.

I can see it now. Well not actually see it. But I can imagine it. Donna and I, together again. Floating the universe in pure mental harmony.

THE SUBSTITUTE

"To your left Lacky!"

Pivoting quickly he snapped off three fast shots. Two of the figures bearing down upon him dropped in their tracks, causing the rest to dive for cover. Mantrat, who had spotted them and shouted the warning, hit one who had been slower to react than his fellows.

"Quickly! Into the car."

They bundled in. Mantrat in the driver's seat. And were cornering on two wheels before the would-be assassins managed a few wasted bullets in their direction.

Try to ambush Lacky Macey would they? He grinned wolfishly. Well there were a few who wouldn't be telling their children about the attempt. "We've got them worried, Mantrat," he said, not without a hint of triumph. "Just a few expendables this time. But it shows they've started to take me seriously."

"Sure, and it means you never again travel without a full bodyguard. That was a clumsy effort but better and more sophisticated efforts will follow."

Lacky shrugged. "That's the name of the game. The stakes are high. The prize is big. Just the whole damn country. That's all!"

"I wonder if they realise just how high you're aiming?" Mantrat allowed himself a wry chuckle. "From local terrorism to major revolution is a mighty big step."

Lacky settled back in the passenger seat as the car sped deeper into Macey territory. "They might not know yet, but they soon will. That much I promise you."

And the next step would be a raid on the Fallow Arms Depot. That would really set the Bennington Dictatorship on his tail...

***

"Larry! Come along now Larry. You never seem to hear your alarm clock these days. Larry! Wake up at once. Do you hear me?"

"What's that?" Larry Macey opened his eyes and struggled into a sitting position. "Am I late?"

"You will be if you don't get a move on," replied his mother.

"All right mam. I'm awake now."

Getting up he allowed his mother to shoo him as far as the bathroom. "Now hurry. Do you hear me?"

"Yes mam."

"Be quick and you'll have time for a cup of tea."

"Lovely."

"And don't forget to make your bed."

"I won't."

As she went down the stairs Larry pointed two fingers at her back and mimed a shooting action. Lacky would've known how to deal with a bossy woman. Bang! Bang! 'Bye 'bye mother. He blew make-believe smoke from the pretended barrel, grinning self consciously as he went into the bathroom and closed the door.

It was funny the way he, Larry, became Lacky almost every-time he slept. Or even daydreamed. And what a name to choose for his fantasy self: Lackadaisical Macey. Lacky for short. Part freedom fighter. Part underworld mobster. A revolutionary with Mafia tactics.

First Walter Mitty, then Billy Liar, and now me, he thought

ruefully, plugging in his electric razor and starting to shave. But he just couldn't help himself. Especially since things were really heating up for his alter ego. Those bully boys had probably been sent by Louie Riccio, Head of the Secret Police in Dictator Bennington's oppressive Government. Mantrat was right about the bodyguard. Lacky was going to have to watch his step.

Ablutions finished, he checked to make sure he left the hand basin as clean and tidy as he'd found it. Then back to his bedroom to dress before making the bed.

Lacky never had to see to such menial tasks.

But he was Larry. Not Lacky. He was a Cost Clerk. Not a Revolutionary Leader. Lackadaisical Macey was nothing more substantial than a dream world creation. More's the pity.

Hurrying downstairs, Larry managed to gulp his promised cup of tea before rushing off to catch his bus.

"Don't forget you and Maureen are babysitting for Norman and Diane this evening," called his mother from the front door.

Larry waved a silent acknowledgement as he sped down the street. Yet another thrilling episode to look forward to. He and Maureen were engaged and saving to get married. Norman was Maureen's brother, and an evening when they baby sat while he and his wife went out was an evening with no spending. Maureen was budgeting very carefully towards their trip down the aisle.

Yet another situation Lacky would never have got himself into.

He reached the bus stop just in time, for which he offered thanks. Mr Huxton, the Works Accountant, was very strict on time keeping. And on everything else for that matter. Larry preferred not to cross swords with him if possible. But he usually did, at least once a day.

Not that "crossing swords" was a very accurate description. That implied a two-sided clash with at least an active defence on Larry's part. What actually happened was that Mr Huxton would look for, and find, a reason to reprimand him. And Larry would suffer in virtual silence, only rarely managing to do other than nod dumb but angry agreement.

Mr Huxton was in fact a bully. Like all of his kind he preferred a safe target, and that was Larry Macey. Not that the other office employees were immune from his vitriolic outbursts, but none suffered quite so often, or for less reason.

"Larry!"

Startled from his private reverie he knocked a number of sheets of paper onto the floor as he quickly tried to look busy.

"Pick it up! Pick it up!" Mr Huxton advanced to stand alongside his desk. "Don't dawdle, man!"

On his knees, Larry snatched at the fallen sheets.

"From the way you've been sat, staring into space for I don't know how long, can I take it you have finished the Canteen Accounts?"

He knew, and Larry knew he knew, it was a two day job that had only been started that morning. "No, not yet," he mumbled, retrieving a ruler which had also fallen.

"Then stop day-dreaming and get on with it. We can't afford to carry slackers in this office."

Back on his seat, having picked up all he'd knocked down, Larry shuffled through the sheets, reassembling them into their correct order while Huxton looked on critically. Finally the Works Accountant turned and stalked back to his own office.

"You idiot, Larry," said one of the other clerks good-naturedly. "Stop your mooning. You only give the old sod a reason to pick on you."

"I know," agreed Larry ruefully. "But the Canteen Accounts are so boring." Planning and executing Lacky's raid on the Fallow Arms Depot had been much more interesting and exciting.

***

The place had been better defended than had been anticipated and the attack had been touch and go for a while. But Lacky's men had won through in the end. Though not without casualties. Even Mantrat had been wounded. Not seriously, thank goodness, but his left arm would be in a sling for a spell.

Lacky himself had led a charmed existence with bullets whining all around. Some missing him by only inches. But they had pulled it off and that was what counted. The biggest Government Arms Depot in the area had been overpowered and was in their hands. Not only had Lacky extended his sphere of control but his weapon capability had been considerably increased.

***

"There you go again Larry. Snap out of it before old Huxton comes back."

With an effort Larry redirected his attention towards the work on his desk. A little self-conscious and bewildered, he shook his head in slow bemusement. He really was going to have to do something about the way this dream-world character was invading even his daytime hours.

***

It was like a pre-set alarm. Every time Larry felt he and Maureen were approaching the sort of situation an engaged couple could consider right and natural, one of the kids they were baby-sitting for would wake and demand attention.

Jumping to her feet and hastily tidying herself, Maureen would rush to the bedroom, leaving a frustrated and annoyed fiancé sprawled upon the settee.

After the third such interruption Maureen made coffee for them both and decided it was time to settle down to some television viewing. Larry didn't really agree but knew better than to argue once she had made up her mind.

"Good looking French film on BBC2," he suggested hopefully while glancing at the evening paper's programme guide. If it was anywhere near the critical assessment it might help put Maureen back in the mood for some more heavy petting.

"No," she decided with a finality he well recognised. "There's an ITV documentary I particularly want to see. About homelessness in the north-east. It should be both interesting and educational."

"Oh yes, very," said Larry without much enthusiasm. He could picture it already, without bothering to switch on the set. There would be a fearless television reporter, a dedicated social worker, a crusading churchman. Almost certainly an inept housing official or two, and streams of faceless people moaning either bitchily or self-pityingly about their particular plight. Maureen loved such programmes. She would do nothing about any of the problems investigated but it satisfied her social conscience to view in a sympathetic manner.

As expected, Larry was bored to tears and found more entertainment in sulky contemplation of the possible state of undress of the heroine of BBC2's French film. An actress he had long admired, and not only for her thespian talents.

It wasn't long before his chin dropped forward on to his chest as he nodded off.

And when Larry slept.

Lacky lived!

**

She stood before him. Proud, beautiful, her eyes flashing with a passionate anger that over-rode any fear she might have been experiencing. "'Ow dare you 'ave me abducted and brought to ziss place?" she shouted, tossing her mane of auburn hair defiantly.

Lacky signalled the two men, who stood one on each side of her; he remained silent until they had left the room.

"I apologise for any inconvenience mademoiselle. And for any unwarranted fears my men might have inadvertently given rise to. Your personal well-being and safety are guaranteed."

"Zen why am I 'ere? Is it a political abduction?" A distasteful expression crossed her face. "Or 'ave I just been kidnapped to be 'eld for ransom?"

"Wrong on both counts," replied Lacky, getting to his feet. He nodded towards two easy chairs that faced one another on either side of a homely log fire. "Let's sit," he suggested, "and I'll tell you all about it."

With an aloof nod she stalked regally to the nearest chair and sat down.

"Drink?"

"Cognac."

"Of course." He poured two, gave one to her, then sat in the other chair.

"You were going to explain, monsieur."

"First let me introduce myself. Though locally of some notoriety, I doubt that my name will have been heard of in your country, yet. I am Lackadaisical Macey."

She glanced at him with sudden interest. "But yes, your

name it is known to me. Not back 'ome, but since I 'ave arrived 'ere. Something to do with an attack upon an arsenal, no?"

He nodded. "The Fallow Arms Depot. That was my most recent acquisition."

The woman laughed sharply. "I disagree Monsieur Macey. I would say that I am your most recent acquisition."

It was Lacky's turn to laugh. "Oh no, Mademoiselle Chabon. You are a guest, not an acquisition. If only you were. But no, it is the other way round. Though you have been brought here against your will, it is you who control the situation. This evening you will dine with me, I hope, as my guest. But after that you will be free to leave, if that is your decision."

"If zat is so, why bring me 'ere at all?"

"Because I am your most devoted admirer."

"Indeed?"

"Only last week I sat avidly through the showing of one of your films on our television. *Darkness Be My Friend*, starring Catherine Chabon. I was glued to the screen and you were as marvellous as always. So when I heard that you were arriving in this country to promote your latest epic I just had to meet you, and the cloak and dagger routine seemed the only way. I do happen to have a price on my head, so could hardly have turned up at your hotel with flowers in my hand."

"You surprise me, Monsieur Macey."

"Call me Lacky. All my friends do."

"Lackee…" She toyed with the name." I am 'onoured zat such a renowned bandit should find my acting so enjoyable."

Her eyes sparkled. No longer with anger, but with delight and interest.

"Then you will dine with me?"

"I will."

"And after?"

"Ah well, let us wait and see what afterwards will bring."

"Then let us drink to favourable circumstances."

Lacky went across to where she sat and as he took her glass their fingers touched lightly. For a moment they paused, motionless, looking deep into each other's eyes. She was even more beautiful, here and now, than the screen goddess he had desired so strongly.

"Catherine," he whispered huskily.

"Oh Lackee!" she exclaimed, clutching his hand and pressing it to her breast...

***

"Oh Larry, it's your turn. Go on, be a love."

"What's that? Go on where?"

"To see what little Billy wants. He's woken up again. Didn't you hear him call?"

"No." He shook his head. "I must have dozed off." Larry heaved himself to his feet, a little cross at having been disturbed just when things were looking interesting with that Catherine Chabon.

"Thanks Larry. I didn't want to miss the end of this programme."

"That's all right," he said with a shrug. "The little devil probably only wants a drink of water."

***

It was ten to one when Mr Huxton brought the Invoice Register to Larry's desk. "I must have last month's figures for this afternoon's meeting," he said. "Everyone else either eats at the canteen or goes home. But you only ever sit over by the tennis courts with your sandwiches. So it won't be any loss for you to get these totalled and have a late lunch."

Only that I'll be completely on my own, thought Larry with tired resignation. During the summer months he always sat with a few colleagues from other offices who also brought packed lunches. They chatted a bit and watched members of the tennis section who spent their hour on the courts.

"All right Mr Huxton."

"And no mistakes Larry. I'll not have time to check. When you've finished leave the Register on my desk. Right?"

"On your desk."

He watched while everyone else got ready to leave.

"Head down Larry. No mistakes now," ribbed one of his fellow clerks. Then they were gone and he settled down to the job given him. A straight forward task demanding nothing more than an ability to tot up columns. For every type of invoice entered he had to provide three totals. One each for Nett, Value Added Tax and Gross.

Hoping to get over to the tennis courts while there was still someone there, Larry got stuck in. Then: "Pssst!" He looked up and saw a shadowy figure in the office doorway.

"Where are the others?" asked the man.

"Gone to lunch."

"Lunch? Bodyguards don't have meal breaks."

"Pardon?"

"It's a good job I decided to come over."

Larry stood up. "Who are you and what do you want?" Old Huxton would blow is top if the figures he wanted weren't ready for his meeting. Larry couldn't afford interruptions.

The man stepped out from the doorway and into the office, and Larry could only gape in surprise.

"It's me. Mantrat. Who the hell did you think it was?"

"How's your arm?" asked Larry without thinking. Somehow

registering the fact that it wasn't in a sling now.

Mantrat patted it. "Sore but okay," he replied. "Never mind that though. Look, taking over large industrial plants is all to the good. I'm not knocking the strategy. But infiltrating the places yourself is damned stupid. Only expendables should be used."

Larry tried hard to control his tumbling thoughts. To make some sort of sense from what was becoming a crazy situation. But the more he tried the more insane it appeared.

All he could manage to say was: "But I'm not asleep."

"Obviously," retorted Mantrat.

"I'm not even daydreaming."

"So?"

"So you shouldn't be here."

"Maybe not, but from the strange way you're acting it's a good job I am."

"But you don't exist. Not in the real world."

A worried frown crossed Mantrat's face. "Snap out of it Lacky."

"My name is Larry!" He felt hysteria rising like bile in his throat.

"Never mind what you are calling yourself here. There's no one around to hear me use your real name."

"For God's sake stop it," shouted Larry, making one final attempt to restore believability over this fantasy. "I don't know who you are or who you're pretending to be. But I've got work to do and Mr Huxton will have my guts for garters if I don't finish it in time."

"Yes, Huxton, that's the one," agreed Mantrat, nodding vigorously. "I know you have already listed him as a strong Bennington supporter, but what we've just discovered is that he is an undercover member of the Secret Police. This Huxton is one of Louie Riccio's boys."

Larry's jaw dropped.

"So do you see what I mean about you taking part in works infiltration yourself? If this Huxton had got just one whiff of who you really are, you'd be either dead or rotting in some stinking cell by now."

"Old Huxton can be a right swine at times," said Lacky – no wait – said Larry. "But I can't believe he's one of the Secret Police."

Mantrat snorted. "This has come from our agents in the capital, and they don't mark anyone unless they're right. You know full well that Riccio has his men posted under all sorts of cover."

"I suppose so."

Good Lord, realised Larry with a start, I'm starting to accept it. This just had to be a dream. Soon the others would arrive back from lunch, wake him up, and he'd be in all sorts of trouble for not getting the Invoice Register totalled.

But it didn't seem like a dream.

Always, in the past, when he'd slept he had *been* Lacky. That was what was different. This time he knew he was Larry, but was being mistaken for Lacky. Didn't that prove he was awake? But if so, how come Mantrat was suddenly a real-life flesh-and-blood person?

He was good at questions, but poor on answers.

"How are we going to handle it then, Lacky?" asked Mantrat, interrupting Larry's feverish train of thought. "It might be best if you headed back to HQ and left this Huxton to me."

"I don't know yet. Let me think."

Mantrat winked, man to man. "Don't let it influence you, but Miss Chabon is pining for your return."

If anything was likely to tempt him into full acceptance of the Lacky role, it was the thought that Catherine Chabon was as real as Mantrat appeared to be. But he didn't know where this HQ was so couldn't return until guided. It was totally beyond his comprehension, but maybe he *was* Lackadaisical Macey, Revolutionary Leader. Maybe it was Larry Macey, Cost Clerk, who was the dream character. Trouble was, he still felt he was Larry.

He was going to have to play it very carefully until the real him, whichever it was, could obliterate the other. "How do you suggest we deal with Huxton?"

"As if you hadn't already decided," replied Mantrat, studying the ledger he had been working on. "Very clever and rather apt."

"The Invoice Register? Nothing clever about that..." But then he noticed the wires and intricate mechanism which fitted neatly into where the book's pages had been hollowed.

How...? When...? He had been totalling columns not making bombs.

"Perfect," said Mantrat admiringly. "It will make a great booby-trap. Big enough to get him without doing too much other damage."

"You mean it will kill him?"

"Of course it will kill him. We always kill Riccio's men."

Larry was aghast. But he knew that Mantrat was right. As Lacky he had personally despatched more than he now cared to remember.

"I'm not going back to headquarters until this site has been taken over," he said. "Then we can return together."

That took care of one problem.

"For now I'll retain my Cost Clerk cover."

"If that's the way you want to play it," agreed Mantrat.

Larry – or was he now Lacky? – nodded. "You continue your watching brief while I get over to the tennis courts."

"Right, but plant the bomb first."

Lacky watched Mantrat slip stealthily through the door. Then, with extreme caution, he carried the booby-trapped ledger into Huxton's office and placed it carefully on his desk. Returning to collect his lunch box, he rushed from the office block and hurried over to where the tennis courts were situated. There was, he checked his wrist watch, only ten minutes of the normal lunch break remaining.

"Hullo Larry. Late aren't you?"

"Hullo Sid. I had to finish a rush job for old Huxton."

"Proper slave driver, that bloke. I don't know how you lot put up with him."

"Got no option, Sid."

"I suppose not."

Lacky smiled to himself. If you only knew, Sid my boy, if you only knew. He opened his box and bit into a tomato and cheese sandwich. He had to act natural. Play it cool. Keep up his cover.

"How are the lads performing today?" he asked.

"Harry is bang on form. Serving ace after ace. Giving old Jack a bit of a drubbing."

Harry was both captain of the works tennis team and secretary of the sports section. As Lacky watched he got to the net and put away a thundering overhead forehand smash.

"Good shot Harry," called Lacky.

"See what I mean," said Sid.

It all seemed so normal here. No dream-world characters coming to life. No talk of revolution and murder. Maybe he had been dreaming again back in the office. And would be in big trouble when he went back for not having completed what was only a routine task. In a way, he hoped that would indeed prove to be the case.

Lacky – or was he back to being Larry again? – nodded and took another bite from his sandwich. "No good Jack trying to lob when Harry's in that sort of form."

Sid chuckled contentedly. "Jack's not looking very happy about it all," he said.

Shortly afterwards the players called it a day, much to Jack's obvious relief, and made their way to the changing rooms. Then Sid decided it was time to wander back to the Progress Department, leaving Larry completely on his own. Come what may, he was determined to have his full hour lunch break. Only then would he face the music over the totalling he hadn't done.

"Old Huxton will flay me alive," he murmured, amazed at himself for being thrown so completely off balance by what he could only put down to an over-active imagination. He might even lose his job because of it.

Larry panicked at the thought. Maureen would be absolutely furious.

Maybe if he went back straight away there would still be time to finish the job before Mr Huxton's meeting. His watch said the lunch hour was ten minutes over, which meant – a faint but definite explosive bang reached him from the general direction of the office block – which meant it was too damn late to worry either way anymore.

He had done it! And the jubilation he felt was almost pure Lacky.

He could see people running pell-mell in every direction. Putting on a worried frown he ran all the way back to join them.

"What's happened?" he asked Price from the Pay Office, grabbing his arm.

"It's your boss. He's dead!"

"Mr Huxton! How?"

"An explosion of some sort. Someone said it might have been a letter bomb."

"Good Lord." He let Price go and moved on through the panic stricken crowd.

With a peculiar sense of detachment Larry/Lacky noted the blank and dazed expressions on most faces. And the aimless movement. Little groups kept coming together, splitting, then reforming. He alone stood apart from this general aura of bemused and worried pointlessness.

"Will everyone please return to their own offices. Except for Cost and Buying personnel who are to go to the Training Centre."

Larry/Lacky recognised the voice of Mr Watts, the Assistant Works Manager. With him was "Old Smokey" Pipe, the Office Manager. They moved quickly from group to group, asking that calm and good sense should prevail.

"Back to your offices, there's good chaps."

"The police are on their way and they will expect good order to have been maintained."

"That's right, to the Training Centre for Buying people, and Costs. The accident area must be kept clear."

"A terrible tragedy. But we must all keep calm."

Just then Mantrat appeared from nowhere and sidled up to where Larry/Lacky stood alone. "It's Riccio's boys been sent for. Not the ordinary constabulary," he hissed. "This Works has turned out to be a real rat-nest of Secret Police activity."

"What do you suggest?" hissed back Larry/Lacky.

"Sneak away and get back to where you've been staying. But you'll need more confusion than this. Got anything else up your sleeve?"

"Naturally," said Lacky, feeling the Larry role fading. "A number of larger devices. All due to go off soon if not deactivated. A precautionary measure for just such a situation as this."

"Great! I'll join you later and we can hightail it back to headquarters together. Got a weapon? Just in case."

"My little snub nosed automatic."

Mantrat nodded, then slipped silently away.

Lacky knew he couldn't simply march out past the Works Security Officers at the main gate so headed instead towards the smaller and unattended rear entrance.

"Hey Larry! Where are you going?"

Damn! He'd been spotted by Tony Maund, one of the lunch time tennis players. Trust a Work Study Engineer to notice. Maybe he too was a member of the Secret Police.

Lacky walked faster. Pretending he hadn't heard.

"You'll be in trouble Larry. Come on back."

Glancing over his shoulder he saw that Maund was hurrying after him. Automatically he slipped a hand into his coat pocket and gripped his pistol. As he did so the full implication of his action hit him like a slap. Mantrat would use the gun, he knew, and so would Lacky.

"But am I Lacky or Larry?" he asked aloud. But kept his hand on the weapon, which maybe was some kind of answer.

"Wait, Larry!"

I will use it, he thought wildly, but then a number of separate but closely consecutive explosions drowned out all else. Lacky saw smoke and flames billowing from points in both the office block and the works offices. Maund, he saw, had thrown himself to the ground.

For a moment Larry could only stare at the scenes of destruction, full of panic and worry. But Lacky, elated, was gaining ascendency again. Taking advantage of the situation, he turned and ran.

***

The house was empty when Lacky got to the place he'd been calling home. He went to his bedroom, feeling more secure there than anywhere else. Things were happening fast. Too fast. Nothing was going to plan anymore.

He wished Mantrat would hurry up. Things would be better back at HQ. He just didn't seem able to cope at the moment. Then the doorbell interrupted his worried thinking.

Running into the front bedroom he peeped through the curtains, hoping to see his right-hand man standing below. But it was Maureen, not Mantrat.

Going downstairs he let her in. Quickly shutting the door when she entered.

"Larry," she exclaimed with relief, throwing her arms around his neck. "I've been so worried."

For a moment he wanted to snap at her to exercise self-control, but then he remembered that she thought he was Larry. So he played along, just standing there while she held him tight.

Finally Maureen let him go and stepped back a pace. "Mr Newland let me leave the shop as soon as we heard about the explosions. I dashed straight around here to see if your mother knew what was going on."

"Mam's not here."

"But you are. Thank goodness!"

Lacky could hardly credit her obvious relief. During his time as Larry, Maureen had always been so calm and self-possessed. So in charge of their relationship. This was a previously unseen side of her. One more in keeping with the emotional state of Catherine Chabon, when aroused by Lacky.

"What happened, Larry?"

Best to stay in character, he decided. Play it dumb. Stick to outlines. "There were a number of explosions throughout the site," he said. "I don't know how many casualties, but Mr Huxton was killed."

Her hand flew to her throat. "How awful," she whispered.

"Someone mentioned a letter bomb but I think it was just a guess. Anyway, the police are there now. Nothing I could do to help, so I came home."

"I'm glad you did," she said emphatically.

"Are you going back to the shop or staying here?"

"Oh I'll stay, I think, if only for a cup of tea. I still feel too shaken to get back behind that counter straight away."

"Let's go through to the kitchen and I'll make us both a cuppa."

Maureen followed meekly and sat quietly while he made the drink. Small stuff maybe, but it felt good having her leave things to him. Normally he had to play the Larry role and let her lead.

It was while pouring a second cup that he heard a tell-tale noise from the hall. Someone else was in the house. "Won't be a minute," he said, splashing tea from the mug as he placed it before her then rushed from the kitchen.

It was Mantrat, on the stairs. "Into my bedroom. Quick," hissed Lacky. It would be best if Maureen did not see him.

"Those other bombs sure did the trick," said Mantrat with a chuckle, leaning against Lacky's wardrobe.

"What sort of casualties?"

"Two dead in the Pay Office and an unspecified number in the factory itself. Plus a large number of injured. The Pay Office was a neat touch. Money blasted all over the place, so they are saying."

"Who were the two killed there?"

"How the hell would I know their names, Lacky?"

"I just wondered."

"Anyway that's history now. What about the present?"

"Back to HQ I suppose. But I can't leave right at this moment."

Mantrat winked. "And I know why."

Does he suspect I'm really Larry, worried Lacky. He'd been playing the milksop for too long. Sometimes being unsure of his true identity himself.

"How do you do it, Lacky?" he asked, twisting his face into a leer. "I mean, that is Miss Chabon you've got downstairs isn't t? There was me thinking she was pining for you back at headquarters and all the time you've spirited her all the way here just to make your life a little bit sweeter. I take my hat off to you. I really do. It's no wonder you command such respect amongst your followers. You're a man's man Lacky."

And Mantrat was right. Of course he was. Only he, Lackadaisical Macey, would have the audacity to conceive and execute such a plan. This current setback would soon be erased once he got down to planning their nest move.

"We'll move out tonight. Under the cover of darkness."

"Right, Lacky."

"You go and scout round now. Make sure all our men have got clear from the Works and spread the word for them to head home."

Mantrat nodded.

"Off you go then, and watch out for Riccio's boys."

Mantrat saluted. "Back at eleven then."

Lacky grinned. "No, make it midnight."

On his own, he lay back on the bed and closed his eyes. He felt more his old self now. Back on the ball. Making his own decisions. Taking the initiative. Funny that he still couldn't remember how to get back to headquarters though. But even there, if something should detain Mantrat, Catherine would be able to show him the way. Odd too that he had forgotten she was really called Maureen. Catherine being her professional name.

His thoughts were interrupted by a knock on the door.

"Enter," he called and Catherine came in.

"I was wondering where you were," she said.

He smiled. Confident in the knowledge that this beautiful woman worshipped him. "Come and sit down," he said, patting the bed alongside where he lay.

She did so with a shyness he found quite becoming, even though unnecessary.

"So this is your bedroom," she said, looking around.

"Sure. And this is my bed. And this is me lying on it."

"You're in a strange mood Larry."

"No! Not Larry. You must call me Lacky, Catherine."

She stared, open-eyed. "Lacky? Catherine?"

"Oh all right, Maureen – if you insist upon me using your proper name." He sat up. Reaching out he touched her dress, his hand stroking the material that covered her breast. She stiffened momentarily, but then relaxed. He could feel the rise and fall of her breathing grow more pronounced.

"What are names anyway?" he continued. "Only tags upon

which to hang our personalities."

Leaning towards her he allowed his free hand to slip beneath her dress to where it could massage the inside of her thigh.

"Larry! What are you doing?" But she didn't try to stop him. Instead she leant forward, lowering her mouth onto his. Kissing him. "Oh Larry. I've never known you like this before," she whispered in his ear. "But no more than this. Please. Not all the way."

Moving his hand from her breast to her back, Lacky started to unzip her dress.

"Oh Larry … Larree … Lackee..." she moaned huskily, burying her face into his neck as his fingers sought to undo the hooks that held her brassiere in place.

Then: "No," she shouted as the straps fell free. With an effort she pushed herself away from him. Standing, visibly trembling, holding her loosened clothing in tightly clenched fists.

Lacky looked at her with surprise. They had been lovers for over a month now. So why this sudden and misplaced show of virginal fear?

"Get on the bed with me," he ordered with a slow and deliberate menace.

"No!" She took two jerky backward steps. "We agreed to wait until we were married. I realise it's not a fashionable stance, but it's how I wanted it. Please don't make me."

"Until we're what? Stop spouting nonsense." Lacky clambered to his feet. "And stop calling me Larry." He delivered a cruel backhand slap across her mouth.

"Larry," she screamed, stumbling against the wall and bursting into tears.

For a moment he considered taking her forcibly. But anger

had now replaced his earlier desire. Striking swiftly he landed three hard blows before she fell to the floor. Dazed and hurt.

"That's your acting career put on ice," he said, laughing harshly. "Let's see you face the camera looking like that!"

So much for the film she had just signed to make about homelessness in the north-east. But Catherine Chabon was no longer any concern of his. None whatsoever. He had to find Mantrat, quickly, and get back to headquarters.

Pulling on a coat he hurried from the bedroom and down the stairs. Just in time to hear the turning of a key in the front door lock.

Riccio's boys!

They'd found him and were closing in. Well, Lacky Macey wouldn't be taken easily. That much was for sure. Pulling his snub nosed automatic from his pocket he crouched by the hallway coat stand. Pumping three quick bullets into whoever it was entering.

With blood seeping from the gunshot wounds, the woman, whose son he had been posing as, slumped dead upon the tiled floor.

Lacky looked down at the body. Of course it was a pity, but loss of innocent lives was an unavoidable consequence of revolution. Circumstances had dictated that this should happen and Lacky could not help but feel a strong relief that it had turned out not to be the Secret Police after all.

The finding of Mantrat was becoming more and more important.

Stepping over the dead woman, Lacky pocketed his revolver as he left the house. Proceeding along the street at as brisk a pace he could risk without drawing attention to himself. Determined to come out on top. As he always did.

One moment he was Lacky. Hurrying along. Looking for a way out from his current predicament. The next, he was Larry. "Oh my God," he whimpered, slowing to a stop. "What have I done?"

The floodgates burst open.

Mr Huxton and others at the Works, bombed: by him.

Maureen, battered to unconsciousness: by him.

His mother, shot: by him.

"Mam," he cried aloud. "I didn't mean to!"

Sobbing hysterically, Larry dropped to his knees. He was still there, grovelling and crying on the pavement, when the police car screeched to a halt alongside him. Hands reached down. Grabbing, lifting, bundling him into the back seat.

They could get no sense from him at the station. "I'm Larry, not Lacky," he babbled. "Lacky doesn't exist, but he did it. Not me. Him and Mantrat. I wouldn't hurt a fly. Not Larry."

Finally a doctor had to be sent for and a sedative administered. Even case-hardened policemen were amazed. "The bombings were bad enough," said a still shaken Detective, "but when we reached his home and found his mother dead. I could have puked on the spot."

***

Everything was hectic at the station so, during all the hullabaloo, nobody noticed a young constable leave and slip quietly to a call box on the other side of the road. He dialled a very special number and was carefully vetted before being put through to the person he wanted.

"Whitcomb here, Mr Riccio," said the young constable. "Attached to the St Paul Street Station, Things are breaking big there. Lackadaisical Macey has been arrested and charged with multiple murders."

THE FLIER

LaRocca sat in his chair, twiddling his thumbs while the woman sobbed quietly. Standing up he strolled to the window, looking down at *The Happy Coconut Bar*. He had been drinking there the evening before and wished he were doing so now.

Turning slightly, he looked at the crying woman. Expensively dressed and still fairly well proportioned, but late middle-aged and fading to old. As she wept she clutched the photographs LaRocca had given her. Photos of her husband and his secretary, unclothed and intimate. This was the part of his job he didn't like.

"I'm really sorry, Mrs Hawkins," he said, and meant it. "I wish it had been a different outcome."

"Not your fault, Mr LaRocca." She sniffed a couple of times then blew her nose with a dainty lace hanky. "It is the twenty-first century. Couples don't stay together like they used to."

"I guess not."

"But Mr Hawkins will pay for the privilege," she stated, placing the photographs back into the large envelope LaRocca had provided. "He will most assuredly pay."

"I guess he will."

"Do I pay you now, Mr LaRocca?" asked Mrs Hawkins, getting to her feet.

"No," he replied, shrugging. "Let's keep it official. I'll bill you in the post."

"As you wish."

She held out a hand which he hurried over to shake, then guided her towards his office door. Another dissatisfied/

satisfied customer, he thought as she left.

Alone, he sat at his desk and pressed the play button to listen again to the CD that had been delivered the day before. First was a little surface noise, then the voice.

"Are you an honest man, Mr LaRocca? Will you just keep the money sent with this recording? Or will you accept it as a retainer? I need a Private Investigator, Mr LaRocca, and your name came out of the hat.

"My name is Paul Townsend. At least, I think it is. I'm not completely sure of anything anymore. But I do think I am Paul Townsend, and I think I have something to do with flying.

"I need you to find me, Mr LaRocca, before I disintegrate totally. Before I stop being me. If it costs more than I've sent, I'll pay it. No problem.

"Just find me. Please. And quick!"

Mrs Hawkins had been the last case on his books. Sure she would pay, but the office rent was due and he had to eat, not to mention drink, and with an empty in tray. Also, this was intriguingly different from his usual runaway teens and messy divorce cases. Plus there was no return address, so he couldn't just send the money back.

An honest man? Well, sort of.

All right, Paul Townsend, he decided, case accepted. Let's see about finding you.

***

The four roomed apartment – living room, bedroom, bathroom, kitchen – had an unoccupied feel to it. The bed looked unslept in, the oven uncooked on, the bath unbathed in, the solitary easy chair unsat upon.

It had taken LaRocca a week to find where Townsend lived, or had lived, whichever scenario fitted, and at first glance it looked like seven days wasted effort. The cold sterility of the place reflected his initial disappointment. But he was still methodical, however pointless it seemed.

There were no clothes, no food, and no odds and ends of personal occupation. Just a fine film of undisturbed dust. Then, under a pillow on the apparently unused bed, a yellow cardboard folder. A single item to suggest an earlier presence.

Inside the folder were photographs. Mainly of the same man, both in and out of uniform. Others featured various shots of a crashed plane, all seemingly quite a few years old. Well none of them looked modern anyway, and a news report looked old too.

Tucking the folder firmly under his arm, LaRocca left the apartment as quietly and discreetly as he had arrived.

***

He had hoped against hope the photographs would be of Paul Townsend himself, with the report offering possible whereabouts, but that would have been too easy. This case was a bit more complicated than snapping silly old roosters with fluffy young chicks.

The images were, it appeared, of an American. A Captain Thomas F. Mantell. An Air National Guard pilot who the report said had crashed and died on January 7 1948. The wreckage of his F-51 Mustang fighter aircraft had been found on a farm, his body still in the cockpit. There had been no attempt to bail out.

LaRocca sat at his desk with the pictures spread out before him. The Townsend CD had suggested a flying connection. A link now established, but all the way back to 1948! And was it just a coincidence that he had an interest in that particular period due to an enthusiasm for classic film noir and bebop jazz? Or had he been hand-picked for this specific case because of it?

***

A sharp knock on his office door interrupted thoughts which were leading nowhere anyway. "It's open," he called.

She was tall, statuesque, not unlike the young Lauren Bacall, and was even dressed in a style reminiscent of that era. *Posh broad enters seedy Private Eye's office*, he thought. It was so film noir it should have been happening in black and white.

Dick Powell, Cagney. Mitchum.

Charlie Parker and Dizzy Gillespie at Minton's Playhouse.

George Raft, the gangster's gangster, who reputedly turned down the lead in *Double Indemnity, The Maltese Falcon, High Sierra* and *Casablanca*. Clearly George was not the best judge of a script in the business

It brought to mind Bacall's first ever meeting with Bogart. If this good looker would only say that LaRocca was shorter than she had expected, then he could snap back that he would soon cut her down to size.

Great dialogue.

Trouble was that though she was tall, LaRocca was taller. So pop went that particular bubble.

"Tom Mantell," she said, looking at the photographs on his desk and recognising the man even though only seeing them upside down.

LaRocca was surprised that she should be familiar with someone from so long ago. "You know him?" he asked.

"I know of him," she replied. "He was in all the papers. You must have seen them. I wouldn't have done it though, that's for sure."

"Done what?"

"Why, chased after that flying disc. That UFO thing."

"UFO?"

The woman shrugged. "I know the official explanation was that he died from oxygen starvation, but many people believe he was shot down by a ray gun or something, and it wasn't the only case that year."

"There were others?"

"Sure were!" This seemed to be something she was interested in. "Chiles and Whitted, said to be very experienced pilots, said they saw something big and round. Then there was a flier called Gorman, said it was like one of those wartime dogfights, and the UFO seemed to be toying with his aircraft. All in 1948, but Tom Mantell was only fatality."

"All very interesting," decided LaRocca, "but I don't think you came here to talk about flying saucers."

"No," she agreed. "Word has it you are trying to find Paul Townsend."

"Could be," said LaRocca, masking his interest.

"Then try *Café Society*."

"*Café Society*?"

"He's said to be a regular."

"What is this?" asked LaRocca, his tone hardening. "The only place with that name was in New York from the late 1930s to the early 1950s."

She held his gaze. "I don't know how you can say when it's going to close, but that is where you should look."

"Wrong city! Wrong country! Wrong time" he thundered angrily.

"Hey! Don't blame the messenger."

"Who sent you?" he demanded. "Was it Townsend himself?"

"Never heard of him before today," she said, backing towards the door. "Look, I was just doing a favour for a friend of a friend."

"And just who might—?" he started to ask, but she slipped swiftly through the office door and was gone from sight by the time he got there. Frustrated, LaRocca walked back into the room and looked again at the photos on his desk. Then brought his fist down heavily, scattering them in all directions.

Just what the heck was going on?

***

Townsend, frightened, struck out wildly, hitting nothing. There were no walls, no ceiling, no floor. Leaving him trapped, suspended in an awful limbo. Seeing nothing, feeling nothing, but audio sensibilities continued to function. He could still hear that damned radio.

Through the crackle and hiss of increasingly turbulent atmospherics, a voice kept breaking through. Sometimes rising, sometimes falling, but making itself heard.

"This is the control tower at Godman Air Force Base, Kentucky. Sergeant Blackwell calling the Air National Guard Flight Leader."

"I'm not him!" shouted Townsend.

"Come in, Flight Leader…"

"You've got the wrong man!"

"Come in, Flight Leader…"

"It isn't me!"

"This is the control tower at Godman Air Force Base, Kentucky. Sergeant Blackwell calling the Air National Guard Flight Leader."

Moving his arms and legs was like flailing through treacle. Whether or not he did manage to cover any distance he didn't know. But if he did, then that never ending entreaty moved with him.

"Come in Flight Leader…"

Was he dead?

Was this hell?

Could this monstrous existence be his eternal punishment? To listen to these same words repeated over and over again for the rest of time?

"Come in Flight Leader…"

Where the heck was LaRocca? What was keeping him? If this wasn't his personal damnation, then how difficult was he to find?

Townsend howled a wordless amalgamation of fear, frustration and anger, knowing that nothing he said or did made any difference. Damn you, LaRocca, he thought bitterly, when are going to start earning your corn? And the radio continued to crackle and hiss.

"This is the control tower at Godman Air Force Base, Kentucky. Sergeant Blackwell calling the Air National Guard Flight Leader."

***

Going through his desk drawers, LaRocca rummaged around until finding *Strange Fruit* by David Margolick, the story of the anti-lynching song, composed by Abel Meeropol and famously sung by Billie Holiday. The first time at Café Society, New York, in early 1939.

Meeropol, a white American Jew who wrote under the name Lewis Allen, was an unlikely composer of a song that became so totally associated with the black civil rights movement. Lady Day herself sometimes, though wrongly, claimed at least part authorship, and schoolteacher Meeropol became better remembered for adopting the two sons of executed spies Julius and Ethel Rosenberg.

All interesting stuff, and LaRocca remembered how impressed he had been when first reading the book. Settling himself as comfortably as his hard wooden chair allowed, he thumbed the pages, looking for specific references to the nightclub *Café Society*, and there were many. It had been one of the first fully integrated night spots in any of the United States. Maybe even the very first.

"But that was New York, America, back then," he muttered to himself, "not Plymouth, England, now."

Whoa, you Muppet! Why had he said that when he lived in Cardiff, Wales?

This whole case was weird, and getting weirder. The CD and cash. The unlived in apartment. The folder and photographs. The girl who had looked, spoken and acted as if part of a Forties-Fifties film noir. If he saw her again LaRocca would push a grapefruit into her face like Cagney did to Mae Clarke in *Public Enemy*. And now he was even mixing up which city he was in!

It was getting to him and suddenly he felt he had to get out, breathe fresh air, walk with people. Had to make sure just where he was, outside of his shabby office. The lift being out of order, again, he ran down the two flights of stairs to street level. Stepping out into Leeds he was immediately faced by a bright sign directly opposite. It no longer said *The Happy Coconut Bar*.

It said *Café Society*!

***

Dodging traffic, crossing the busy Glasgow road, he paid more attention to the building he was making for than the cars tooting their horns. Rehashing an obscure old club name did not seem all that clever. But, what the hell, someone was pushing him in this direction, and he was quite willing to go with the flow.

It was late afternoon, and the place not yet open for business, but a man was unlocking the door. "Hi," he said as LaRocca stopped beside him.

"Hello."

"You're early," The man laughed. "I haven't even got my rags on yet."

That was really taking historical data on board, realised LaRocca. He had read that the doormen dressed in rags and stood to one side and let the customers open the door for themselves. It was part of the quirkiness the place was known for. But back to business. "I'm looking for someone," he said.

"And who might that be?"

"Paul Townsend."

The man with the key laughed again. "You're a card, Mr Townsend. Looking for yourself! What next?"

"I'm not Townsend."

"Come on now. You've been a client here for years, Mr Townsend."

"Years? This place wasn't here yesterday. It was a bar, *The Happy Coconut Bar*. No doorman in rags. No music and entertainment. Just a bar for drinking, and my name is LaRocca. Martin LaRocca."

A third man had joined them now. "Hello Paul," he said with a nod to LaRocca, then turned to the other. "Any problems?"

"Not really, Mr Josephson. It's just Mr Townsend having a bit of fun, pretending to be someone else."

Josephson? The newcomer did indeed look just like a photo in the book *Strange Fruit*. A photograph of Barney Josephson, a former shoe salesman from New Jersey, proprietor of *Café Society*. But that was the 1940s. Not now!

"Hey," said Josephson, spreading his hands. "We take the stuffing out of stuffed shirts. It's the wrong place for the right people. We can stand a bit of fun."

"My name is LaRocca," he said again, loudly.

"Rocca! Bocca! Mocca!" exclaimed the man who had unlocked the door and was now holding it open. "Whatever name you want, Mr Townsend."

"I – am – Martin – LaRocca!"

"Sure, Paul," said a smiling Barney Josephson. Either him or the man who was his double. "Billie's touring just now, but we've got Lena Horne doing a spot tonight. Should be good."

This just couldn't be happening in downtown Bristol.

With a gargling sound at the back of his throat, LaRocca spun on his heels and started to run along the Belfast street. It was either madness or conspiracy, and he wanted no part of either. So he ran, past Big Ben, on and on through Manchester city centre. Until, gasping for breath and clutching at his shirt collar, he staggered to a halt in Halifax.

A big black hole spread out before him in the Haverfordwest pavement. With a cry that was partly fear and partly relief, LaRocca fell forward and into it.

***

Paul Townsend experienced no actual sense of movement but the voice of Sergeant Blackwell, and the crackling static it emerged from, was growing gradually fainter, moving away in a downward direction. Either the transmitter was dropping or he was rising. Not that it mattered who was going where, just as long as that series of calls kept fading. Just as long as it would finally stop.

Which it did, to his immense relief.

But if the voice had not dropped, then he must be rising. If so, where? And would it be to a place where that stumblebum LaRocca could finally find him? Private Investigator, he called himself. Well there would be no bonus payments for this case. Knucklehead!

***

LaRocca was falling in blackness. Expecting, at any time, to land in the fires of hell. The last thing he could remember was pulling up, panting, in Preston. Then diving into that spreading inky hole.

This was death. Had to be. A crowd would be gathering around his body as it lay on a cold Wrexham pavement.

"Is he dead?"

"Looks like it."

"Heart attack?"

"Probably."

Someone would have phoned the emergency services. An ambulance on its way. While all the time his awareness was spinning out of control. But it didn't somehow feel like being dead. Where were the bright lights? The long tunnel? Friends and loved ones waiting to greet him? The things he'd read about.

And why was he falling up?

A startled LaRocca suddenly realised the implications of his last thought. How was it that having dived head first into the blackest hole imaginable, he was now not falling at all.

LaRocca was rising!

***

Captain Thomas Francis Mantell Jr, a twenty-five year old Second World War veteran, said goodbye to his wife and children. Going to work as a Flight Leader with the Air National Guard was no hardship whatsoever. All he had ever wanted to do was fly so being able to pilot an aircraft on a daily basis was a dream come true.

Tom Mantell was, first and last, a flier.

***

The F-51 Mustang, designated P-51 prior to 1947, was generally considered the best piston-engined fighter developed in America. Now, thirty months after World War II had ended, main Air Force Units had been given jets, but the Mustang was still giving good service with the Air National Guard.

Of the four planes originally asked to investigate the usual sightings, one had been short on fuel and two were not equipped for flights to altitudes requiring oxygen. This left only the plane piloted by the Flight Leader to try and complete the mission.

When he reached a height of fifteen thousand feet, the pilot radioed: *"Object directly ahead and above and moving about half my speed."*

Then: *"It appears metallic and of tremendous size."*

A little later he radioed: *"I'm still climbing. Object is above and ahead, moving about my speed or faster. I'm trying to close for a better look."*

His final words were: *"My God! I see people in the thing!"*

The UFO beckoned, merging Earthbound concepts of time, place and identity. Ready to absorb. To accept or reject.

This was the stuff of dreams, of fantasy. Mythology in the making. The flier – Tom Mantell/Paul Townsend/Martin LaRocca – pointed the Mustang's nose upwards, and flew to his/their destiny.

PRISON

The fine drizzle seemed never ending. Sweeping down, blown this way then that by gusty winds. More than mist yet less than proper rain.

Aislewood tried to compress his body even deeper into the folds of an army topcoat. "I hate this drizzle," he muttered. "It gets in everywhere."

"What's 'at?" wheezed the old man.

"Nothing important," shouted Aislewood.

The old man grimaced. "Awful weather," he said conversationally.

They circled the Whip, turned left at the Coconut Shy, passed the Figure Eight and walked around the Wall of Death. As far as Aislewood was concerned, there was something both dismal and creepy about an empty and derelict fairground. But Watko liked it, and that was what counted.

"You sure you know where yer goin'?"

"Of course I do," Aislewood replied loudly. "Deaf old bastard," he added under his breath.

"Eh?"

"Nearly there."

"Good. I'm soaked to the skin."

Aislewood just shivered. He didn't like the drizzle and he didn't like the place. Watko did, and he probably liked the drizzle too. Bound to really, realised Aislewood with a flash of insight. Yes, Watko would definitely like it when it drizzled.

As they neared the Ghost Train, Aislewood whistled a few bars of "Knees Up Mother Brown". Watko considered it very much a fairground-like sort of tune and had insisted they adopt it as an approach signal.

Janet came out and stood by the pay desk. "Tickets please." She giggled as they filed past.

"Get stuffed," said Aislewood tiredly, causing the girl to giggle all the more.

"Station Master?" she yelled. "Passengers!"

Watko stumbled out through the doors into which the track led. "The two fifteen for Cardiff will leave platform three at five past ten," he boomed while waving a little red flag.

"Is he a nutter?" whispered the old man.

"Hear that?" Janet said. "He wants to know if you're a nutter."

"What a delightfully old fashioned turn of phrase," said Watko. "Nutter! I haven't heard that used in years."

"'Ere..." The old man turned to Aislewood. "Where've you brought me then?"

"To meet friends, like I told you. We'll have tea soon, and if you like it you can stay, rent free."

Watko strolled over and put his arm around the old man's shoulder. "All pals here, Pop. A great place to live, a derelict fairground. You'll see."

"Sounds barmy."

"Vanquish the bewilderment from your wrinkled brow. Once you see how well we live, you'll never want to leave."

The old man was not very convinced. He had just collected his old age pension when Aislewood had struck up a conversation. They left the Post Office together and sat for a while under the shelter of the Bandstand in a local park. Aislewood had spoken feelingly about the ostracizing of the aged by today's society. His sympathetic handling of the theme had soon broken down the other's embittered reserve. His grumpiness, long matured by years of lonely bed-sitter existence, melted away. As a drowning man grabs at a lifebelt so he clutched at this unexpected hint of companionship.

"I live with some friends," Aislewood had explained. "We have that much in common with you old timers. We want nothing more than to be allowed to live our lives in the way we see fit. But, because we don't conform to the accepted norm, society has cast us out. We are the present day lepers, and this is why we can see the tragedy age brings. We are able to appreciate your position because we share it."

The invitation to accompany this new friend had seemed a natural progression from the proceeding conversation. Meet the others, have some tea and, as a soul mate of sorts, maybe even move in with them. The old man could join their tiny community, living outside the chained bondage of an unfeeling way of life. Anything, at that moment, seemed preferable to returning to the solitary confinement of his dingy bed-sitter.

Now, however, instead of being concerned and involved, Aislewood appeared bored and distant. The old man felt let down. A previously offered friendship now seemed withdrawn and a sense of alienation substituted. He found himself now trapped within the confines of a derelict fairground. Surrounded by a bored man, a crazy man and a giggling girl.

The old man was beginning to regret his decision to come.

"Janet?" called Watko. Big, blonde Watko, with the face of a cherub and the body of a bull.

"Yes sir?" she said, then spluttered into ill-controlled laughter as if at a private joke.

"Where are we dining this evening?"

"I thought one of the Side Shows might be cosy."

"Which one?"

"The Fortune Teller's hut."

"Ah yes, our guest should like it there." Watko turned away from the girl. "See how difficult it was for me to get a direct answer from her?" he said to the old man. "I lack adult companionship, something you may be able to supply. You will be staying, won't you?"

"Eh?" The newcomer cupped his ear. "Will be what?"

"I said: You will be staying, won't you?" repeated Watko more loudly.

The old man scratched his bulbous nose. "But I haven't paid my landlady this week's rent yet."

Janet clung to Aislewood for support as a spasm of orgiastic laughter left her helpless. "He hasn't paid his rent." she said.

Aislewood shrugged her off. "Poor bastard," he muttered, more to himself than anyone else.

Watko patted the old man's shoulder and smiled down at him with a look that bordered upon affection. "No rent here, Pop," he told him. "But come, our tea awaits."

The three men sat around a green topped card table while Janet served the meal. Mugs of steaming tea, cheese and onion sandwiches and chocolate sponge.

The booth was small and only dimly lit, both factors helping to create an atmosphere of subtle intimacy. Bodily contact was impossible to avoid as Janet performed her waitress duties. And she, with a complete lack of pretence, sought such contact without favouritism. All three were subjected to bodily pressure as she squeezed past.

Watko seemed to ignore it while Aislewood appeared irritated. The old man, apparently the only one of the trio, experienced long forgotten desires he'd thought himself long since incapable of feeling.

They ate their fill and drank the hot, sweet tea.

"Isn't she goin' to have none?" asked the old man, indicating Janet.

"She has hers when she prepares the meal," replied Watko.

"Oh."

In the centre of the table, covered by a square of black satin, was a crystal ball. Janet sat down and fingered a corner of the material. "Anyone want more?" she asked.

Nobody did, so they lit cigarettes.

Watko exhaled noisily. "Plain ordinary fare, but plenty of it," he said. "That's the secret of true contentment."

"An occasional taste of caviar wouldn't upset my stomach," grumbled Aislewood.

"Those are the words of a troubled spirit. You spend your days not being at peace with the humdrum existence that is your lot, but in secret yearnings for that which lies beyond your allotted scope."

"Don't waste your cod psychology on me, Watko. I'm guilty of being human, which means I feel the usual jealousies and needs common to the species. There's a lot around, and I'm not getting my share."

"So speaks Man the Animal. What do you think, sir, as a relative newcomer to our circle? Should we desire that which we cannot have?"

"I don't know. I s'pose it's only natural to want." The old man remembered the reawakened feelings he had experienced as Janet squeezed against him while serving. "I did think 'at after all these years I was past things." He paused to glance at the girl. "But now I ain't so sure."

Watko surveyed his fingertips. "You feel that this perpetual want is what distinguishes man from the other animals. Is that what you're trying to say?"

"Something like that, I s'pose."

"A very profound viewpoint." Watko nodded wisely. "I can see you are going to add intellectual stature to our little group."

Aislewood pushed back his chair and stood up. "I'm going to catch a breath of fresh air," he muttered, and hurried out from the booth.

"What's up with 'im?"

"Take no notice," said Watko. "Aislewood is a mere philistine."

"I always thought he was British!" Another bout of laughter shook Janet from head to toe.

"Ignore the rabble," said Watko while removing the square of black satin from the glass ball. "Let us see what the future holds."

"I only ever 'ad my fortune told once," the old man said. "Back when I was a young feller."

"What happened?"

"Nothin' much, Mr Watko. The gypsy said I would make a pile, be rich as a King. The very next day I lost my job, and I've never seemed to get back on me feet ever since."

"While there's life, and all that. It still isn't too late for her words to achieve actuality. I have a certain flair for prophecy myself. Let's see what I can see. And, by the way, just plain Watko will suffice. We have no titles here."

"Right you are, Watko."

Outside, the drizzle had stopped at last. Aislewood stood by the Hoopla Stall and ground his cigarette under a heel. His tall sparse figure, merging with the falling dusk, stood silent while he studied the grotesque silhouettes that surrounded him in every direction.

"Pssst!"

Aislewood looked around quickly, startled as the sudden hiss interrupted his reverie. "Who is it?" he called, though he knew who it was likely to be.

A small shape detached itself from the shadows and moved towards him. "It's only me, Renfrew."

"Of course it is," said Aislewood, relaxing as the hunchback drew near.

"I failed again, as I nearly always do. No wonder Watko derides and abuses me. Just a miserable little creature of the night, is one of his kinder descriptions."

"You take too much notice of him."

"Not without good reason I assure you. If I were tall and straight things might be different, but as it is..." Renfrew shrugged. "But I notice even you do his bidding."

It was Aislewood's turn to shrug.

"But as I said," continued the hunchback, "I failed again, so have kept out of the way, waiting for darkness and the chance to catch you alone. Were you more successful than me? I hope so, for if not his anger will be such that I will have to hide all night and try again tomorrow."

"No need to hide," said Aislewood bitterly. "I did our master's bidding. An old chap I found in a Post Office."

"And Watko is satisfied?"

"He appears to be."

Renfrew performed a drunken dance of delight. "Well done, Aislewood," he said. "What's he like, this old chap of yours?"

"Just a typical pensioner. Going bald, wispy grey moustache, big nose, wire frame spectacles, face a mass of wrinkles."

"Anything else?" prompted Renfrew eagerly.

"He's all alone, lives in a bedsitter, and is deaf."

"Sounds just the job! Where is he now?"

"In the Fortune Teller's hut, with Watko and Janet."

Renfrew traced a finger around the outline of his own face. "Don't think I'll disturb them," he said.

"Do as you please," said Aislewood, turning away.

"Find some food and get some sleep. That's it. See you."

"So long then," mumbled Aislewood as the little hunchback scurried away in the direction of the Ghost Train.

After a few moments deep in thought, Aislewood strolled through the desolate area of past pleasure until he stopped beneath the lattice-like framework of the Figure Eight. From inside, etched against the darkening evening sky, it impressed as being part of a totally alien landscape. As he stood there, Watko sprang to mind. He could picture him, getting his kicks by mocking an old fool who lacked the wherewithal to realise it. No wonder he felt at home in this unused pleasure park, scene of long forgotten amusement. It presented a bizarre distortion of normal concepts that blended well with Watko's strange mentality.

And he himself, Aislewood, felt sickened for being a part of it. A member of the cast. One of the henchmen in Watko's kingdom of nightmare and fantasy. What had brought him here? And, more importantly, what made him stay?

Renfrew's reasons were simple. Here, his deformed body took on an obscene normality. He would probably stay even if the others left. The derelict fairground was as one with his derelict body.

Janet, on the other hand, did not appear specifically tied to this particular place. For her, it was a refuge from a mundane world that refused to accept her nonconformity, but any other refuge would do just as well. She tottered from one crisis to another, a victim to her own emotional extremes. Poor beautiful Janet.

Aislewood experienced the familiar tightening of throat and quickening of pulse that always accompanied thoughts of the girl. Her flowing auburn hair, elfin face and supple body. So beautiful and yet, by the standards of an uncaring society, so insane.

Could he too be involved in a form of escape? He had drifted unwittingly into Watko's realm and stayed, he'd always believed, because of Janet. Circumstances being what they were, he took her physically as was his due, but kept silent about the spiritual need he felt. One day things might be different, but for now Watko ruled.

But could it be that this in itself was just another elaborate hoax? One he perpetrated upon himself?

"Aislewood?"

At the sound of her voice he allowed the doubts and fears to recede into the corner of his mind that comprised their normal habitation. "Over here," he replied softly.

"Oh yes, I can see you now." She came across and stood alongside him. "You always come and stand here, under the Figure Eight, when you're moody. Especially on evenings when a new guest is present. Why is that?"

"It could be only habit, or it could be a private ritual."

"Make it a ritual," she said, clapping her hands excitedly. "Tell me what you mean."

"Well, it's like this," he told her, stroking his chin thoughtfully before taking her hand in his. "I feel that in our efforts to throw off the chains imposed by the society we seek to escape, we have done no more than substitute others in their place. For all our talk of freedom, we are trapped within the confines of the boundaries we ourselves create. This is something I feel at all times, but never so strongly as when a guest is here. Then the realisation overpowers me to such an extent that I am drawn to this place. I stand within this criss-cross structure and it personifies, for me, every manmade trap ever constructed. The whole damn world is a prison, and our derelict fairground is nothing more than a smaller one within the larger. But this, in these moments of acute depression, is my own personal prison, and I come here almost as an act of penance."

They were silent for a while.

Then, "I always knew you were a moody sort," said Janet, "but I never guessed it went this deep."

"Just shows how well we really know each other."

"Funny, the way different people react to the same situation. You are depressed by the old man's presence while I bubble over with joy. Not because of the reason for having him, that is only a by-product as far as I am concerned, but because it is what Watko wants."

Aislewood let go her hand, taking a backward step and feeling his stomach muscles twist violently. "What is Watko? Is he God?"

A hurt expression shadowed her small face. "Don't shout, Aislewood. Not you. He does, but not you."

He stood, clenching and unclenching his fists, staring up at the sweeping trajectory of rail above him. Starry pinpoints of light flickered amongst the maze of frail supports. He could almost hear it hum with life, flinching at screams of false fear emanating from past pleasure-seeking riders.

"Watko isn't God but he's all I've got for the moment. At

times I hate him, but I need his protection. I dread to think what would happen to me otherwise."

"Do you hate me too?" he asked harshly.

"No."

"So you hate him but not me, yet he has first call on you. Whatever I feel, if he beckons you break away and run to him."

"But of course." She was surprised that he didn't understand. "I might prefer you as a person. But you, Renfrew and myself are only set-up members. Watko runs things. His is the power, so his is the right."

"And if someone else took over?"

"Then I would transfer my allegiance to the new leader."

She came close to him then, fingers lifting his t-shirt and caressing the flesh beneath. "One of the reasons I rejoice in the arrival of someone like this old man of yours, is that Watko only wants to enjoy the newcomer's company. I am able to search you out with no fear of interruption."

Clinging together, they sank to the stony ground. "Replace him, Aislewood," Janet said. "Kill Watko and make me yours by choice."

The next day followed the usual pattern. Watko lauded the old man until the mid-day meal had been eaten, then told Janet to instruct their guest in the delights of the Tunnel of Love. The old man virtually drooled with anticipation as they left, while Janet seemed totally unconcerned at the task ahead.

Aislewood found himself suffering new depths of jealousy and anguish. For one wild moment, as they pair walked away hand in hand, he hovered upon the verge of challenging Watko there and then. Even defeat, and maybe death, seemed preferable to what he was going through.

But he held back and the moment was gone. Maybe even he,

Aislewood, was beginning to accept the mythology of Watko's supremacy. More suffering yet was required before a decisive step could be taken.

"Right," said Watko, once Janet and the old man were out of sight, "down to business."

"How's it going to be this time?" asked Renfrew.

"We haven't used the Coconut Shy in a long time."

"The Coconut Shy?" repeated the hunchback. "Yes, yes, yes!"

"What do you say, Aislewood?" asked Watko.

"It's your party," he replied.

Watko studied him thoughtfully. "I remember when I first came here," he said slowly. "I haven't always been Head Man you know. There were others here then, as there will be others in the future. I remember too, how it was with Janet in those days. Somewhere along the line we've lost what we had then. Inevitable, I suppose."

"That's your problem," snapped Aislewood.

"True," Watko said, nodding. "But for how long will it remain only mine? Just let me know when you can answer that. She's quite a girl, out Janet."

"I'll let you know," said Aislewood, turning away.

"Fair enough."

"The Coconut Shy then, is it?" butted in Renfrew.

"That's where I said," replied Watko.

It wasn't all that long before Janet and the old man returned. His eyes were glazed, his legs rubbery, and he didn't appear far from total exhaustion.

Renfrew tittered obscenely as the old fellow sat down heavily on the Ghost Train steps. Gulping air greedily, wheezing loudly with each lungful. "You were too much for him, Janet." The hunchback grinned. "Much too much, too much, too much!"

Both Janet and Watko laughed.

The old man looked up. "You did say I could stay, didn't you Watko?"

"Indeed I did."

"Well I'd like to. I really would."

"Then you shall, Pop." Watko went across and patted his shoulder. "There is a little initiation ceremony we perform. How about right now?"

The old man beamed with pleasure. "As long as it won't take too much puff," he said with a cracked laugh.

"Not for you, Pop, I promise." Watko led the way to the Coconut Shy.

The old man, though a little surprised, allowed Renfrew to bind his feet together and his hands behind his back. He started to get nervous, though, when they knelt him behind one of the coconut holders, placed his chin in the cup, and tied him to it.

"What's all this then, eh?" he asked worriedly.

Then he started to scream.

Watko's first two balls missed, but the third shattered the old man's wire framed spectacles. Broken glass lacerated his tired flesh while a ruined eye dripped down his face. Watko's first hit was the signal for the others to join the game. Renfrew squeaked hysterically, but missed more often than hit, while Watko himself exhibited no more than an average sort of ability. Janet though, threw with an apparently wild abandon, as if a demonic bloodlust had her in its grip. But her aim was deadly and true, nearly every wooden ball she threw striking home.

The last of the four to actually throw a ball was Aislewood, and his first few were purposefully cast wide. He wanted to turn and run, get away from this mad place for ever. To find a quiet corner and vomit.

He wanted to, but he didn't. Instead, the wrecked and dehumanised face drew him hypnotically. His aim improved, to hit the target, and as the balls did so he started to throw faster and faster.

Then, suddenly, it was Watko's face he could see resting in the cup, blood spurting with every missile that smashed it. Watko who had been tied, bound and executed. And Aislewood exulted as he threw with as much force as he could muster.

Watko! Watko! Watko!

Kill! Kill! Kill!

Kill Watko! Kill Watko! Kill Watko!

And all the time not one of them spoke. Nothing could be heard but their heavy breathing, inarticulate grunts, and the thud of the balls.

Aislewood wasn't even aware that tears were streaming down his face.

REMNANTS

Mallard hid behind a stunted tree that overlooked the snow-covered beach. His breath frosting, his hands clenched with cold. It was pure chance that he should have come across Crompton in this way, but since he had, he would watch. Whatever was interesting the other might well interest him. So he hid, and waited, and watched.

Crompton had found a large black box. For fifteen minutes it had foiled his every attempt at forcing the lid, and the rising tide was lapping at it hungrily. Soon the water would reclaim what it had earlier relinquished.

With what seemed to Mallard to be every ounce of his energy, Crompton dragged the box beyond the zone of freezing sand and up to the snowline. His lips were twisting and it was obvious to the watcher that the man was cursing volubly. Icy cold wind blew off the sea and Mallard huddled up as he peered through the trembling branches of the tree. The light growing worse as dusk approached. Already the huge red sun was gone and the twin moons were skating into the north-eastern sky.

Still the box would not open. Then suddenly Crompton's frustration erupted into a vicious kick as he swung his foot at the cause of his anger.

Whether his foot had activated a hidden mechanism or whether a sharp blow anywhere was designed to trigger the thing wasn't obvious. All Mallard knew was that as Crompton's foot had landed an almighty explosion had blown both man and box into a zillion fragments.

All that remained was a sandy crater which rapidly filled

with water as the tide rose.

Mallard turned from the beach and headed inland. He felt no sorrow at the man's death. Surprise, yes, but nothing more. In all probability he and Crompton might well have clashed, sooner or later. That was the way of things. Hardy had saved him the trouble, for Mallard thought he could recognise Hardy's handiwork in the booby-trap. The power source from the wrecked ship, useless outside the ship and highly dangerous. A very effective mine. The initial cold knot of fear faded from his stomach as he realised it did not necessarily mean Hardy was armed. Not with conventional weapons anyway. Mallard knew that.

He strode along at a steady loping pace. His feet sinking noisily into the crisp new snow. All around him the land was white. White and still. Not a sound other than the sighing of the winter breeze. The dusk-light made it look like Christmas Eve in New England.

He stopped suddenly as a thought occurred to him and refused to go away. If only he could one day catch Hardy like that. He nodded to himself, smiling slightly at the thought of seeing that one die. He would dance and sing on that occasion. He could even set out to find the others, those that remained. Put an end to the conflicts once and for all.

If Hardy could be killed.

If…

Though he walked on, the thought refused to return to the back of his mind. Daniel Hardy, the man in possession. Mallard pushed on through the beachside forest. His breath a cloud of white. His eyes almost shut against the cold of winter. Hardy! The name, the man, stuck in his mind. Crompton had been no more than a potential rival whose removal was no more than an inconvenience struck from Mallard's list. But Daniel Hardy was something else. Another colour of the spectrum entirely. Apart from being the most dangerous individual of them all, he held the key to making life at least partially bearable on this godforsaken world. He had what the rest of them wanted. What at least six men had died trying to gain.

Hardy had the women.

The only women on the whole damned planet.

Emerging from the trees, Mallard stopped and regarded the raised township in which he lived. Out of the corner of his eye he could see the graves where he had buried Addler and Li Chan, the only ones he, himself, had so far killed. And because of nothing more serious than a squabble over food. But food had been more important back in the early days of the "colonisation".

The winter then had been ten times as strong as now, at the time they had crash landed. Now, spring was slowly approaching and edibles were growing but back then their pitiful rations were like gold. They had stripped the ship of everything remotely useful, then slowly they drifted apart. Hardy had already gone, taking the two surviving girls with him. In those early days, food and shelter had been more important than sex. Now though, with food becoming less of a problem, the idea of female company became more and more desirable.

Mallard grinned wryly as he walked to his stronghold. The utter silence of this deserted world was no longer as depressing as when they first arrived. Now it was a godsend. It made the house in which Mallard lived a virtual fortress. For none could approach without sound and the silence made it easier to hear.

Mallardville, he called the place, living in a tree-house

surrounded by the natural ruins of the native township. The tree grew in a place where once a village green might have been situated, and he felt reasonably secure in the structure he had built up amongst the branches. Though he had searched far and wide, nothing had ever been found to give any clues about the former inhabitants. The place had been without animal life for what appeared to be thousands of Earth years.

The ruins were booby-trapped and he lived up a tree. Mallard felt as safe as was possible.

Snow-blasted and frozen by a terrible winter, which they had calculated before the crash to have lasted for three hundred Earth years. It was at least fortunate that they had arrived at its end and not the beginning.

After swallowing a vitamin concentrate from his dwindling supply, Mallard heated what he called vegetable soup. Though selecting what he thought might be vegetables was a matter of trial and error. Some tasted too vile to ever try again, but at least he had not poisoned himself yet. Later he would chew on a few berries.

"Spring will be better," he said aloud, between mouthfuls

***

Much time had passed since he'd seen Crompton die in the explosion. How much he wasn't sure. Time no longer had any significance for Mallard and he kept no calendar. But one important change had taken place. He was no longer alone.

Vasily Chukovsky squatted across from him. Unsure, unhappy, but ready to trust the older man for the sake of companionship.

"It's good to talk to another person," the Russian said. "The solitude was driving me crazy." The slight accent in his voice rankled Mallard a little. It always had. He would have preferred the Russian's use of English to have been guttural and barely understandable.

Chukovsky had approached Mallarville openly, under a white flag of truce. Mallard's first intention had been to kill him. Honour and rules were gone. A part of a past that existed only in brief, soon forgotten memories. The man's white flag was an anachronism, but curiosity had won. He had wondered what it would be like to experience again a contact with a fellow human being.

"You know," said Chukovsky, while eating the vegetable stew Mallard had offered him, "we should never have split up. We should not have let things go the way they did, huh? Communal life would have given us more … more stability, more purpose."

Mallard laughed bitterly, inching closer to the fire in the middle of the floor. "Purpose," he exclaimed. "We had no purpose other than to survive the terrible conditions we found here. Communal existence can never work when each is thinking only of how to stay alive." He threw another log onto the fire. "We had no group purpose, Vasily. Not ever. The split was inevitable."

Chukovsky finished eating, wiping his mouth with the back of his hand. "That is just defeatism, Mal. You always were a defeatist. Even before things went wrong."

"Well, isn't that what we are? Defeated?"

Chukovsky shrugged. "I don't know, Mal. I used to think that at least we had a chance. But now, sometimes, I feel we are at the dying end of something once great but now slipping into oblivion. Defeated? Yes, I suppose we are, and we definitely are if we accept it. One man cannot win, nor just two. But all of us, fighting together. We could win this world." His face was tense, drawn, a half shadow in the light of the fire. He looked old, wasted. The body was aging faster than the man within. That was the way with them all. "Mal, spring is coming. The winter, all the hardships, they're ending. Surely you cannot acknowledge defeat. Not now, surely."

Mallard saw the tears in his eyes and felt immediately helpless. Chukovsky was right though. They could be more than the remnants of a failed expedition. They could survive, and even thrive. Winter was ending and a hundred-year spring cycle was about to begin. They could live out their lives in sunshine.

"But we need…!" He dropped his voice as he realised he was shouting. "For there to be a proper future, Vasily, we need the women. And how do we get them, eh? Just walk and say, 'Hello Mr Hardy, we want the two girls to take part in a breeding programme'? In the first place, we don't even know where they are, and secondly…" He paused at the memory of the broken bodies of those who had challenged Hardy's right to the women. Bones broken and faces black with strangulation. And within those dead faces: something, an expression, a look of utter desperation. As if they had come within touching distance of that which they had been willing to risk death for. Then Hardy had vanished, and with him went the only hope for a colony. "And secondly, we would have to get past Hardy."

"I was always more than a little afraid of that man," murmured Chukovsky. "Maybe we could reason with him, Mal. Maybe he would see the sense in reforming as a group."

"Reason with Daniel Hardy?" Mallard snorted derisively. "He killed to get the women and he killed to keep them. Our only hope would be for him to die in his turn. And are you and I men enough for that? Could we find and then kill the son-of-a-bitch? Easily said, Vasily."

"But not so easily done," added Chukovsky, completing the thought.

They both sat there, leaning forward into the light of the dying fire. "Those women, we need them badly, huh?" Chukovsky spoke softly, looking down at his hands. "There can be no possibility of creating a colony without them?"

"None that I can see, and time is not on our side. Look at me, Vasily. Really look at me. How old do I look, eh?"

"You look old, Mal."

"Yes, I'm old, and weak. And so are you. Yet in terms of age I should be in my prime and you are merely a youngster. This planet is aging us, and that includes the women. If we are going to establish a proper base, if we are going to provide future generations to take on and conquer this world... Then we had better get started."

He threw more logs onto the fire. Spring wasn't here yet.

Chukovsky nodded. "I guess we had better get cracking, huh?"

"I guess so," said Mallard quietly.

***

More time passed and as it did, so grew Mallard's realisation of just how lonely an existence he had led before Vasily Chukovsky had joined him. Together they embarked upon a series of scouting trips which took them far and wide in their search for Daniel Hardy. The two men rarely took part in long conversations but gradually he built a picture of Chukovsky's life before he had turned up at Mallardville.

Unlike those who had opted to strike out alone, the Russian sought company, teaming up with Ricardo Parsonage, the youngest spacer on the crew. Someone ill-equipped to deal with the horrendous situation circumstances had thrown them into.

They had trudged far before making a base in the wind-swept ruins of what might have been a farmhouse, being the only building in a bleak and desperate valley.

Parsonage, in spite of Chukovsky's best efforts, was in both mental and physical decline from the outset. Having convinced himself that they had been at the forefront of a major Earth force, he spent his time scanning the heavens for signs of the ships that would rescue them. Right up until the time he slipped into an unconsciousness from which he would never awaken, Parsonage believed that they would be saved.

Unable to face life there without his friend, Chukovsky buried him then left, becoming a wanderer. Mallard had been the second former crewmate he had found. The first had thrown rocks from behind cover and had not let him get close enough to even talk. He wasn't able to find out who it had been. So he had decided upon the white flag of truce plan when he stumbled upon Mallardville

"Poor Ricardo, he died of a broken heart," said Chukovsky as they trekked through the melting snow and ice-fields near the valley where he had lived with Parsonage. "Hoping against hope. Really believing that Earth would send a rescue party."

"Well why not?" Mallard was tired and grumpy. Not in the best mood for idle chitchat. "I don't mean specifically to save us. But why shouldn't someone come to check out this planet?"

Vasily Chukovsky was silent for a long moment. His breath came in clouds. His goggles reflecting the light of the large red sun that was now halfway to zenith. "Why would they come, Mal? Why would they come *again* to somewhere they have *already been*, huh?"

"What do you mean?" Mallard thrust a menacing expression in the Russian's direction. "I've never let it become the all-consuming focal point of my existence the way Parsonage did. But hey, haven't all of us got a little hope at the back of our brains that another ship might show up here?"

Chukovsky unslung the home made bow he carried and fingered it thoughtfully. "Did it never occur to you that the ruins we find are not the remains of a lost civilisation? That they might be the decayed remnants of a failed human colony?"

Mallard shook his head vigorously. "No! Never! It can't be…" But now that he thought about it, he could see how terrestrial were the buildings' design. Even the township layouts. "But they're primitive," he said, as much to himself as his companion. "I thought that Earth colonies would be … I don't know … more advanced, aesthetically modern. Do you follow me?"

"It's only a theory, Mal, but I am convinced by it. They arrived in summer or autumn, not knowing what weather was to come. They quarried the rocks of the valleys and built their houses out of grey stone and the wood from the forests. True pioneers. Huh? But they, or their children, or their children's children, were not prepared for the winter. And they perished."

"But it's only a theory."

"Yes, but it fits. For me, anyway. And it doesn't alter our plans. We won't see the next winter, thank goodness. But if there are to be descendants, they will be prepared. This time."

Carrying on their trek in silence now, Mallard tried to assimilate his reactions to Chukovsky's words. They came to the top of a rise, both finding it heavy going, with the effort of struggling through the soft underfoot, and looked down into the valley.

It was green!

They both gasped with surprise, Chukovsky on the verge of

tears. The valley was a beautiful vista of leaf-covered trees and sparkling brooks. The water would be icy, the ground hard as steel, but the valley was alive. And in the middle, a ruin. The grey-bricked building where the Russian had lived with Parsonage. Tumble-down and shattered, but somehow less sinister than the snow covered townships beyond the vale.

"Look! There!" Chukovsky pointed and Mallard saw a blue flag fluttering free from the ruin. A ragged banner that had marked his previous occupation. "I thought it would have blown down by now."

They stared down at the now more friendly ghost-dwelling, and the green slopes of the valley walls. At the waving trees and sparkling water. They stared for a long time and a new hope began to stir within their hearts. The valley must have been a heat trap. Winter left early and probably came late. Here, between the towering walls of the glacial channel, here the winter would be the shortest.

Mallard looked up into the sky, screwing his eyes behind the goggles as he looked into the glare of the late winter sun. "Spring is coming," he said. "Spring is coming."

After a while they turned and began the long hike back to Mallardville. Next time they came they would bring what they needed and stay. Neither man had said a word, but both were thinking precisely that.

And then, on a planned detour during the return journey, they found what they were looking for. Closer to the valley than Mallardville, which made their move to the former even more of a necessity, their days of careful searching were finally rewarded. They had found the stronghold of Daniel Hardy.

He had established his base amongst a small cluttering of buildings on a solitary hillock. The surrounding ground was flat, still under a cloak of snow, and with very little cover. It was well booby-trapped, though, and only Mallard's skill in the art of survival enabled them to retreat undiscovered. He had spotted a disguised pit only moments before Chekovsky was about to step into it and a careful search had revealed an intricate series of tripwires and traps which almost certainly encircled the whole hillock. Though there was no sign of life, Mallard knew without doubt that this would be Hardy's doing. He had set up some defences back at Mallardville. Nothing as good as this, but he'd not had anything valuable to protect. Hardy had the women.

They carefully swept snow into their footprints and settled to wait under the cover of a small group of stunted trees a reasonable distance from the stronghold. An hour's patient watching finally paid dividends with a glimpse of the man himself. High, looking down from his citadel, within the circle of tripwires and traps. Probably on a tour of inspection.

The brief glimpse had been enough. It was Hardy all right. A big brute of a man. The man in possession. Up there, hidden and guarded so well, were the only two women alive on this whole crumbling world.

***

Back in the relative safety of Mallardville, sorting what they could reasonably take with them for their switch to the valley, Vasily Chukovsky was visibly elated while Mallard remained silent and withdrawn, seeming not to notice his friend's high spirits.

"What are they? Early thirties?" Chukovsky was saying. "Still young enough for conception. If we can just get them to the valley we will be able to get a colony started. I know it."

Mallard watched him, taking in the white hair and heavily

wrinkled skin. The Russian's hands shook visibly. Whatever his true age, he was old. "What if they've aged like us?" he asked. "What if they're old hags?"

Chukovsky laughed. "Well they've got no competition," he replied. "We can't be choosy can we, huh?" He stopped packing his rucksack and shrugged, his eyes narrowing. "We'll have to find the others, those who've survived. As many as we can. Make our own small start on the necessary population increase. The colony will need numbers in preparation for the next winter." He looked at Mallard. "This is our purpose, Mal. Don't you see? A reason for living."

"Of course I see," he snapped, then continued more calmly. "I've got a dream, Vasily. Deeply buried and sometimes almost forgotten, but not quite—"

"Dreams!" interrupted Chukovsky. "What are you Mal? A mystic? This is a time for practical issues, not dreams. Either we attack Hardy and win the women for ourselves…" his hand swept down to strike his own thigh with a hard slap, "…or we don't!"

There was a long silence, broken finally by Mallard. "From the moment we awoke on board ship with the warning sirens ringing," he said softly, remembering, "from the moment we realised what sort of trouble we were in, Hardy took command. Even though there were more senior crew members amongst the survivors. After the crash we seemed, I don't know … to lose interest in anyone or anything bar ourselves."

"Our big mistake," said Chukovsky.

Mallard nodded. "We let Hardy keep the control he'd assumed without so much as an argument." He paused, his face alive with the flickering flame from the fire. "And by the time others got around to wanting their share of the girls, he was ready…" He trailed off, once again remembering the futile attempt to oust Hardy from his position of power. The dead men who had tried. And the next day Hardy and the women were gone. Soon after, Mallard himself set off from the wreck and struck out on his own.

"Time has not softened the memory of Hardy's murderous brutality," he continued. "But I always felt that the time would come when our paths would cross again and I would have to make up for not joining that initial attack on him. My involvement might have been sufficient to swing things against him." He looked sharply at Chukovsky. "It seems that time has come. Two of us, working to a plan, might succeed. But Hardy is an animal and there won't be any mercy shown. If we fail, we die."

"You think I don't know that?"

"I think we all, in the beginning at least, shared the hope that another expedition from Earth would find us. Too much so for Parsonage, but I have kept that hope at the back of my mind. It's a dream that has helped me survive. Even now Vasily, although I accept the possibility of your theory, I cannot dispense with it entirely."

"Oh I do understand, Mal," said Chukovsky. "I'm not all Russian practicality. We all use whatever we need to get us through the day. But until it actually happens, a dream is just a dream. Huh? We can't wait for an off chance."

"Just me being moody, I guess." Mallard returned to packing gear into his rucksack. "Trying to verbalise but not knowing the right words, eh. I want those women too, Vasily. Whatever they're like now. Having located them, I know we have to try."

Outside the tree house the wind whipped up strongly and the fire burned low and fierce. The flames dancing violently and licking upwards through the suddenly swirling ash. It was snowing again. Winter having a final fling. Chukovsky hoped that Mallard's spirits would rise when they returned to the greenery of the valley. "We could both be right, Mal," he said. "Even if the ruins are what's left of a failed human colony. That doesn't mean that another expedition won't come this way. But we can't simply wait and see. We have to proceed as planned."

"And we will. Take no notice of me and my moods. We'll set out for the valley in the morning."

Alone, neither would stand a chance against Hardy. Especially the Russian geologist. Not that Mallard, who had adapted to the physical hardships more successfully, would have had better prospects in a one-to-one face-off, either. Hardy might no longer be the killing machine who had seen off his challengers before disappearing, but they had regressed too. Everything was relative. Their only advantages would be surprise and stealth. Together they would have to outwit him.

If only they were better armed. The few weapons that survived the crash were all laser based and were rendered useless when the power faded and they had no means of recharging them. The homemade bow that Chukovsky carried was poorly constructed and inaccurate over any sort of distance; a psychological prop rather than a practical aid. Mallard carried a cudgel, but would need to be close to use it.

Brain over brawn was their only chance. Careful planning and the nerve to carry it out.

***

After moving their main base to the valley, they set up a camp where they were hidden by the stunted trees at the edge of the open ground that surrounded Hardy's stronghold. He was, their spying revealed, very much governed by a regular routine.

Regular inspections of his hillock perimeters were carried out like clockwork at specific intervals.

They were soon confident enough to take advantage of snow showers, to obliterate their movements, to scout the lower part of the hillock nearest them when they knew him to be on the opposite side. This way Mallard mapped the booby-traps and they built up a plan based on his movements. Since Hardy showed no sign of being aware of their presence, surprise remained their biggest advantage.

"It's strange," remarked Chukovsky, just after viewing one of Hardy's anticipated appearances at one of his vantage points, "the way he keeps it up. Round and round with a regularity that borders upon obsession."

"Don't knock it," said Mallard. "Just pray that he doesn't change his routine the moment we make our move."

"I think not," said Chukovsky, looking up at the fence-like structure Hardy had built around the hillock, creating a sort of compound. "The veneer of civilisation may be tarnished, but even with a man like him it can never be completely erased. Huh! He has set a certain semblance of order for his day-by-day life and will stick to it, come what may."

Mallard just grunted. The reasons for Hardy's action were of little interest, only their physical reality. One point had struck him though. "We've not seen a single glimpse of the women," he remarked.

"Which would suggest Hardy keeps them shut away."

"Which in turn suggests they are not with him willingly."

Chukovsky laughed. "And if we extrapolate one more time, we could be greeted as their saviours."

Even Mallard grinned at this extravagant line of reasoning. "Which if true would make things a lot easier for us." He clapped the Russian on the shoulder. "But we'd better not depend on it, Vasily."

One particular section of the hillock was more densely scattered with traps than the rest and they had pondered long over possible reasons. It could be pure coincidence. But it could mark the weakest point in the stronghold above. In the hope that the latter might prove correct it was up this section they had decided to advance when the attack took place.

The lower half of the hillock offered no problems. They knew every trap and tripwire. The higher stretch would be more difficult since their knowledge was sketchy. Mallard was confident enough in his own ability to find a route to the top. It was what they would find beyond the traps that bothered him. Apart from knowing that what looked like the ruins of a house and two out buildings within the ramshackle fence, the internal layout could only be guessed at. They would have to play it by ear.

Chukovsky tested the tension of his bowstring, shaking his head at the crudeness of the weapon. "If only the armoury hadn't exploded during the crash landing," he muttered.

Mallard shook his head. "If the armoury hadn't been destroyed then Hardy would be armed as well. He might even have taken all the weapons. It's better this way."

"Maybe." The Russian would still have preferred a hand held missile blaster to the poorly made bow and arrows he carried. He gave Mallard a sideways glance. "A lot of work went into fencing the hillock and booby-trapping the slopes. Sometimes I wonder if he had help. If there are more than just Hardy and the two women up there."

Mallard shrugged. "It's a possibility, and if there are other men then we don't stand a chance, but I don't think there are.

Maybe he did solicit help, but even if he did I doubt that there are more than three living people up there. Hardy wouldn't have been colony building. He just wanted everything for himself."

Chukovsky was getting edgy and Mallard knew there was nothing to be gained from postponing the first phase any longer. The women were up there. Waiting. It was time to go and get them. "We'll go tonight, Vasily. Not a practise, we've done enough of those. The real thing, tonight."

"Tonight," echoed the Russian.

***

Following Mallard's example, Chukovsky tied his sleeping roll around his waist and secured his hefty club, along with his arrows, further round his belt. Dusk was approaching when they left the valley and was closing rapidly as they reached their main observation post amongst the bedraggled trees. This, they concluded from many days and nights of watching, was when Hardy rested. This was the longest period between his obsessional tours of inspection. White coloured over-suits blending well with the crisp snow, they left their hiding place and started up the slope.

Mallard led the way confidently. This part at least had been well planned. They crawled on all fours. Rising to step over some tripwires and squirming under others. Squeezing past one trap then circling round the next.

As they climbed so the twin moons rose above the horizon, setting the white snows alive with stark flames. Shadows became more solid and the trail the two men left became a black tracer leading back to the trees. No need to cover their tracks this time. The slope was becoming steeper now. Hardy's stronghold a dark and sinister monolith waiting above them. The two men continued to climb.

The initial familiar section posed no real problems. They knew it well enough and made good time. When they reached higher than they had previously been able to probe, their speed lessened. But there was nothing new. The traps were similar in design and distribution. Hardy was not an imaginative man. At one stage Chukovsky, careless in the mix of fear and anticipation running in his blood, pushed ahead and almost fell into a concealed pit. Mallard spotted it in time to pull him back, signalling angrily for the Russian to stay behind him.

Finally, stepping over a last wire, they reached flat ground. Phase one completed. Seen up close, the construction the two men had referred to as a fence was much more impressive than the name implied. A mixture of wood, rock, and bricks taken from the ruins. It was a defensive wall that drew a gasp of begrudged admiration from Mallard. The work that must have been put into its construction was amazing.

"He must have had help," whispered Chukovsky.

"Don't start that again," hissed back Mallard.

As indicated by the increased number of traps below, a portion of the wall here had collapsed somewhat and would be more easily breached than elsewhere. Wrapping up tightly, the two men settled down to wait out what was left of the night. They would have to move quickly then, better able to see the lay of the land, before Hardy rose to make his first circular inspection.

There was a lot of material strewn around the breach, they saw as the light improved. Hardy had obviously been trying to shore it up. Was either still trying or had given it up. Slowly, with great care, they picked a way through the rubble of the fallen barricade. As they did, a sudden noise like distant thunder echoed from behind them.

"What the devil was that?" Mallard asked softly as both men turned to look.

"I don't know," replied Chukovsky, "but it seemed to come from the direction of the valley."

The sound died away and there was nothing to be seen anyway. "It might have been a rock fall," murmured Mallard. They both turned back towards the compound, hoping that Hardy had not been disturbed, but everything remained as before so they continued to cross into the compound.

As well as the ruins they had made out from below, there were also a number of closely grouped huts which had not been visible. "Look there: those huts!" Chukovsky's voice betrayed panic. "I told you he must have had help!"

Mallard glared at him, eyes narrow and fierce behind the snow goggles. "One or twenty, it doesn't matter now," he snarled. "We knew failure was a possibility, didn't we?"

"I guess," said Chukovsky hesitantly. "How are we going to do it, Mal?"

"Take these huts, or cabins, or whatever they are, one at a time. If we find the women, try to keep them quiet. If we find Hardy, or any other man, swing our clubs like crazy." The place was still silent. "Best get started while they appear to still be asleep."

Reaching the first hut, Mallard whispered some instructions. Nodding agreement, Chukovsky unslung his bow, standing a little back from the building, and nocked an arrow. He aimed for the centre of the door.

Placing himself to the side, Mallard reached with his club until it was touching the rough wooden entrance. Then, taking a deep breath, he pushed.

The noise was deafening as what sounded like empty cans

toppled and fell.

"It's a trap," shouted Mallard as the clatter echoed through the compound. And he realised just how well they had been tricked. "He is on his own Vasily," he shouted. "These are all traps." There were no others here. Just big Daniel Hardy and the two women. "It's us against him. We can still win."

"Behind you," screamed Chukovsky hysterically.

Turning quickly, Mallard saw the shadowy figure bearing down on him through the emerging dawn. He lifted his club, ready to strike, but a rock struck him firmly on the chest.

"Shoot, Vasily," he managed to gasp as he hit the ground, and heard the twang as the Russian fired, but missed.

"Your club, Mal. Pick up your club," yelled Chukovsky, backing off.

Mallard did so, scrambling to his feet just in time to throw himself to one side. The lumbering figure of Hardy, bellowing like an angry bull, thundered past, unable to stop. Mallard was able to get in one blow to Hardy's back to help him on his way.

By the time Hardy staggered to a halt and turned, Mallard was gone. But Chukovsky was still there, like a rabbit caught in a flashlight. Managing to act in spite of his terrible fear, he fired off another arrow which hit Hardy's left thigh. But the man just pulled it out and threw it away. Treating it as no more than an irritant.

As Hardy charged in his direction, the Russian turned and ran.

I should have known Vasily would freeze, thought Mallard angrily from where he hid in a gap between two of the huts. Too late to worry about that now though. Survival was all that counted. Maybe he could sneak away while Hardy was occupied with Chukovsky. Carefully, trying to make no noise, he stepped into the open. But suddenly froze.

Had he just heard a whimper? A cry? Yes, there it was again. A high-pitched moan coming from the hut behind him. Mallard had found the women!

In a way this was an unwanted complication. Alone he had a chance of escape, but with two women along the odds in his favour decreased considerably. Mallard thought back to their training days on Earth. He'd been very attracted to Yeoman Alice Tsonga. Had even hoped that they might've paired up after an eventual planet-fall. And Alice had been one of the two female survivors.

Damn the odds!

The door to this hut, unlike the one he'd tried earlier, had three bars across the door. So Hardy kept them locked in. Which was good because they would almost certainly welcome freedom. Working as quietly as he could he removed two of the bars and was just reaching for the third when a roar made him spin around.

Hardy was standing no more than ten paces away.

For a moment the two men were motionless. Hardy, in the growing light of the new day, was a grotesque sight. Wild and white hair and beard framed a face that looked more animal than human. A damaged face with one eye missing, the empty socket criss-crossed with deeply etched scratch-like scars. He was still big. Still powerful. But his face was that of someone twice his actual forty-odd years of age.

Mallard took all this in, then dived for the club he'd put down when tackling the door. But Hardy was on him before he could straighten, lifting Mallard high and then throwing him.

Down he crashed, the force of his landing knocking every bit of breath from his body. Gasping painfully he managed to stand. Only to be hit back down by a savage punch to the face. Lying in a heap, Mallard knew he was finished. He would stand again, if he could, and was trying hard to push himself upright. But he knew it was a fight he could not win. And to lose meant only one outcome.

Hardy advanced. Stood over him, growling deep in his throat, but paused when a sound of mechanical thunder, similar to that heard by Mallard and Chukovsky earlier, broke the silence.

Then: "Here, Hardy! Take that! Huh." The Russian's first blow bounced off the side of Hardy's head; he was able to club him twice more before a backhand blow sent him sprawling. Hardy, nonplussed, was slow to react, allowing them both time to regain their feet. This was the way Mallard had planned it in his mind. The two of them, circling. Whichever one Hardy moved for, the other could get in some blows. But even like this, with Hardy seemingly immune to the damage being done to him, they were tiring quicker than him. The tactics were right. Had offered their best chance of success. But Daniel Hardy was not like other men.

Chukovsky slipped then, trying to evade a lunge, and Hardy was on him like a flash. Mallard rushed forward to try and draw him off but was floored by a punch while Vasily was still being held with his other arm. As he struggled to rise he could see his friend was caught in a ferocious bear-hug, having his life squeezed from him.

The women, thought Mallard. If they were free Hardy would have them to contend with them too, and they might well be more important to him. Why hadn't he have thought of that sooner?

But first there was Chukovsky to help. Vasily, his friend,

who had overcome his blind terror to come back to help him. Who was being slowly squeezed to death. Instead of going for the head, which hadn't seemed to work, Mallard smashed Hardy's kneecaps, hearing bones crack. Hardy toppled over and Vasily rolled free, gasping for air and spitting blood. But Mallard was tangled with Hardy on the ground.

"Let the women out," he shouted at the Russian. "The hut behind you. Let them out!" Then Hardy had him in an iron grip and he was fighting for his life.

But Chukovsky had grasped what had been yelled. Staggering to the hut in question, he removed the last bar. The door swung open and two creatures rushed out. Matted hair, drooling mouths, imbecilic eyes, making strange and unintelligible cat-like noises. Chukovsky fell back with a strangled cry of horror as he saw what the two women had become. And the stench coming from the open doorway made him retch. But he braved the inside when spotting a potential weapon. A pole with a sharpened end, which maybe they had fashioned to use against Hardy.

Meanwhile Mallard, involved in a losing struggle for survival, was suddenly cast aside as the two screaming and mewing monstrosities threw themselves at Hardy. Mallard scrambled to his knees, watching with a horrible fascination as they attacked with manic venom. Seeing them clawing at his one good eye.

Hardy, his guttural screams joining with their high-pitched whines, grabbed the one who had been Yeoman Alice Tsonga by her scrawny neck, ruining her throat. As he tossed her body to one side the other, having concluded her grisly business with his eye, leapt away. Running and shrieking until out of sight and hearing.

Hardy, though bloodied and blinded, could still hear and followed the sound of Mallard's laboured breathing to reach again for one of those who had brought this calamity upon him.

"Get up Mal! Move," shouted Chukovsky.

But Mallard was too slow and beaten to even dodge the waving arms of a blind man. Hardy had him, circling his throat as he sought to strangle him as he had Alice. Then, again, came the thundering metal-on-metal noises they had heard before. Even louder this time. Hardy, bemused, paused momentarily, cocking his head in the direction of the strange sounds and giving Chukovsky sufficient time to act.

The Russian ran forward in an act of desperation and plunged the homemade spear into Hardy's back, the sharpened tip bursting through from his chest.

Mallard lay alongside the dead man for a long while before recovering enough to crawl away and regain his feet. Chukovsky sat beside, barely able to believe what he had done. When Mallard stood he did also.

They found and raided Hardy's food store when they were sufficiently rested and made a meal. Though Chukovsky barely picked at his food.

"So much for the colony idea, eh?" remarked Mallard ruefully.

"At least the winter's ending, Mal. We'll be able to live our lives out in springtime."

Later they left the stronghold. Clambering down the hillock slopes, picking a return path through Hardy's traps. They found the body of the second woman in one of the disguised pits, pierced by wooden stakes and quite dead.

"All this for that," said Chukovsky bitterly. "For nothing!"

"At least we tried," said Mallard, just glad to still be alive. If nothing else, he could now put to rest the worries he'd had about Alice Tsonga.

"Come on, Vasily. Let's go home."

***

It was slow going. Both were bloodied, bruised, and the Russian was sure he had a couple of cracked or broken ribs. Psychologically they were shattered too. They'd thought they would either succeed or die. Come away with the women or succumb to Hardy's brute force. Neither had really considered the possibility that they would defeat Hardy but come away empty-handed. Though Mallard, of the two, seemed more able to accept the way things had turned out, both knew they were going to have to rethink what lay ahead.

They were well into retracing their steps when the sound and thunder of grating machinery started up again. And they were close enough to realise it was indeed coming from the direction of the valley. The two men looked at each other, wordlessly. Baffled, bemused, not knowing what it could be. Though the possibilities were starting to make themselves felt.

Another ship from Earth had arrived? But these were not sounds of a landing. They were more … well, sort of industrial.

This planet did have an indigenous population? A species somehow missed by the human newcomers. A species only now making itself known, however unlikely that theory might once have seemed. Hurrying as fast as their conditions allowed, they reached the top of the rise and looked down into the valley. Both Mallard and Chukovsky gasped in total amazement.

Below they could see dozens of people – humans! – working. Renewing the ruins, erecting new buildings. The whole place looked like a construction site. Large machines moved sluggishly from two huge caves in the valley's western slope, the jaws of the massive metal doors just visible. A group of men stood to one side, pouring over maps and apparently issuing instructions.

The two wasted men could only stand, supporting each other. Gaping in pure wonderment. "They locked themselves away," exclaimed Mallard through cracked lips.

"Underground," added an astonished Chukovsky. "They were here all the time!"

"They must have arrived as autumn ended and worked out what was to come," said Mallard.

"Probably utilised their ship's sleeping chambers," suggested the Russian.

"Converted the whole bloody ship!"

They both laughed, a touch hysterically. "Slept through the winter with a wakeup call set for spring," continued Mallard.

Chukovsky removed his goggles and picked up a handful of snow that still remained here on the rim of the valley. This he rubbed into his face, cleaning away the blood and sweat and grime. Trying to make himself as presentable as possible.

Mallard quickly followed suit when a small rover vehicle left the valley floor and started to climb towards their position. "They've seen us," said Chukovsky, stating the obvious.

The rover came to a halt alongside them and two men got out. "That," said the first, a man with Commander written all over him, "was one hell of a winter!"

"All three hundred years of it," agreed Mallard with a grin. "You're rebuilding already," he added.

"Can't waste time," said the second of the newcomers. "Got to get things shipshape."

"The ladies will want everything neat and tidy," said the first.

Mallard and Chukovsky exchanged knowing smiles. Maybe their abandoned dreams of colony building could blossom again!

"To be honest," admitted the Commander type. "I wasn't sure you would still be here. It was a long time for you to stay in orbit." He turned to look down into the valley as some louder noises echoed up at them. Then back at them again. "Since we knew that winter would be raging by the time you caught up with us, we were worried that you might have assumed the worst and that rather than remain in orbit you might have continued on to the next planet on our list of possibilities."

"If we hadn't lost radio contact we could have kept you informed," said the other. "But the planetary conditions here ruled that out."

Neither Mallard nor Chukovsky understood what they were talking about, but that didn't matter. Spring was coming. A colony would be growing. And hadn't someone just mentioned ladies…?

"We crashed here three Earth years ago," said Mallard, hoping to explain their ravaged appearance.

"Three years," said the Commander. "Why did you leave your orbit? Why didn't you wait till winter was over?"

"We weren't in any long-term orbit," said Chukovsky. "We arrived here then crashed on landing."

"You crashed on arrival?" The Commander sounded amazed. "Then brother, you sure took your time getting here!"

"Never mind," said the other man. "We can sort all that out later. The important thing is that you are here. It would all be rather pointless without you."

"Where's your hold-out?" asked the Commander. "Nearby?"

Mallard shrugged.

"All over, really," said Chukovsky. "We sort of split up."

"Mainly by the coast," added Mallard.

"Well, you can start moving all your people over here now. This valley will be our main base."

The Commander removed his Polaroids and winked. "And when he says all, he means *all*."

Mallard and Chukovsky exchanged puzzled looks.

"It's time we met the women," decided the Commander. "Jump in the rover and give us the directions."

"Eh?" said Mallard.

"Huh?" said Chukovsky.

The Commander and his companion both looked uneasily from one to the other. "You are from the second ship in our convoy aren't you?" asked the former.

"The one carrying the female colonists," added the other.

Chukovsky dropped to his knees and started to sob. Mallard turned his eyes upward and cursed the alien sky.

Down in the valley even the machinery stopped. As if recognising a minute's silence.

NASTY

He stood, feet planted solidly, secure in the knowledge that he held a gun and I didn't. He inhaled deeply and audibly, letting the air escape his lungs in a slow even-paced hiss. Gimlet eyes held me while I stared at the barrel of the revolver pointing straight at me.

I have heard it said that the past life flashes through the minds of those about to die. The edited highlights at least.

I watched as his finger tensed, starting a slow squeeze on the trigger…

***

My baptismal name was Henry. Me, for God's sake, a Henry! Not for long though. By the time she died only my mother still used it. Henry Cecil Bush. My middle name was supposedly after my father. But since he disappeared straight after ma's pregnancy was confirmed, I only had her word for that.

Henry Cecil Bush.

Man oh man! That was no name for a wannabe teenage tearaway.

At fourteen I was over six foot tall, built like a brick shithouse, and expelled from school for beating up the woodwork teacher. Mr Rightmore thought that handing out cigarettes to his pupils made it okay for him to squeeze the cheeks of their arse. He knew he couldn't press charges, and the Head knew it too, but still gave me the big heave ho. And you know what, that suited me fine.

Big, strong and young. Maybe with sawdust for brains. But only ma called me Henry. Everyone else used my surname.

Bush this. Bush that. Bush is the lad if you want some bother. Lots of water, and lots of bother, flowed under the bridge since those days.

Funny thing, as it happened. Even though education was for wimps, I always liked reading. A secret vice I kept to myself, private like, devouring book after book. Science fiction and horror were favourites, though I was more than willing to try whatever I managed to nick from W.H. Smiths.

Bookworm Bush?

Not a nickname I wanted. So kept it quiet.

Bully Bush. Bash 'em Bush. That was the way reputations were made, and in our part of town that meant coming to the notice of Dicker Robling. He even showed a profit with his legit business dealings, but the real money came from his many illegal operations. Locally, he was The Man, and it wasn't long before I became a fringe player within the scope of his organisation. I ran errands, did some fetching and carrying, that sort of thing. Then one day a foot soldier with more ambition than sense objected to me on the grounds of my youth.

"Why we got this boy on a man's job, Mr Robling?"

The boss looked in my direction. "You a man or a boy?" he asked.

So I beat the dumb-head to a pulp.

"Boy, you're man enough for me," said Mr Robling with a laugh, and everyone called me Boy from that day on.

Robber Robling, some people called him, but never to his face. Me? I called him Mister. Knew which side my bread was buttered. Doing everything and anything, whatever was asked. And doing it well. Smart career moves.

Good lad, Boy Bush.

Good at breaking bones.

That too.

But is he just stupidly loyal or quietly cunning?

Either way, he's good in a ruck.

And Mr Robling appreciated the fact, making me an established enforcer within his outfit by the time I hit my twenties. People in the neighbourhood gave me respect; and only my mother called me Henry.

***

He was big and strong himself, the boss, though losing some of that hard chiselled definition as he entered his forties. I sometimes thought he might have seen something of his younger self in me. Either way, as well as the enforcing side of things he used me as muscle in the background on a pretty regular basis, and I wasn't complaining.

If Mr Robling dined at a good restaurant, the muscle dined at a good restaurant.

If he was out for the evening at a classy club, the muscle was there as well.

If he had his pick of the girls who operated under his protection, well the muscle kept his trousers on and watched the door. But hey, two out of three ain't bad, and the muscle could always call round when he was off duty.

On the house, big boy.

Of course it was.

Boy Bush was living the good life that old Tony Bennett sang about. I knew my singers. Sinatra, Tormé, Ella Fitzgerald. None of that X Factor crap. Sometimes Mr Robling would talk to me about them. Seeing Frank live in Vegas, that sort of thing. Or about any new vocal talent he'd heard of.

"Best bib and tucker tonight, Boy," he told me on this one specific occasion. "New girl doing a spot at The Satin Doll

Supper Club. Said to be worth a listen."

Yes sir.

No sir.

Three bags full sir.

Little did I know then...

***

Annie O'Clare was a Shirley Bassey wannabe. She could hold a tune okay but her voice was too thin for her to be anything more than a reasonable club act. Never going to hit the heights of her heroine. She was, though, a real looker, and I could tell the boss was impressed. From the moment she bounced on stage, before she'd even opened her mouth, his jaw dropped and he couldn't take his eyes off her. The fact that she was nothing special vocally didn't matter. Mr Robling was smitten, and I could see why.

If there was one word to sum up Annie O'Clare, it would be vivacious. Small, petite, energetic. Hair so black it shone and ruby lips you just wanted to crush with your own. If only her voice had been more layered she would have been a star.

To my eyes there was something vaguely Oriental about her delicately porcelain features. As if a Chinaman had popped up sometime in the past and dropped a smidgeon of DNA into the gene pool. Whatever it was, it worked. Mr Robling was smitten. And so was I.

For her part, as I found out later, she didn't know us from Adam. Not even the boss. If she had, then Annie would have realized from the beginning that she'd hooked a big one in Dicker Robling. But since he was nothing more than just another drooling forty year old at that stage, she let her gaze move on to me.

Mr Robling and I were both looking at her, but Annie

O'Clare was only looking at me.

This was new. Something that went beyond sex, but didn't exclude it.

This, I could only assume, was love.

***

She was summoned to our table between singing spots, and had obviously been brought up to speed as to the identity of the man doing the summoning. Dicker Robling represented power and money. He was not someone to cross or treat lightly. Also, as with many of his underworld contemporaries, he liked to dabble in show business. So could be useful to an aspiring singer.

Annie O'Clare was savvy enough to know the score. Turning on the charm for the man who mattered, though still managing to catch me with an occasional secret eye. I sat there in that unblessed place, trying to ignore and dislike her pale junky face, but failing. I sat there, immobile like granite, while emotions I'd never before experienced raged throughout the cauldron of my inner being.

I could see the way things were stacking up. And I didn't have to be Mystic Meg to foresee that there wasn't going to be any happy-ever-after for Boy Bush. What Dicker Robling wanted he got, and he wanted Annie O'Clare.

***

It was not by accident that he had got where he was. Mr Robling brooked no opposition, stomping on whoever or whatever stood in his way. The fact he had a wife and twin daughters at home was of little consideration. Within the blink of an eye he had Annie settled in a top of the market apartment. A luxury love nest boasting everything a girl could want.

Everything? Well, not quite. When she was with the man paying the bills, Annie O'Clare didn't just lie back and think of

England. She lay back and thought of me.

***

Dicker Robling was not a comedian. The nearest he ever came to a joke was "Howard Marks can be Mr Nice. I'll be Mr Nasty." It was a line he was fond of repeating and though we dutifully laughed each time we knew it was basically true. Not just in regard to him, but the rest of us too. There were no real nice guys in our line of business. Wouldn't have lasted five minutes. So it wasn't out of any sense of loyalty that I tried to keep my hands off Annie O'Clare, in spite of the invites implicit in her eyes. It was because if I succumbed, as I wanted to, and he found out, I would be a dead man.

Come on, said Annie's eyes.

Don't do it, said my brain.

Come on, please, said Annie's eyes.

Come on please, now, said Annie's eyes.

You'll be a dead man, said my brain.

Our secret, said Annie's eyes.

Well you know the crack about a standing prick having no conscience. Good sense went flying through the window.

Annie's eyes had been devouring me from the word go, but the first time she actually touched me was like pure electricity. I thought I was going to explode. Thought I was going up in a multi-coloured flash. Light the blue touch paper and retreat. But there was no retreating after that. Not for either of us.

We would often talk about making a run for it. But, in the final analysis, I guess we both had selfish reasons for maintaining the status quo. In spite of the fact that I hated the thought of him and her being together, and I no longer looked up to him in quite the same way as before, I was nevertheless firmly entrenched as a member of the Robling organisation.

Good at my job, never short of money, envied and respected by lesser hoodlums. I couldn't see myself starting again elsewhere.

Annie too. Whatever her vocal limitations, she still had show-biz ambitions and Dicker was not without useful connections. Call in a favour or two here, pull a couple of strings over there, and career opportunities could open up.

I didn't like it that she was Mr Robling's bit-on-the-side. Or that I had to keep my feelings a secret.

She didn't like being Dicker's bit-on-the-side either. Or that she had to keep her true feelings quiet as well.

So we talked.

Even made plans.

But we did nothing. Just kept on keeping on.

I think it was love we felt. Real love. I knew that I couldn't picture life without her, however limited my call on her time. I suffered at the thought of them being together, but the rest of my life was lucrative and easy. For Annie, it was the prospect of good club dates being lined up and the promise of recording company interest. So we stayed put. Did nothing to rock the boat.

One thing we did occasionally discuss was what we would do if we were ever found out. There would be no other option for me other than to run. Annie thought she could handle her Sugar Daddy, even though it would mean throwing me to the wolves. "I would blame you completely, lover," she told me. "I'd tell him how you threatened me, pressured me, how it's him I really want. Then, assuming you had got safely away, I would join you at the first opportunity."

It sounded easy. The way she said it.

But as long as we were careful. And we were.

So we thought.

As it happened I was on an evening off when the balloon went up. Having a Chinese meal at a local restaurant and hoping to hear from Annie that we could meet up later. So I was pleased when a text popped onto my mobile. Until I read it.

He knows. Run. Contact you when I can.

An eight word message and my life was in pieces. But Boy Bush wasn't who I was, or what I was, for nothing. Once the initial shock subsided, survival mode kicked in. I had made certain provisions for just such an eventuality. Even though hoping I would never have need to use them.

If old Robber Robling knew, then a team would be on its way to the house I'd first bought for my mother, then moved into when she'd died. So that was off limits. But I did have a lockup garage in a different part of the city, bought under a false name. As well as a car it contained an overnight bag, a suitcase full of bank notes, various firearms and five passports with a different alias in each.

I phoned for a taxi to pick me up at the Chinese eating house, leaving my regular car where it was parked a little further up the road. I'd never told Annie about the plans I had in readiness in case we were ever found out. What she didn't know, she couldn't tell. I just hoped that she had prepared as well and that she would be able to twist Dicker around her little finger. Since I knew how she could get me to do whatever she wanted I'd always assumed he would be putty in her hands too. But now, with a heavy dose of reality seeping through, I had some doubts. The boss was no fool. I could only hope that Annie was his one weakness. But in the meantime, my safety was of primary personal importance. And my future wellbeing.

One advantage to being a trusted lieutenant in the Robling

outfit was being aware of the total logistics necessary for the smooth running of each individual segment. Money was accumulated from various sources, both legal and illegal. Plus his cut from activities he allowed others to carry out in his corner of the city.

Money waiting.

Money in transit.

Here.

There.

And I knew each and every location. I knew where each and every bundle of cash was at any given moment. Not even clever Dicker would expect me to still be hanging around. He would assume I already had my running shoes on.

***

My first two hits went like well oiled ball bearings. The third was messily violent, but successful. When I arrived at the fourth, it was just in time to see a posse of tough guys scramble from two cars and rush into the building.

They'd worked out what I'd been doing. Time to go.

When added to the money already stashed in my lockup, I had a very welcome six figure sum to help me on my way. All I had to do was drive halfway across the country to an airport that would not have Robling's men looking for me, and decide which of the five forged passports to use first.

***

Annie and I both had mobile phones we used only for each other, but her number was now unobtainable and mine remained silent. While not proof of anything, intuition told me the signs were not good. After landing in Italy, and keeping away from big cities and flashy hotels, I did quick hops to Spain and Portugal. Wherever I was I looked out for English language newspapers, and it was while I was in the Portuguese city of Cavado that I saw a small tucked-away headline which stated: POPULAR CLUB SINGER'S SUICIDE.

Annie O'Clare, I read, had overdosed on sleeping pills while deeply depressed following an unreported attack which had left her with badly slashed facial disfigurements. She had left no note so the attacker, and the reason for it, remained unknown.

So he'd cut her. The bastard! Or had her cut. Whichever. Same result.

Poor Annie.

Poor me.

I broke a strict rule and got a little drunk that evening, and flew to France the next day. My wanderings became even more aimless than before. It wasn't that I hadn't suspected she would fail, but having it confirmed was something else. And with such finality. Her being dead was a door slammed shut in my face.

I could see it. Picture it. Annie lying dead on the bed. Cold stiff fingers wrapped around an empty tablet bottle. Other hand over her face, hiding the terrible injuries that had propelled her into free fall.

Well, something like that.

***

Italy had been excitable. Spain and Portugal sort of dusty. France had been, well, French. Germany was Teutonic and Greece in the grip of austerity. I toured Europe in a second class but comfortable manner, keeping away from places where I might possibly be recognised, however unlikely, and making use of all five names in my forged passports. Not only had I betrayed him with Annie, but I had stolen a lot of his money. Dicker Robling wouldn't forgive nor forget. So I played it careful.

Trouble was, I never did care all that much for foreign holidays. Give me Blackpool over Paris any day. One of my best childhood memories was a fortnight with ma in a caravan at Barry in South Wales. Maybe it was a touch of the homesick blues. Whatever it was, I just wanted to get back to the old UK.

My old haunts were naturally out of the question, and I thought it best to keep away from all the big cities. Keep to places more likely be under the radar of organised crime. I travelled for a bit, looking for somewhere to put down roots, before finally settling for a sleepy backwater on the English-Welsh border which had the added attraction of a bookshop owner in need of some investment. I still had a reasonable amount of cash but it seemed sensible to look at potential business opportunities.

***

I bought a house, did my turns behind the counter, and settled into a life as part owner of a bookshop. An occupation that lent itself to my old love of reading. I still had a liking for science fiction and horror and at my partner's prompting started to dip into some of the classics. It was through the shop that I heard of a small independent publisher who was inviting submissions for a short story anthology to be called *The Albany Press Book of Modern Ghosts* and I developed a sudden urge to step beyond reading and try my hand at writing.

"Singing Sad Songs" was the story of a wannabe singer's suicide and her inability to move on through the various stages of death until she had recorded her music for the world to hear. It had her creating all sorts of havoc and disturbances at a recording studio and featured a guitar playing Buddhist poet who senses her ghostly presence and helps her on her way, even though it leads to his own death and the studio being burnt to a cinder.

And it was accepted. Really! My first ever story. They must have been short of submissions.

The anthology came out just before Christmas, probably hoping to sell as a stocking filler. It received some good online reviews and even Alan Morris, the name I now used, had a couple of nice mentions. Though small time enough to satisfy my need for a low profile, it was nevertheless all rather flattering and good for the ego. But then the story was selected for reprinting in the annual *Year's Best Ghostly Chills* anthology, which was a bigger deal. I could have said no of course, but that in itself might have drawn attention. Anyway, I reasoned, nobody was going to link Alan Morris with Boy Bush.

My partner, seeing the potential for a sales bonanza in our little shop, insisted I should attend the anthology launch at a large Manchester store. Not that I needed much prompting. My only claim to fame in my previous life had been an ability to inflict pain and damage to order. This small slice of success with a short story pandered to my sense of self-worth. I was a published writer, and it felt good.

The launch itself went well. There were glasses of wine, cucumber sandwiches, and the other contributors and I signed copies of the book. I seemed to fit in and even received invitations to submit stories for future publications. Whether or not I had it in me to continue writing was something else, but it was nice to be asked.

All in all, it was a good day.

I didn't even notice the photographer.

***

It was only a smallish news item but I did panic at the

accompanying picture appearing in a couple of the dailies. It was a group photo though. Not just me on my own. And not a subject anyone connected with Dicker Robling would be likely to read.

Should be okay, I reasoned, but maybe my writing career should stall as a one-story-wonder. No point in pushing my luck. For as long as we were both alive, I would be a nasty presence gnawing away at the back of Robling's mind. Not only because of Annie, but maybe even more importantly because of the money. He could shrug off being cheated on by a woman, especially after dealing with her the way he had. But being robbed, having to fund my subsequent getaway and lifestyle, that would have been a bigger insult to his professional standing amongst his peer group.

He might be Robber Robling but I was no Robin Hood. There had been nothing altruistic about my actions. Nor would there be about his.

A couple of weeks went by and I began to feel more relaxed about things. Then, on a Tuesday, it was, I saw Doug Henderson drive slowly past the shop. He couldn't have seen me, back behind the counter as I was, but there was only one reason why one of Dicker's goons would be in our sleepy backwater town. And that reason was me.

I had once considered, back when I was travelling through Europe, having plastic surgery to alter my appearance. Too drastic, I decided, settling for a change of hair style and a moustache. Maybe I should have spent the money. Not that I hadn't put some preparations in place in readiness for an eventuality such as this occurring. The man with a plan, that was me.

***

I saw Doug Henderson on a Tuesday and it was two days later on this very evening that they came for me. To my house. I knew who it was of course. I always checked before answering when my door bell rang. Three of them, and one more still sat in the car.

The door crashed inwards as I opened it, sending me staggering backwards. All three were in before I recovered, and they were all packing artillery.

"Boy Bush, as I live and breathe, nifty tash an' all."

Smug sod, Henderson. He'd obviously crawled up the ladder a bit during my years of absence. With him was Lenny Barker, a seven foot Jamaican whose boxing career would have been a lot more successful if he hadn't kept getting himself disqualified. Best punch he threw in the ring kayoed the referee. Got a life ban for that one.

"Hi, Lenny," I said.

"Just business, Boy. Just business."

"Never mind the pleasantries," interrupted Henderson. "Move over there. Legs spread. Hands against the wall."

I did as ordered, allowing him to frisk me.

"He's clean," he said. "Go tell the boss, Reg."

The third guy, who I didn't know, grunted and left. When he returned it was with Dicker Robling himself.

"Come on in, Mr Robling. Make yourself at home."

"Don't get clever with me, Boy. Not at this stage of the game." He shook his head, almost in sorrow. "I had great plans for you, once. But then there was Annie, and all that money you stole. We've all got to pay for our sins in the end, and your time is now."

"How did you find me?" I asked.

"An old retired teacher. William Rightmore by name. He

knew I was looking for you, had been for years, so he brought me a paper with a photo in it. He wasn't positive but thought it looked enough like you to warrant checking. He was the teacher you beat up wasn't he? The one you got expelled over?"

I just nodded. That dirty old fucker Rightmore. Paid me back in the end. Paid me back good.

Robling lifted his right arm then, and I knew the gun he held was pointing straight at me. He was psyching himself up for the big moment.

When that bonehead Henderson had frisked me, he had only been looking for weapons. Fair enough, that was all he'd been told to check for. Little did he know that the fancy iron cross on a chain around my neck was far more potent than any gun or knife.

Little did any of them know.

***

As Dicker Robling's finger tensed on the trigger, so did mine on the jewel at the centre of my fancy iron cross.

"Pay back time," he said, squeezing the trigger. Sending a bullet spiralling from the barrel. Spinning towards me.

As he squeezed so did I. Detonating my booby trapped house. Starting explosions which would blow the whole building and all in it to kingdom come. As to which was going to get me first, bullet or bomb. Well, I didn't really give a fuck...

POEMS #5

OLD BATTLES

Hey you Welshman:

Crouched in darkness
Scorched by furnace
Dulled by future

Sing songs
Tell tales
Fight battles old and new

Ecstatic in victory
Despondent in defeat
Ever cursed with false hope

Where is the trendy balladeer
To sing your history
Into folk-rock chart success

***

FINDING NINA SIMONE

Listening to firmly struck keyboard
And voice capable of horny seduction
Able to bludgeon or soothe
From song to song
From mood to mood
She can grab me by heart or balls
I don't complain
Just as long as next tune kicks in
The chords and structure
Of her interpretations
Sweeping me to an orgy of adulation

Praise be to you Nina
I hope in death you found your god
I've found your music
And that will have to do for me

***

SOULO BEATA

Tell me a story
Blue
Tell me – Baby Blue

Talk the talk
Beat the drum
Crack the ice

Soulo Beata
Soulo Beata

Your stories jar – they're not mine
Your life implodes – it's not mine

Oh you Fool Daddy
King Daddy Fool
Where is the wisdom?
Where is the jazz?

Give me your pain – your hurt
Pile it on these foolish shoulders
Give me your intensity

Soulo Beata
Soulo Beata

I hear discord

Where is the jazz?

MESS OF BLUES

In a search for solid
Within delusional opaque
Howlin' Wolf vocal patterns
Plunder what sense remains

Or maybe I just messed up

***

BLOOD LOVER SANDWICH

You
Between the slices

YOU

Garnished
Seasoned
Worthy of the Ritz

You
Should be a sandwich just for me
Let Geldof feed the world
Let Bono pump platitudes and cakes

Cut thumbs press hard
Blood drips on bread

Blood lovers

YOU and ME

Lying between the slices
Spread
With relish

Peppery hot

THE PAWN SHOP WINDOW

One moment there was nothing. The next: his head was throbbing, throat dry, mouth evil-tasting, eyes blinking as light poured into them. First his body adjusted to waking. Then his mind, as he grudgingly accepted the unfortunate circumstances of his existence.

It was the evening of Friday the ninth of July, 1971, and today they had buried the greatest trumpet player to have ever hit a Top C. Louis Armstrong, having died three days before at his home in the Corona district of Long Island, had been laid to rest at Flushing Cemetery.

The light made him close his eyes again. Eccentric patterns of colour erupting onto the inner curve of his eyelid. He had not meant to actually sleep. Had just stretched out to rest awhile. Which was how come the light was still on. Moving his head a little he reopened his eyes, focussing on a jagged crack running across the ceiling. Then, with a sudden burst of movement, he swung his legs over the side of the bed and sat up.

Dull ache exploded into pain as he succumbed to a bout of disease-filled coughing. When that subsided he clambered onto stiff legs and moved unsteadily to a chipped basin in the far corner and splashed water onto face and head.

He was sixty-eight, three years younger than the man buried earlier that day. "I could've been number one," he muttered hollowly, looking up at the mirror. But the reflection he saw threw the words back in his face.

Armstrong had always loved life. Living and enjoying it to the full. But his music had been the supreme high. No contest.

Had remained so right until the end. Ordinary mortals might have set out with a similar dedication but they lost it somewhere along the way. Which was why they were never tagged with the title of Genius.

After drying and tidying himself he glanced around the rented room he – no, didn't call home. It was just a place he occupied. Faded walls, bare floor. A subtle essence of shabbiness seemed spread over everything in it. Himself included.

It was evening and time to go. Regular as clockwork. At the door he switched off the light. Exchanging the rooming house for a busy Chicago street, he shuffled lethargically until reaching the bar. Cheap and seedy, it well matched the room he'd just left.

The saloons and dance halls in the Third Ward district of New Orleans had been no better in reality, but had appeared wondrous places to wide-eyed youngsters. He had been seven when ten year old Dipper Armstrong had formed a vocal quartet with Happy Bolton, Little Mack and Big-Nose Sidney. They'd sung around the Rampart Street area. Doing a few songs then passing a hat round. They would let him hang out with them sometimes. Even hold the hat while they sang. Other times they would hang around outside the Masonic Hall, listening to all the great ragtime bands playing inside.

Buddy Bolden, Freddie Keppard, Joe Oliver. Horn men supreme. Young Louis: Dipper, Dippermouth, Gatemouth. Nicknames which would evolve into Satchelmouth and then finally into Satchmo. Young Louis would listen to those giants and his eyes would gleam. And he himself, three years younger and standing near, had felt the same. As if even then, before either of them had blown a single note, they knew where their futures lay.

The beer he bought was lukewarm and lifeless. Leaving a sour taste in his mouth. There was a warehouse he knew that took on casual labour when special consignments came in. The foreman would often nod in his direction, but there had not been anything lately so there would be no bourbon chasers tonight.

Then someone started to play the piano. Play the blues. Slow, mournful, suffering. His hand tightened around the glass as the notes pierced his mind. His eyes shut tight. No escape. The music surrounded and hurt him.

In his mind he could picture a pawn shop. In the window was a trumpet. His trumpet. In his pocket was a ticket. Out of date. Unredeemable. Facts he only vaguely acknowledged.

Chicago streets were full of bars. Some with music, some without. But that was what drew him to this particular location. Weren't many places where you could still hear those genuine ever-loving always-hurting blues. Where soul stirring chords could slice you like a knife and beat you like a hammer.

The slow blues having finished, the pianist stomped off into what would once have been called a fast western number, but was today known as boogie-woogie. Short percussive right hand work improvising over the steady pounding of the left.

A surge of life oozed through the listener and he looked, for the first time that evening, at the wizened old black man hunched over the keys. The two blank orbs where his eyes should have been stared sightlessly in no particular direction. Somehow giving the appearance that he looked everywhere else, but never at whomever was looking at him.

Blind Tiny Lester had been every bit as good as those now honoured as legends. But he lived in poverty now, no-one knew where. Alone and forgotten. Every evening he arrived at this bar and played the piano for free drinks and tips. Then later he would return to wherever it was he had come from. Wretched, wasted, tip-tapping the stick he held like a badge of office.

Yet even he had more to his life than the man who came here every evening just to listen. Many bars had a piano that virtually anyone could sit at and play. But none provided a trumpet for casual use. A horn man had to have his own instrument in his possession. Not on show in the window of a low-life pawn shop.

His mind wandered back again. Thinking of earlier instruments he had owned. Of his lovely toned cornet, back before the almost obligatory switch to trumpet. Remembering those New Orleans cutting contests. When the advertising wagons would lock wheels and the bands they were carrying tried to play one another off the street.

All those Big Cats would carve you good. And those younger guys: Buddy Petit, Louis Armstrong, Johnny Dunn, Jabo Smith and himself. All blowing, learning, dreaming. Having themselves a time. Drinking with Buddy, who could have been a star but instead drunk himself to death by 1931.

Him and Louis both made it to the funeral to say a sad goodbye. Little Dipper was never going to do it the Buddy Petit way. Not even when they were kids. Louis could party like anyone else, but he knew control. Nothing came between him and his horn.

His mind leap-frogged back to the present as the fast boogie went striding to a thundering conclusion. Then: "For Louis," muttered the pianist hoarsely, going into "Sleepy Time Down South", the old Armstrong signature tune. A personal tribute to the man whose casket had been lowered into the ground earlier in the day.

When the Navy had closed the Storyville "Red Light" District in 1917 it had been the start of a gradual migration north for many of the New Orleans jazz musicians. He had followed a well worn path by first working the riverboats and then answering a call from Chicago. He had become a member of Blind Tiny Lester's Ragtime Kings in 1923. One year after Louis had followed the same route to join King Oliver's Creole Jazz Band.

He could still picture Tiny as he'd been back then. A permanent smile. A quick laugh. Always sharp in his neat tuxedo. He had not heard of him in many a long year until, quite by accident, finding him playing in this bar. Still blind. Still little. But no longer smiling and no longer sharp.

Tiny had no idea that one of his old sidemen was a regular member of his bar audience. How cruel for both of them to realise that the other knew just how far down the line each had sunk. That would have been too unkind.

What a bunch they had been though. But not one business brain amongst them. Not in Blind Tiny's band. Nor in his own outfit that he'd left the Ragtime Kings to form. Not one of them had foreseen the growing importance of records. They had looked on it as more of a joke than an industry. A passing fad.

Just once his own group, The Bayou Blues Band, had been invited to cut some sides for a new label. On the day of the recording session they had all got drunk and failed to turn up.

They were never asked again.

If only…

But there was no "if", just the fact that they'd got drunk and their one chance was gone. Not that they realised it at the time. Not with the good business they were doing in clubs and dance halls. With a horn at his lips, a jug at his side and women at his feet. He had lived the part to the full. For as long as it lasted.

Louis, though, had known better and had recorded at every opportunity. First as a sideman with King Oliver and guesting all over the place. Want a sweet trumpet to enhance a blues vocalist's record? Send for Louis Armstrong. And then there were his own Hot Five and Hot Seven sessions. New York had come calling as well. Young Satchmo, star soloist with the Fletcher Henderson Orchestra, was already The King. A crown he would never lose.

And today they had lowered him into the earth.

The image of the pawn shop loomed again as he remembered how his own career had crept gradually downhill. Almost as if a counterbalance to the blossoming Armstrong extravaganza. But he forced the thought away by finishing what was left in his glass and buying the only other beer he could afford that night.

Blind Tiny Lester was playing one of his own compositions now, "Blues in a Bucket", and he mentally picked out the trumpet lead he had played to it all those years ago. Maybe it was just his mood. Maybe it was all the memories triggered by today's burial at the Flushing Cemetery. Whatever the reason, the blues coming from the piano seemed the most poignant he could remember in a long, long time.

Taking an automatic sip from his beer, he let all else slip from his mind until there was nothing left but the music. It surrounded him. Filling. Lifting. Until he was out of his earthbound body and floating high.

He filled the universe.

He was the universe.

And everything in it was blue.

Blue for the *blues*.

His shell, the aging husk, was sitting in a rundown bar listening to an old blind pianist. But the real him. The essence. The soul. The formless spark that constituted the individual self. That was expanding far beyond terrestrial boundaries. Swollen with the blues, and not just piano but full orchestra too.

Then, suddenly, above it all, he heard a trumpet. Soaring. Full toned and beautiful. His trumpet. Playing blues of such a hurting intensity he knew that glorious immortality would be his if only other people could hear it. He could make a comeback. Earn his rightful acclaim.

With his trumpet at his lips again he could...

But wait.

Stop!

If the trumpet was no longer in the pawn shop, how had he managed to redeem it?

And the answer, when it came, was devastating. There, sat in the centre of the pawn shop window, was himself.

The old man came there every evening. He sat at a table. Had a couple of drinks and listened to the piano player. Nobody took any notice of him. At least, not until Friday the ninth of July, 1971, the day they buried Louis Armstrong, Not until he suddenly jerked to his feet making strange strangling sounds, then collapsed to the floor.

And died.

CROSSING THE SNOWLINE

Walking the dismal night-time streets of a shabby northern city, my internal rhythm section couldn't decide whether it was backing a honking tenor sax or the plaintive blues of a sad but mellow cornet. The two leads switching as my mind raced.

Where were the disenfranchised when you needed them?

Where were the robbers and muggers? The alienated youth said to roam in feral packs?

Seeing an approaching group on the opposite pavement, I held my mobile phone in plain view as an inducement of sorts to attract a criminal response. But though boisterous and loud they ignored me completely, fading away into the distance.

I walked on. Passing as many boarded-up shop fronts as those still seemingly operational. A mixed-up sad-faced individual moving through the dark heart of a disillusioned and dispirited metropolis with only artificial lighting to gleam a visual accompaniment to my heavy footsteps.

Was I really looking for trouble? Would I fight back if attacked? Would I just hand over what was demanded if mugged? Or would I hang on to my mobile phone, struggle with the robber, and maybe get my fingers broken in the process?

I would probably run a proverbial mile. But broken fingers did sound promising. A solution of sorts. A piano player with incapacitated digits was no piano player at all. And so typical of me. Seeking to force an answer rather than coming to an evaluated decision.

On the one hand was Marion, my wife, who loved me unconditionally. Who fully supported my musical ambitions.

Even working in various dead-end jobs to help out financially when gigs were scarce. A wife who I still loved, in spite of my quandary.

On the other side of the coin was Estella, who I wasn't even sure if I actually liked. But who I desired with every ounce and fibre of my bedraggled being. And I could have her too. But not on the side. Only if I committed.

Ah, there was the rub.

The problem.

Where were the robbers and muggers when you were trying to convince yourself you were looking for them?

Beyond the street lighting there was only darkness. A starless and dreary night in a dump of a city where I knew nobody and had never been before. So much had happened in so short a time. So much had happened since I first met Estella.

***

"Hi, you must be Tim Henning. I've been told that had you been American you would have been regarded as a Jazz Piano Great. Or even as a Brit, if you had moved to the USA your career would have blossomed more than it has here."

Typical transatlantic gabbiness, I thought. But bloody gorgeous with it.

"Yes, I am indeed Tim Henning," I agreed with both a smile and a nod, taking hold of the hand she held towards me. "The rest of your statement is pure conjecture and I could not possibly comment."

"I'm Estella Kemp."

"I'd rather guessed you were."

For the past few months my foursome, the Tim Henning Quartet – piano, guitar, bass and drums – had held down a residency at The Hangout, a quite well regarded part of the

London club scene. We would have our own spots and also provide backing for booked-in guest singers and/or instrumentalists. Mostly British. It wasn't quite in Ronnie Scott's league. But with an occasional smattering of foreign performers.

Estella Kemp was a Canadian thrush who had worked small-time in America and was in Europe to push a debut CD for a very low-key label. After being told she would be doing a full week at The Hangout I was relieved to discover that both her music and voice were very jazz orientated. Some of the talents we had to work with were less than inspiring, but this girl sounded as if it would be a good gig.

"Hold on there buster," said Marion, laughing, after seeing Estella's photograph on the CD cover. "Let's not get too enthusiastic."

Oh sweet Marion. Sweet and trusting Marion. If only she had known just how enthusiastic I was becoming about the delectable Canadian songbird.

***

We gelled musically. "The Tim Henning Quartet is the best group I have ever worked with," she told the audience every night. Repeating it to anyone else who would listen. And she liked some of the little tweaks I suggested to the way she sung some of her numbers, and their arrangements.

"Gee, Tim," she would say. "I wish you had been there laying the tracks down with me." And I found myself wishing that I'd been there too.

As well as musically, it seemed to me we were hitting it off on a personal level also. But, surprise surprise, I soon found out there was a hard self-centred streak to Estella Kemp. Something I guess most wannabes have in spades. Estella was beautiful, true, but knew it and used it. Already causing a little stir in jazz circles, my advice would have been to consolidate that early promise. To have mastered walking before trying to run. But she was already thinking in terms of a crossover success. And she was soon seeing my input as becoming an integral part of her planned strategy.

Marion only came to see Estella at The Hangout once. "The girl can sing," she agreed, "but she's got you in her sights." A suggestion I poo-pooed, but Marion was adamant. "Never mind the sweet-voiced canary bit. During your solos she hovers like a vulture waiting to pick your bones clean. Mark my words, Tim. Whether it's you or your musicianship I don't know, but you've got something she wants, and she's a calculating madam who knows how to get her own way."

My wife had summed her up neatly, but knowing it made little difference. There was no question of loving her the way I did Marion. I didn't even have to particularly like her. But at a stark and basic subliminal level of pure lust, I simply yearned to possess her body.

***

Something I would probably have suppressed if she hadn't dangled the forbidden fruits so openly and tantalisingly.

"Listen," I said at one afternoon practise, playing an example of what I was trying to get across. "Forget the rigid bar -line structure. Let your voice sweep aside the hurdles."

"Tim," she exclaimed. "With you writing the charts we could conquer the world!" And as I stood up from the piano stool she pressed her lips on mine for a quick celebratory kiss, but pulled away when I tried to hold her for a longer version. No," she said teasingly. "I don't do it with married men. At least, not while they're still with their wives."

Her face said, I know you want me.

It said, I want you too, but on my terms.

It said, You won't be sorry…

"One moment you're hot, the next you're cold," I grumbled.

"I'm ice, Tim. Estella the Ice Queen. But ice can burn under the right circumstances."

***

Since she didn't have an actual manager, someone from the record company was acting in an advisory capacity while Estella was over here. A keen young guy who was probably not much more than a filing clerk back in the office, but full of enthusiasm and eager to make his mark. The Hangout dates went well enough to be extended into a second week and a couple of BBC Radio 2 presenters latched onto her CD and were giving Estella Kemp some good quality airtime. This, in turn, helped notch up better than expected sales for the disc.

Danny, the record company feller, quickly arranged a small hall tour covering a number of our bigger cities and towns. It also made sense for him to negotiate our release from The Hangout rather than have to rehearse a new backing band to do the shows. And since we would have our own spot as well, it wouldn't do any harm to the Tim Henning Quartet's reputation.

Estella's eyes were gleaming. She was already thinking in terms of a big second album, in the Amy Winehouse tradition, and was keener than ever to secure my fulltime involvement.

"It's only business," I explained, trying to calm an angry Marion. "It'll be really good for the Quartet. The Hangout is already offering us better terms to go back there when this little tour is over."

"Just you keep out of her panties!"

"Marion, baby! You know you're the only girl for me."

"I know I'm a good ten years older than her. But even saints can be tempted by young flesh, and the bitch wants you."

"Rubbish!"

"A woman knows, Tim."

"Not that old intuition thing," I said with a laugh, trying to combat her fears with good-natured banter.

"I'm not joking," said Marion.

***

Okay, let's be honest. Estella wanted me as her Musical Director. And if that meant having me as a lover too, then fine. She was flying back to Canada at the end of this short tour and the record company, who was seeing her as the artist capable of taking them into the bigger world of commercial success, wanted a second album started straight away. Some top American studios were already being touted as possible recording locations. Estella had a contract for me, all drawn up and ready to sign. The terms were excellent, but it would mean breaking up the Quartet, and Marion was not part of the deal.

For myself, well yes, it could be viewed as a smart career move. But did I really want to take a chance away from my comfort zone? And did I really want to give up my marriage?

Suddenly I wasn't sure.

The only thing I did know for certain was that her physical allure was very real. Both professional and musical gains were a part of what was on offer, but deep down I knew that in reality it was all about sex, and was that sufficient reason to give up all I currently held dear?

Was the promise of Estella's body temptation enough?

On the other hand, what had I achieved in my stay-at-home, play-it-safe career? In the words of the song "Thirty Year Man", lyrics by Clive James, "A brindled crew cut and a silk lined jacket". In other words, nothing of any great note. I had turned down offers in the past when I'd thought the risk factor too great. Maybe it was time to make a change.

Really though, I knew this argument was merely an attempt to justify the madness Estella had brought into my life. I would not be considering the job offer without the added bonus of her body. All this to screw a singer who would probably drop me when someone who offered greater career potential came along. All this for a fuck!

Nothing made sense. Not anymore.

***

This had been our last gig on the hastily arranged mini-tour. Danny, the record company guy, had put it together well. He was no slouch and, knowing what was going down, he too was pressurising me to sign up. He could see in the way we collaborated just what it was I brought to Estella's table.

The last gig and here I was, walking cold and unattractive streets when I should have been back in the hotel we had all been booked in. We had all joined in an end-of-the-tour drink in the hotel bar. Estella, Danny, the other Quartet members and me. A lot of good humour and celebratory back slapping, but the eye contact between Estella and myself was driving me crazy. Then people were saying goodnight and making for their rooms.

"Decision time, Tim," she whispered in my ear. "My room door will be unlocked. Come in. Sign the contract. Stay the night. In the words of Sinatra…" She sang the line: "Come fly with me..." and I was mentally filling in the chords behind her voice. "And stay every night," she concluded.

Tomorrow we would return to London. If I signed I would have only a couple of days in which to break up the Quartet, put my affairs in order, end my marriage. I could not see Marion agreeing to be a stay-at-home wife while I zoomed off to America with Estella Kemp.

So I was out in the cold, walking these stupid streets rather than make this one big decision. Which hotel room? Hers or mine? I couldn't simply toss a coin because both options meant me losing something, and I still wasn't sure which it should be.

The sky above was still dark and uninviting. No guiding star on this gloom filled night, and my mood was compounded when a fine drizzle started to fall. Even the occasional group of late night revellers were more silent now. More intent on hurrying on to wherever they were going. Hatless and wearing only my stage outfit, not suitable for the cold and wet, I started to retrace my footsteps.

***

The hotel was imposingly quiet and only dimly lit when I got back. The drizzle had grown into a more steady rainfall and I was drenched, both physically and mentally. Shivering, I used the lift to carry me to the required floor. There were two doors in the same corridor. Near yet far, and my mind was still helter-skeltering between the pros and cons of which one I should go through.

I stood there, switching my gaze from one door to the other. Time to do it, I told myself. Bite the bullet. Toss the coin. Cross the snowline. I walked, not without some hesitation, to the door of my choice.

Reaching out I gripped and then turned the handle. Opening the door, I entered the room…

PLAYING FROM MEMORY

It was all too easy to coast during these small-time ten-a-penny club dates. To drift off at a tangent. To fall back on licks. Very few real listeners. Most of them the "Go man!" variety who would not recognise anything subtle if it rose up and head-butted them into next week.

It's not the worst outfit I have ever played in, this current quintet, but it isn't the best either. Maybe we have been together for a bit too long, though. Like a marriage. Know what I mean?

Dave Skinner, our pianist and nominal leader, well it's his name we play under, is intricately slow and gentle for the first half of "My Funny Valentine", swopping runs with the double bass and allowing me to indulge in a little brushwork. My sticks are fine. Can fill a hall and will flash a hot cymbal beat when our trumpet and tenor up the tempo for the second half of the number, but I do like to use my brushes now and then.

***

There was a time I played my second wife's body like a snare drum. My brush-like fingers and tongue stroking a seductive rhythm over every square millimetre of her smoothly taut coffee coloured skin. What a skin she had. What an epidermis. It's the one good memory I have of her.

***

A quick change to my sticks as the trumpet takes over, hitting my rim shots with a practised ease. Most of what we do these days is music by numbers. Our tenor sax player is younger though. Still keen, still hopeful, still trying. Sometimes I would summon the energy to spray some hot press-rolls into his solos, propelling him upwards and onwards. Whenever I did he would look at me afterwards; smile, nod, then roll his eyes to heaven.

When I was his age I played drums like that all the time.

***

I had been twenty and playing on my very first tour as a full-time professional musician when I met wife number one. She was ten years older and the singer with the band. I was supposedly engaged to a sweet little girl back home, but within weeks I could barely remember her name. Patty, the singer, based her vocal style a little bit on Ella, a little bit on Billie, and a little bit on Sarah. With a dash of Anita thrown in for good measure. I thought she was totally wonderful.

Though it had started out as just one more fling for her it was love for me and I wanted it to last forever. My inexperienced enthusiasm even carried Patty along initially. Temporarily blinding her to the harsh realities of our ten year age gap and the fact that she did not really love me. I dumped the girl back home by letter, which was pretty gutless, and married my new lover just as soon as a break in tour dates allowed. A drunken trombonist was best man. Someone who I later found out had been my wife's sexual partner a year or so earlier. But that was before me so I could hardly complain.

***

Dave names "Desafinado" as our next number. Bossa Nova time and a big tenor feature as the kid pays homage to the Stan Getz original. It brings back memories of Patty singing the cool chick vocals over a similar Latin rhythm for "The Girl From Ipanema".

***

Patty wasn't made for monogamy. I called her my Nightingale but she was soon singing in more squares than Berkley. It broke me up when she finally left. Though maybe some of the hurt was me being angry because she had been the one to make the decision. I probably should have ended it earlier.

Patty and I didn't last much longer than the Bossa Nova craze itself, but at least she made no financial demands on me. Mind you, as a singer she earned more than a mere band member, so maybe I could have claimed alimony from her.

Our paths crossed on and off at occasional club dates and festivals. Then I heard she was performing on cruise ships and she seemed to drop off the face of the earth. Some time later I found out she had reached Australia, liked it and stayed, and was actually doing okay. But I was heading for my second divorce by then so had more pressing concerns on my mind.

***

"I'm Beginning to See the Light" announces Dave. A feature for our bass player, Bobby Norman.

***

I had thought Patty and I would last forever. But I'd been wrong. Then I thought Aphra would be the one. Wrong again.

With a white Welsh father and a black Nigerian mother she was one of those who took the best from both parents and was stunningly beautiful. They had named her after a seventeenth century English writer, Aphra Behn, whose play *Oroonoko* showed up the horrors of slavery. They were right-on, do-gooding, stand-up-and-be-counted liberals. Their hearts were in the right places but, oh my God, they could both be a pain in the arse at times. Aphra, who didn't have one political bone in all her body, found it hard to keep up with their expectations. A student at the London School of Economics when we met. She was looking for a way out and saw me as her ticket to freedom.

***

Dave Skinner is mentioning me by name now. "A Night In Tunisia", my big number. Showtime for the *Go-Man-Go* brigade.

Not that I'll play it, but even after all this time there are still some who shout for "Skin Deep", which Louis Belson once drummed into the pop charts for the Duke Ellington Orchestra. For years after it had been a big band must. Which had been as good a reason as any for me to stick with smaller sized groups. There is plenty a drummer can do to prove his worth without resorting to the circus act pyrotechnics of a Gene Krupa or Buddy Rich, excellent musicians though they undoubtedly were. But I had debts. I had expenses. So I paid my dues and for at least a part of the solo my sticks will be a blur and the punters will love it.

***

Looking back, my time with Aphra was something of a blur too. But there were moments of compensation, even though her parents blamed me for all their daughter's failings. Someone as beautiful and sexy as Aphra had little need to worry about the sort of racial and gender prejudices that so concerned her mother and father. Her skin, so flawless, drove me wild. I would have been happy to explore it for time without end.

***

"Cottontail", announced Dave Skinner and I went straight into some fast two-handed rolls by way of introduction and then speedy left hand patterns when the two horns started to riff. Sometimes things gelled and it could be oh so good. But not always. Like life.

***

After having been very much the junior partner during my marriage to Patty, I truly thought I had a fuller input in my relationship with Aphra. Whatever we did was decided jointly. So I thought. So it seemed. She quit the LSE, which caused a break with her parents. For which they blamed me completely. We married in haste and she followed me round from gig to gig. The happy little musician's wife.

Then my darling girl became pregnant. Which I later came to realise had been her plan from the very beginning.

The prospect of imminent grandparenthood was more than sufficient leverage to bring both her mother and father willingly to heel. Suddenly Aphra was laying down the rules and an itinerant drummer did not cut it as a prospective daddy. Before I could properly realise just how well manipulated we had all been, she was back in Cardiff with her parents and calling all the shots. As for me; I was heading for divorce number two and a baby girl I would never see, but would pay for. On the dot. Every month.

***

Veteran trumpeter Martin Goodrich blew a well worked coda to see out "Cottontail". A short but telling sequence that laid out his unashamed Chet Baker influences for all to hear. "Nice one, Marty," muttered our young tenor sax player quietly. We were all too often travelling the route of least resistance. So the good moments were to be savoured.

***

I had been five years now married to Kate. So I guess the seven -year-itch had come twenty-four months early. She was a good woman and loved me whole-heartedly. Which was more than could be said for her two predecessors. She did her best to understand and fit in with the strange and precarious life of a jazz musician. And was more than willing to make allowances for the occasional stress and strain of living with my creative temperament.

Kate was the sort of wife I had dreamed of when my first two marriages had fallen apart. So why did I toss and turn sleeplessly, lying beside her? Why was I putting everything I thought I'd wanted under threat? Why was I carrying on a clandestine affair with her sister, who lived only two streets away from us?

Deep down, I knew I still loved Kate. That was the stupid part of it. But one flash of her sister's wild eyes and I was putty in her hands. Good intentions and common sense went flying through the window.

***

Max Roach once said that he wanted to do with rhythm what Bach had done with melody, And he could often sound like any number of drummers playing at the same time. I have never possessed either his talent or his elevated ambitions. But when I am struck by the ironies of my marital mistakes then I too can attack my kit like a man with six arms.

I feel that way now.

I circle my drums, moving from one to another in a manic frenzy. Cymbals crash, ringing out in sharp shimmering waves. The others have to move aside and let me through. So what if I am riding roughshod, drowning them out? Sod them! I am the drummer.

Small tom. Medium tom. Floor tom. My stick work becoming more and more extravagant with every flourish.

Ride cymbal. Crash cymbal. Hi hat. Echoing and reverberating throughout this seedy little club. Throughout my seedy little life.

Bass drum booming. Snare drum rattling. Shifting patterns of accentuation jumping through the entire kit.

I am the drummer!

I ... am ... the drummer!

Sod them all!

DIGGING OF HOLES CONSIDERED AS SYMPTOMATIC OF PERSONAL COMPULSION

The Man

He had something of Tom Cruise about him, only taller and with scars around the mouth. He wore a khaki tunic and black jogging pants. Standing in the pub where Tanner was celebrating his thirtieth birthday, he toyed with a barely sipped pint glass.

Maybe it was Tanner's depression at leaving his twenties that triggered the whole thing.

Or maybe not.

Whatever the reason, from the moment he first became aware of the man, he found himself fixated with ground level indentations. From tiny wormholes to massive craters.

The Task

For days after he did nothing but produce never-ending diagrams of holes. Large, small, all shapes and sizes. If he went outside, the man in the khaki tunic would be loitering at the periphery of his field of activity. When he stayed indoors, the man would be reading the news on television, reporting that the Government had confirmed the construction of a crater large enough to protect the entire cabinet from the after effects of both World War Three and climate change.

The Place

Tanner chose a decaying unit in an abandoned industrial complex as the site for his planned excavation. He had decided upon only a moderately ambitious hole. Circular, ten foot diameter, fifteen feet deep.

Why he was doing it? Why here? And what would follow completion? All were imponderables outside his self-imposed remit.

The Result

The man in the khaki tunic looked down from his vantage point in the cabin of a rusty overhead crane. A smile played across his scarred lips as Tanner swung a pickaxe at the littered floor.

The Conclusion

Confidentiality takes precedence.

THE DYING GAME

The television news anchor-man adopted a suitably serious but concerned expression and read from the autocue. "Show biz tycoon Joe Brent was badly injured in a car crash during the early hours of this morning when his Mercedes-Benz was in collision with a lamppost just after leaving the motorway at Newport, South Wales. No other vehicle was involved and he is currently in the Intensive Care Unit at the Royal Gwent Hospital.

"Joe Brent first made his mark fifteen years ago as Manager of the Welsh Valleys group Billy Reverend and The Worthy Ones. Reverend, real name William Harris, committed suicide when their initial success faded and his former backing band, The Worthy Ones, stepped forward to achieve a worldwide number one with the tribute single, "Why Billie Why?" They remained global superstars until their acrimonious breakup ten years later.

"His management and promotions company, Cutting Edge, has issued a business-as-usual statement, with Marty Jones taking temporary charge. Though it is expected that teenage singing sensation Sarah-Jane will postpone a planned promotional visit to America.

"His wife, Kay, the third Mrs Brent, is at his bedside."

***

They had put a tube into his neck to do his breathing. Bandages covered his head and much of his face. He was connected to an array of life support equipment. Monitor screens displayed and charted the rhythms of a life on hold. A ventilator hissed as it throbbed.

Kay Brent sat alone by the bed.

"So much for the divorce Joe. Thought you could get rid of me just like that," she said, clicking her fingers. "Well you're dying now and the boot is on the other foot. I don't think the doctors know why you aren't dead already. Either way, you haven't much longer. And when you do go, it will be as my husband.

"Till death us do part? Oh yes, I do like the sound of that."

Screw you! Joe tried to shout, but nothing seemed to be working. The words just echoed round and round inside his head.

"Should I bare my soul to you Joe? Now you are on that rocky road to hell? Now you can no longer do anything? I don't suppose you can even hear what it is I'm saying…"

Oh yes I bloody well can!

"…which is a pity because I would like you to know that I won in the end. That in spite of the extra-curricular activity on both our parts, our marriage survived. Only just, I admit. And only because you wrapped that silly sports car of yours around a handy lamppost. But history doesn't give a damn about near misses. Only hard facts. I am Mrs Brent, widow in waiting, and I'll look lovely in black."

Kay got to her feet, pushing the chair back and stretching her arms, catlike. She looked down at her husband through narrowed eyes before continuing to speak.

"Doctor Jessop is quite dishy in an unworldly man-of-medicine sort of way. He's been baffling me with all his talk about brain wave rhythms and levels of consciousness. About EEG and ECG readings. About broken bones and damaged organs.

"Do you know, Joe, that you're not even breathing for yourself?

"All these oh-so-clever machines. I wonder how long I should wait before suggesting they should be switched off? Do me one last favour and save me the bother, Joe. Die yourself, and make it soon."

Die yourself you bitch! I'm going to hang on for just as long as I can.

**

She never had liked hospitals. Neither the buildings themselves nor the disinfectant-like smell that seemed common to them all. She had never liked silences either. Which might well have had something to do with her becoming a singer. And the only non-human sound here was that of the portable ventilator as its spirometer maintained a regular hiss.

"Joe? Can you hear me?"

Yes I can, Sarah-Jane, but you can't hear me.

"I won't be able to cope without you."

You will. Don't cry, Sarah. Marty will look after you.

"Three consecutive number ones. Top of the album charts. Merchandising going ballistic. And all down to you, every bit, and none of it will mean a thing if you're not there to share it with.

"Doctor Jessop tells me not to get my hopes up. He says your prognosis isn't good. But he doesn't know you. Doesn't love you. Doesn't know the empty space that's going to be left in my life if you go."

Hang in there, girl. I haven't gone yet.

"What am I anyway?" continued Sarah-Jane. "A twenty-six year old teenager, that's what," she said, answering her own question. "Oh we fooled them good, didn't we Joe? A twenty-six year old able to pass for eighteen. But when can I put an end to this teen-queen business? When can I be myself? And will it matter anyway if you're not there?

"I've loved you for ages Joe, and you said you felt the same way about me. So why wouldn't you let us be together?"

Believe me Sarah, I'm asking myself that very same question.

"Oh I know all your reasons. How a sleazy little affair between a singer and her manager would soon fizzle out. How you wanted us to wait until you got a divorce so we could be open and above board."

Yes! I really was that stupid wasn't I?

"But if you are going to die now, that means there is no future for us. We might just as well have done it while we could. I didn't have to be Mrs Brent, Joe. Kay was welcome to that. All I wanted was you."

Don't cry, Sarah-Jane. Please don't cry.

***

So, okay, his wife wanted him dead while Sarah-Jane wanted him alive. But both seemed pretty certain that he was going to die. He was in a hospital; that much was obvious. Wired to various machines and unable to move even one tiny muscle. But he could hear and he was mentally aware. As he was, for example, of someone examining the monitors to the left of his bed and then crossing to look at those on the right side.

He even recognised him!

Billy

Billy Reverend turned sharply towards the bed. *Can you see me?*

Billy?!

I guess you can. But can you hear as well?

Of course I can bloody well hear, and see, thought Joe Brent, a touch hysterically. *And you walked* through *the bed! And not only that:* you're dead!

Amazing, said Billy, shaking his head. *We are not supposed to be able to communicate in any way until the moment you die.*

This was all becoming much too much for Joe. *But you're Billy Reverend! You left a pathetic little suicide note and OD'd with a drug cocktail strong enough to have laid low a herd of bloody elephants. When was it? Must be all of twelve years ago.*

Thirteen to be exact. And what do you mean by pathetic?

Come on Billy. You wrote something about not being able to face up to the responsibilities of stardom when your last two singles had bombed and your career was in terminal decline. It was failure you couldn't face.

The dead singer shrugged and pulled a face. *Maybe,* he said. *But it certainly turned out okay for you and my old backing group.*

Joe Brent could only shrug mentally. *Water under the bridge now, Billy. Of much more importance is what is happening now, to me?*

Well Joe... Billy paused a moment. *...you are dying. As a matter of fact you should already be dead. Which I suppose is why you can communicate with me even though a tiny almost non-existent strand of life is somehow refusing to let go.*

Does that mean that if I keep hanging in there, if I won't let go, then I'll survive?

Sorry Joe, said Billy, shaking his head. *It doesn't work like that. You were smashed up bad in that crash and there's no way your body can heal. You've managed to somehow delay things, but don't fool yourself into thinking it can last. That sports car and lamppost did as good a job on you as my drug concoction did on me.*

All this might be nothing but a dream, thought Joe. But the memory of the high speed skid and fighting with the wheel. Of seeing that lamppost come suddenly into view. It was all so terribly real. *But let's say I accept your version of events as true. Then why aren't I dying to plan? What's going to happen next? And what the hell are you doing here anyway?*

I'll answer your questions in reverse order, decided Billy. *Number three: suicides are not allowed to move on beyond Earthly limits before they have paid sufficient penance to earn absolution, and I'm not there yet. My function is to greet the newly dead and guide them to their first port of call.*

Number two: since normal rules are not being followed, I really don't have any idea what might happen next.

Number one: and I'm only guessing here, but I think the reason you have not died to plan is because something very important to you personally was missing from your moment of death. You are maintaining a fingertip hold at the bottom region of a level four coma and you are going to have to let go soon, even if you don't find whatever it is you are looking for. Either that or they will turn the life support systems off for you.

My darling wife is already thinking along those lines.

I probably shouldn't be telling you this, whispered Billy, glancing furtively over his shoulder, *but you could sort of influence her if it became necessary.*

How?

The level four coma you're in is known as the theta region, which is beyond and below where you dream. It's where mystical experience can occur, and that includes telepathy. If you aim a constant stream of thought at someone it might get through and influence them.

If Joe Brent could have rolled his eyes to heaven, he would have done at this point. *I'm having enough trouble accepting that my imminent death is unavoidable,* he thought, *and now you're taking me into sci-fi land!*

Sorry Joe. I keep forgetting you're not dead yet.

Give me a bit of time so I can think things through, Billy. Can you do that?

All right, but not too long. If you need me, just call. And as he finished speaking, Billy disappeared.

***

Marty Jones stared blankly at all the life support paraphernalia before turning slowly to look at the man on the bed. "I don't know why I'm here really, Joe," he said finally. "Apart from the fact that I'm in a blue funk at having to run the business on my own. I was your assistant, not your partner. You made all the decisions."

Come on now, Marty. Clear your mind and think.

"I had to cancel Sarah-Jane's American trip. It wouldn't have looked good and she's in no fit state anyway. I think she really does love you."

Concentrate, Marty. Forget the side issues.

"I know you've been giving some thought about how best to repackage her from teen-queen to a more grownup performer. Not that it will be my problem for long. Once you are gone and the legalities have been sorted, Kay will get rid of me pronto. I could never work for her anyway. She made a pass at me once…"

She made a pass at everyone.

"…made it obvious she was interested. But I wasn't, Joe. Not with your wife. She hasn't liked me from that day to this. I will do my best for Cutting Edge though. For as long as I'm there."

I know that, thought Joe, content that he had made the right move in leaving Marty a 70 per cent controlling interest in the company. With the other 30 per cent going to Sarah-Jane as a long-term investment in case her singing career faltered. Kay would do better than she deserved from his estate, but she wouldn't get Cutting Edge. *It's going to be yours, so listen carefully...*

"I guess it's time to fade out the teen anthems. I bet she'd do wonders with folk and blues-tinged rock material. And how about if The Worthy Ones reformed to guest on her next CD as a tribute from them both to you, the manager who helped them reach the top."

Keep listening.

"The Yanks would just love that!"

Wouldn't they just!

"You always had such great style, Joe."

***

That telepathy thing really did seem to work, thought Joe excitedly. *I thought a few ideas at Marty and he picked up on most of them okay. But more than that, he made me see what it is I am hanging on for.*

Billy was all ghostly ears. *Which is"* he prompted.

Style.

Style?

I'm not Joe Bloggs. I'm Joe Brent! he thought, explaining as best he could. *I've lived my life with glitz. With flair. With a style that was all my own. And that's the way I need to end it.*

Okay, said Billy, trying to match the mood. *But how?*

By turning it into a big production number, thought Joe

triumphantly.

But you'll need props and things.

No Billy, not props. Just people. Sarah-Jane, Kay, Marty, Doctor Jessop. I guess they'll do. Give me a hand, will you? Let's see if we can call them with this telepathy thing. Does it work over a distance?

Only one way to find out, said Billy.

***

"So there is no real chance of him being able to breathe on his own again?" Kay was asking as they entered the Unit.

"An emergency tracheotomy was performed immediately," explained Doctor Jessop, yet again. "Hooking Mr Brent to a ventilator, which has continued to breath for him ever since. There have been no vital signs. No hint of recovery. No indication that the multiple injuries sustained during the accident could possibly improve to a level at which he could undertake respiratory functions for himself."

"Doctor," purred Kay, "do you realise just how sexy you make all that sound?"

"Mrs Brent! Your husband."

"And don't I know it."

Following behind, Sarah-Jane and Marty entered the room. Straight away, the two women locked eyes.

"Cow!" hissed Kay.

"Bitch! retorted Sarah-Jane.

"Ladies!" exclaimed Marty.

"Where?" asked Doctor Jessop.

Better get them started before one of them joins me in Intensive Care, thought Joe and the sweeping strings of a full orchestra played a short introduction under Billy's direction. He then pointed his baton at Doctor Jessop, who stepped into the spotlight and sang:

> *This is for Joe, best guy on the block*
> *I am his Doc*
> *I am a medical medical man, do what I can*
> *It's not easy having to cope*
> *With an ice cold stethoscope*
> *But I keep trying, save you from dying*
> *Do what I can*
> *'Cos I'm a medical medical man.*

As the Doctor stepped back, Marty came forward.

> *This is for Joe, great guy till the end*
> *He was my friend*
> *He was a show-biz show-biz tycoon, dying too soon*
> *He knew every trick in the book*
> *Always knew just where to look*
> *He was a big guy, travelling sky high*
> *Dying too soon*
> *He was a show-biz show-biz tycoon.*

And then it was Kay's turn.

> *This is for Joe, through trouble and strife*
> *I'm still his wife*
> *Not in a lovingly lovingly way*
> *We had started drifting apart*
> *We were divorcing, legal enforcing*
> *What can I say?*
> *Not in a lovingly lovingly way.*

And finally, with choral backing and all the trimmings, came Sarah-Jane.

> *This is for Joe, An angel above*
> *My one true love*
> *I am a torn-apart torn-apart gal*

Lost my best pal
It's not easy carrying on
When the man you love is gone
With halo and wings, those sort of things
Lost my best pal
I am a torn-apart torn-apart gal.

Then all four in unison: *This was for Jooooooooooe...*

***

Joe Brent reached out. Took hold of the waiting hands. And left his body...

THERAPY

The self-help group was theoretically free from official participation or interference. Of those who accepted such guidelines were being adhered to, some nevertheless felt that the mad had finally taken over the asylum. Others thought it likely that covert infiltration had placed sleepers within the group. That way, subtle directives could steer the patients along prescribed lines, towards set conclusions.

McCorte considered that his personal self-help would be impossible until the dark fusion of the Bush/Blair Axis could be persuaded to return and rerun the Iraq conundrum on a time-lapse loop until a successful outcome could be achieved.

Am I a patient or an agent provocateur? A question he often agonised over.

Maps marking the narcotic nation of Afghanistan had been distributed the day before with suggested routs for illegal worldwide poppy-produce exports. Being of specific interest to those with drug-trauma backgrounds, McCorte had experienced mixed Baghdad/Kabul/Morphine flashbacks. Though whether or not they were really his remained to be seen.

"Let me be your therapy," invited Yvette, arms spread in an apparent search for optimum geometric angles. Her whole being seemed to be seeking a positional advantage. Receiving no response from him, she sang Puccini's "O Mio Babbino Cara" in a pure and meaningful soprano. She had a beautiful voice.

Yvette's head and face were enveloped in permanent shadow. Her features blurred in darkness though the rest of her could be seen in natural clarity. A small piece of night that accompanied her at all times. McCorte had first seen her in the hospital library daubing slogans on the walls, but no-one else had commented and he wasn't sure if anyone other than he actually acknowledged her existence. She had sung on that occasion, too, but no library user had asked her to be quiet or even to stop daubing.

"Let me help," she offered after finishing her song. But he continued to hesitate.

Would physical contact prove flesh and blood reality or merely increase the depth of his crushing paranoia? He felt it best not put to the test.

Later, walking in the walled garden, McCorte studied the floral faces of both Bush and Blair, as cultivated by green-fingered patient gardeners. Was I really in Iraq, he wondered. Or Afghanistan? If so, was it as invader, resident or observer?

Was he now an asylum inmate or an asylum seeker?

Were there really secret watchers studying his every move? Recording his personal improvisations?

***

The Playhouse was home to a movement dubbed the Theatre of Normality, where dramas showcased the normal by featuring members of the public on stage while actors became the audience. Trasker went there as often as he could, finding definite parallels between the staged presentations and what was taking place within the self-help therapy group.

Arriving, he saw that the stage had been decorated as a Baghdad open market area. Some, Trasker included, took up stall-holder positions. Others, as potential shoppers, adopted stances best suited to reflect both formal and informal patterns of tension.

Who knew when or where the insurgents might strike?

The actors, when they filed in to occupy the theatre seats, were all wearing George Bush masks. For over an hour the two sections studied one another with a growing sense of unease. Then, as one, the mask wearers rose from their seats and threw cardboard rockets at the stage.

People dropped to the floor, ran for cover, shouted in panic, as if expecting real explosions. Even Trasker couldn't suppress an involuntary shudder as he automatically ducked his head. When they left, many expected a war zone to be waiting and were disorientated upon finding the real-time streets peaceful.

***

The man called Tex nodded slowly. "'Nam?" he drawled. "Now that really was a war." His eyes glazed wistfully. "Saigon?" he continued. "Now that really was a city. Black market fortunes made and lost daily. And all the sex a good old boy from the Lone Star State could want. Slitty-eyed darlings. Hot slitty-pussies, every one."

McCorte doubted he was even American, let alone a Vietnam veteran. "Are you getting any benefit from the self-help group?" he asked.

"No need. I'm okay. But if it keeps the Pentagon happy…"

"Pentagon?" queried McCorte.

"Doctors, nurses, managers. Wherever the power lies."

"Right. I get it."

"So did I, in 'Nam. Lucy Loo I called her. Not her proper name but near enough. There was nothing that girl wouldn't do for me, and I mean nothing."

McCorte studied the man before him. Particularly the alignment of the constituent parts that comprised the whole of his body. Searching for the construction faults he felt certain existed within his overall makeup.

"You ever had a girl like that?"

The question took McCorte by surprise and he replied "Yvette" without thinking. Immediately regretting his automatic response.

Tex lifted quizzical eyebrows, inviting further elaboration, and McCorte wondered if this might be an opportunity to find out if others saw her as he did. "The girl with the night-time face," he offered as explanation.

Tex's expression went from quizzical to puzzled. "Do you mean come-to-bed eyes?" he asked, but McCorte was already leaving the room.

***

Returning to the hospital Trasker found the reception area plastered with Bush and Blair wanted posters. None of the photographs had been selected with flattery in mind. He was immediately reminded of McCorte's recent description of this particular pair.

Bush: a brain operating two sentences slower than his mouth.

Blair: from fawn to poodle in two easy lessons.

Although at first look the scattering had appeared haphazard, a closer examination indicated that specific geometric patterns had governed the placing of the posters. Maybe even endorsing elements of future hostility.

Revenge and punishment were lethal cocktails in unstable hands. But a fuller interpretation was beyond Trasker's present understanding.

The hospital, never the most welcoming of places, suddenly seemed more oppressive than ever. If bricks and mortar were sentient, he thought wryly, such doom and gloom feelings could be credited to a practical causation. But as it was he could blame only his own state of mind.

With disjointed and ill-at-ease hand movements, Trasker hurriedly removed the posters from where they hung.

***

"Korea?" said Tex, dragging out the word. "That really was a war." He stopped pacing. Momentarily lost in thought. "Seoul?" he continued. "That really was a city. Treated us like kings. Defenders of the 38th Parallel."

Trasker nodded encouragement

"Did you get it?" asked Tex.

"Get what?"

"It."

"What?"

Tex shook his head. "I guess you didn't."

"It would seem not."

"I did," Tex carried on. "In Korea. Wang Ho I called her. Not her proper name but near enough. Nothing that girl wouldn't do for me, and I mean nothing."

"Did you love her?" asked Trasker.

"Love?" responded Tex. "Slitty-eyed darlings. Hot slitty-pussies. I loved them all. Each and every one."

"You know," remarked Trasker, "you don't look old enough to have fought in Korea."

"I lied about my age," said Tex.

***

McCorte and Yvette sat on plastic chairs in the walled garden. She was wearing a brightly coloured summer frock. He longed to ask why her head was always in darkness, but was afraid of what the answer might be. Plus he still wasn't sure whether or not she was really there, so he stayed on safe grounds.

"The tyrant was toppled but the people still died."

She said nothing.

"The war was won but the peace was lost."

Yvette bent her left arm in stop-go motions, as if evaluating the different angles.

"The war on terror has no zonal boundaries."

Then she did the same with her right arm.

"Bush and Blair disenfranchised the political intelligentsia with their dangerous over-simplification of the genre," McCorte continued, grinding out the words.

"It's a double-edged sword, our relationship," decided Yvette. "My presence alone has a debilitating effect, while my singing can smooth the worry-lines from your brow."

I know, I know, thought McCorte wearily. If only her face were visible and her reality confirmed. If he could see her beyond the level of paranoiac paraphernalia. But her voice was phenomenal. Her amazing range and ability to soar dazzled him.

"Shall I sing for you now, and try to calm you?"

McCorte nodded. "A 'bel canto' aria maybe?" he suggested, and sat back in his plastic chair as her rendition of Bellini's "Casta Diva" filled the garden.

***

"Why do you spy on him so much?" asked Tex, feeling an awkward watching-the-watcher embarrassment. He stood alongside the man at the window, looking down into the walled garden.

"He is fast approaching a redefining of his potential for violence as opposed to his need for absolution," replied Trasker. "His cross-fertilised landscaping of battle zones has culminated in extreme visions. Which may or may not be his, but will soon reach some sort of conclusion."

"Battle zones?"

"Iraq."

"Iraq?" echoed Tex. "That really was a war."

"Afghanistan."

"Afghanistan? That really was a war."

They looked down at McCorte, sitting back in his plastic chair, eyes closed.

"He sees Bush and Blair as terrorists," said Trasker.

Tex shook his head slowly. "Aren't they giving those two some sort of award?"

"They are indeed, my military-minded friend. Specially struck medals to honour their contributions to World Peace."

"To what?"

"I know, it beggars belief doesn't it? There is going to be a big presentation at the Royal Albert Hall."

"McCorte won't be too pleased about that."

Trasker nodded agreement. "It might even be sufficient to trigger some sort of endgame," he said.

***

The van was a metallic blue Diahatsu Hijet diesel with twin loading side doors and a fully opening back. Not that such trivia mattered. The van was functional. Which was all that mattered. From A to B and X marks the spot.

"That's it then, soldier," said Tex, now dressed in army fatigues. "I knew my old contacts would come in handy one day."

"Thanks, Tex," said McCorte through the vehicle's open window. "I still don't believe you fought in all the wars you claim, and I think you might be more Tyneside than Texan, but none of this could have happened without you."

"My pleasure, trooper."

As McCorte started the engine Tex stepped back, came to attention and saluted as the van began to move.

From his high vantage point, Trasker felt a twinge of regret that his function had now been reduced to that of an observer. The shaping of events was now beyond him. "Normalism, pure normalism," he muttered quietly, switching from binoculars to telescope in an effort to keep the van in view for as long as possible.

Tex still stood at attention, ramrod straight while the sounds and explosions of battle raged through his head. "Give that man a Purple Heart," he said aloud as the van was lost to sight.

***

As McCorte drove through the open hospital gates he glanced at the woman sitting alongside him. "Just you and me then," he said.

"It always has been," Yvette replied.

"Only your singing has kept my total obliteration at bay." He paused for her to respond, but continued when she remained silent. "You should be singing professionally. You really should. Giving recitals, concerts, making records. You can outdo Callas. Sutherland and Caballe stand in your shade."

"Hold on there, buster!" she interrupted with an embarrassed laugh.

"But you are that good," he insisted.

"If I aspired to any of the greats it would be to Tebaldi or Kanawa. Voices that can calm and sooth. That, my friend, has been my purpose with you."

This, he realised, might be his last chance to establish the facts of her reality. In a sly and quiet movement he edged his left hand towards the woman sat next to him. Closer it crept.

"Both hands on the wheel, McCorte!" she ordered.

"But I only wanted…" he started to say, though doing as she had demanded.

"I know what you were doing, and why, but it doesn't matter. Can't you see that? Whether I am real or a figment is of little consequence in the final analysis."

He gripped the wheel hard, concentrating keenly on the road ahead. "Will you sing me one final song for the journey?" he asked.

"Of course. And since this will be my final performance, you can choose."

"Then I would like it to be Mozart's concert aria 'Popoli di Tessaglia'."

Yvette's tinkling laugh filled the van. "Ah ha," she exclaimed. "So you want to test my upper register."

"It's just a favourite," he said, almost to himself. Then felt the tension leaking from his mind as she started to sing.

She was, as ever, absolutely note perfect. McCorte felt an almost righteous divinity sweep through the very bones of his construction as the God-given voice carried him to a far better place than the one around him. It no longer mattered whether she was real or not. Nor did he need to know why her face was shrouded in darkness. Her vocal glory was sufficient in itself and by the time the singing ended there were tears of joy in his eyes.

"Are you coming all the way with me?"

"I think not," she replied. "This journey encapsulates an area of your most personal and private needs. To stay would be an intrusion."

She said no more and when McCorte glanced in her

direction the passenger seat was empty. Yvette had been right though. He could see that. It was all about his acceptance of the role now thrust upon him.

It was about him, them, and the Accuracy International Super Magnum Lapua Rifle hidden in the back of the van.

Driving carefully yet purposefully, McCorte headed into London. Towards what awaited him at the Royal Albert Hall.

POEMS #6

ROCK & ROLL DAMNATION

Kill your teachers
Kill your parents
Kill your leaders

Screaming guitars
Torn bleeding teen-lyrics
Harley Davidson mock-up
Customised
Sleazy glitzy
A glorious jumble of ballooning excess
And it's like: Wow!

Kill your elders
Kill your priests
Kill your neighbours

Beneath the beat
Within the groove
In and out of the fast fingered
Squeal of tortured strings
The subliminal inveiglement
Of the unknowingly compliant

Kill the deaf
Kill the dumb
Kill the blind

The future wears black
Carries a Fender Strat
And has no soul

Kill all who fail to heed the word

***

SINGING

Went through door X
"Sing," said man
Give him both barrels
Watch greenback sludge
Ooze from wounds
"You're good
But it's not singing,"
Said corpse
So machinegun whole room
Splash petrol
Strike match
Taught us well at Academy
Captain Getaway waiting
Foot down
Seatbelts flapping
High-speed whine
"Now THAT is singing,"
Said Captain
Crashing the barrier
Scattering scorpions
"Damn insect cops!"
He shouted
Driving out and over
Into space
And a three mile drop
Time to die again
A song I knew how to sing

***

SUCKERS

Born in the heat
Of a Saturday night
In the truth
In the lies
Of misplaced reality

Waits a fictional body
Sprouting lines of decay
Waits the mothman
The croupier
The dealer of cards
To the suckers
And fools
Corruption that hangs
On the turn of an ace
A sinister shadow
In flickering light

Turn away in confusion
Turn away
While you can

***

I SEE MANY DANCERS

In the land of flashing strobes
Big-time jive-chief: Me

I – Dealer
Can feel your needs before yourself

A tab of E
A line of C
Uppers downers
All over towners

I – Dealer
The man to see

In the land of hard-core heaven
I see many many dancers
But none before like you

Just a kid

Jail-bait meat

But what a mover what a turn-on
Got myself a hard-core hard-on
Watching from the side

I – Dealer
Lord of Clubland
I see many many dancers
But none sweet child like you

Ask – and I will deal you in
Name your dreams…

Bring me the head of John the Baptist

***

KNOW THE BLUES

She's a rambling Miss
Bad luck charm
She's Old Nick's gal

If you know Black Angel you know the blues

Left Oakland plinth
For a Delta scene
Crossroads : Midnight : Halloween

Mercy Lord
Mercy Lord
Help the man

If you know Black Angel you know the blues

Signed in blood
Covenant scaled
Crossroads : Midnight : Halloween

Voodoo handshake
Hellhound trail

If you know Black Angel you know the blues

Signed and sealed
For Delta throne

But here's the catch
First you die

If you know Black Angel you know the blues

You really do
Know the blues

SHREWHAMPTON NORTH-WEST
(a continuation)

The man with the military moustache. The one who had appointed himself interrogator-in-chief but whose interrogation had ended. The one who had offered to carve Mr Ash and had actually done so. He, not wanting to relinquish a position of importance, took it upon himself to switch from interrogation to butchery. As carver-in-chief he would slash, slice, hack and provide everyone with their mealtime portions.

Some initially found the consumption of raw human flesh indigestible. In spite of having been stuck at the Shrewhampton North-East station for three days, the man who had obsessed about my sweets before having one, and was obviously more in need of nourishment than the rest, vomited noisily following his first chewed morsel. The equally thin lady also regurgitated the first piece of Mr Ash that she attempted.

"It should be cooked," she complain shrilly.

"You must cast aside the trappings of civilisation, madam." said the military-moustached man as he paused from his butchering duties. "Does the lion ask that his wildebeest steak be medium rare or well done? He does not. The King of the Jungle partakes of his meat raw and bloodied. The way nature intended. And we must be as a pride of lions."

He smirked a little at that, I noticed. Rather pleased with his own choice of analogy. A bit of a puffed up fellow I thought. Probably prone to covering up his own shortcomings with bombast and bluster.

The man who doubted the existence of Shrewhamton North-East was one of those who ate with apparent relish. No-one else had noticed, only myself, that he had inherited the late Mr Ash's premonition of impending speech. At that early stage he would not have realised it himself, but would do later. As would the others. And when they did they would, not exactly ostracise, but keep him at a distance.

"What?" he'd go, unable to resist a glance over his shoulder. "Eh!" he would exclaim. "What was that?" he'd continue. "Oh not again!"

"It's not a fatal condition," he would shout. Trying to convince himself as well as us. "That Ash guy didn't die from it. You don't die from thinking you're about to hear a voice."

But nobody offered the hand of friendship. Even my mother kept her distance. No-one wanted to become pally with a future meal.

By the time Mr Ash had been half consumed, even those initially queasy had adapted to the diet circumstance had forced upon us. And the man with the military moustache had become more expert with the knife. At first he had chopped and hacked with a distinct lack of skill. His work being haphazard at best. Sometimes no better than a back street abortionist. Not that I was aware of their specific level of competence. But practise, as they say, and if his primal cuts were not always totally uniform then he trimmed them most professionally.

"I know it's the means by which we are staying alive," said the lady who resembled the second porter, who had not been seen since depositing the canteen of cutlery in the waiting room. The porter that is, not the lady who looked like him. She hadn't deposited anything anywhere. "But I never once thought in all my life that I would one day practice cannibalism."

"Oh no, it's anthropophagi," insisted the man who no longer worried about my sweets, which were all gone anyway, and no longer checked the station buffet. After his bad start he was now eating well. The two words meant the same thing, eating the flesh of your own species, but some were squeamish over the term "cannibal". I suppose they pictured missionaries being boiled alive in large African native pots. Even being likened to lions, the King of Beasts, didn't remove the stigma completely.

The man with the military moustache, in between his butchery, organised periodic Hunt-the-Porter searches. The second one that is. The first being somewhere else entirely and whose actions I could still bring to mind — he had stacked, scratched, picked and grinned — but whose features were now well and truly forgotten, except that I had labelled one of our company as looking a little like him.

The second porter was never found. Nor did those looking expect him to be. It was similar to an army training exercise in that they went through the motions but it wasn't the real thing.

"I believe only in what I can see and touch," said the man we secretly expected to be our next food source. "There is nobody standing behind me about to speak. Ash thought it would happen and so it did. Or he became convinced it did. But not me!"

His voice would end on a note of triumph. But then: "What?" he'd go. "Eh?" he would exclaim. "What was that?" he'd continue. "It was nothing. Really! Nothing!" he would finish.

The equally thin lady would cross herself and everyone would turn away from him.

"I will beat it," he would mutter, more to himself than anyone else. "I will. I will."

"Do you think there might be a Shrewhampton North-West?" I asked him once, thinking he'd be grateful for a little conversation. A foolish question really since he often doubted the existence of the North-East version. Which was where we were supposed to be. And without the one the other was unlikely.

"Come away. Come away," fussed my mother. "Don't bother the gentleman."

The man himself just glowered.

The one thing we lacked in our constant diet of Mr Ash was variety. "A couple of 'taters would go down nice," remarked the man who reminded me of the now forgotten first porter.

"Or just some salt and pepper," added someone who I hadn't likened to anyone.

"Mustn't grumble," our military-moustached self-appointed leader would insist, keen to quell any possible mutiny in the ranks. "Just give thanks for what we have."

It did turn out, however, that though we were being held in a form of captivity our grumbles were sometimes listened to. Not the big issues like: why can't we get out of here? But smaller matters of comfort and taste. For instance, the next time the second porter put in an appearance he brought with him a selection of sauces and condiments.

Mr Ash had been reduced to a pile of bones and some totally indigestible scrag-ends of what had once been a plump and rosy body. It was obviously time to replenish the larder. The man who doubted the existence of Shrewhampton North-East was beside himself with worry while none of the other adults would meet his gaze eye-to-eye, acting as if he wasn't there. Which made him even more paranoid.

I would still have preferred a more physical ailment, as I had with Mr Ash, but it did have an added psychological twist to it now. "What's it like knowing that you are probably going to hear a voice and then die?" I asked, but he just buried his face in his hands.

"Now now, my boy," said the man with the military moustache, trying to head off a potential scene. "We all have to die some time."

"But we don't all have to know about it," I insisted. "And I wondered what it felt like to know you are going to be eaten."

"Out of the mouths of babes," said the equally thin lady, which I thought inappropriate since I was long past the baby stage.

The man who only believed in what he could feel and see, who had buried his face in his hands, started to cry.

"Come here! Sit down and be quiet," my mother told me.

"Let's try and keep calm about everything, shall we?" suggested the man with the military moustache.

"Keep calm," repeated one of the men who resembled no-one of my acquaintance. "We live in a station's waiting room, converted to an abattoir. We live on raw human flesh and play Hunt-the-Porter. We wonder when it will be our turn to experience premonitions of impending speech, because surely it is going to come to all of us one after the other. I think it understandable that calmness should be in short supply."

I thought he was chatty enough to be Welsh. Which he was, trying to form a Choral Society to help pass the time. But nobody else wanted to sing.

Anyway, the second porter turned up with the sauces and condiments just as we finished Mr Ash. "Mr Leckwith only believes in what he can see and feel," he said. "But knows nothing." Then he disappeared again.

Mr Leckwith, when we all turned towards him, was in the process of hearing the impending speech he had long denied existed. Which made me feel there was hope for Shrewhampton North-East after all. And maybe even North-West.

Mr Leckwith, as with Mr Ash before him, smiled contentedly and rolled over. The man with the military moustache pronounced him dead. He then proceeded to strip the corpse and cut around the digestive tract to prevent faecal contamination. His butchery technique was much improved by now.

"Hmm. Tastes like chicken," suggested someone after our first meal from the new source.

"Pork," declared somebody else.

"Venison,"

"Goat."

"Ostrich."

I was pretty certain that some of the people concerned had never tasted the flavours they suggested. Alligator was one I dismissed out of hand. My mother favoured the opinion that it tasted like pork. She was sure she'd read in the past that one cannibal tribe referred to the people they feasted on as long-pigs, and that was good enough for her. My mother, prior to all this, had been best described as scrawny. Which was why I had thought one of the other ladies to be as equally thin as her. But both had benefited from our rich fleshy diet and neither could be called skinny any more. Which was just as well since it was the equally not-so-thin lady who took up the mantle of impending speech.

No wonder that first porter had grinned knowingly when I poked out my tongue. No wonder Mr Ash, the plump man, had smiled so contentedly when finally hearing the voice. No wonder the man with the military moustache tried to hang on to a position of authority. Had my mother known any of them in a previous life? Could any or either be my father?

My father who art in…?

An on-going question and one my mother had so far refused to answer. "When you're older," she would say if and when I pressed the issue. "When you are old enough to understand."

Sometimes I thought I might be the illegitimate son of royalty. The secret heir to the throne. Maybe my mother was not my mother at all. Maybe she was my nurse who, loving the blue-blooded babe, was given the job of bringing him up permanently. And I did have vague babyhood memories of being called Prince. But whether it was as a term of endearment or a title I couldn't be sure.

Sometimes…

But at other times not.

The equally not-so-thin lady dealt with her acquisition of the impending speech syndrome in a much different manner to her predecessors. She accepted the condition as having been bestowed by Someone Up Above and turned it into a religion. Her turn would come and she would relish the sacrifice to be made.

The Welshman who reminded me of no-one soon became the most ardent member of her congregation. Mainly because it enabled him to sing "Bread of Heaven" with full revivalist fervour, and in a surprisingly pleasant lyric tenor.

Others joined in too. More because it provided a break from the monotony of our existence than because of any genuine conviction. Even our military-moustached feeder and leader saw the sense in letting the movement flourish unopposed.

So things drifted along. Mr Leckwith's bones and remains

joined those of Mr Ash in a corner of the platform outside the waiting room. An area we called the Knacker's Yard. And Miss Babbington, as the second porter eventually named her, listened joyously to the voice and died a happy woman. Misguided maybe, but happy all the same.

The Welshman tried to keep the religious aspect alive after her death but lacked the necessary zeal Miss Babbington had brought to the task. His only real interest was in the hymnal side of things. Also, the latest to twitch and turn and gasp with a premonition that had again become unwanted, was a man who looked like no-one and sat morosely on his own. And who did not welcome his prospective elevation to becoming part of the food chain with the same acceptance Miss Babbington had brought to the role.

Our resident Taffy, however, did not give up easily. With a similar selling technique to that employed by the Welsh Outside Half Factory in their non-stop supply to northern Rugby League clubs, he offered a quest. Maybe my unanswered question had not gone unnoticed after all. He offered the Holy Grail of Shrewhampton North-*West*!

It caught on to a certain extent. And in reality was little more to him than an excuse to sing songs such as "It's a Long Way to Tipperary" (World War One ditty), "The Long and Winding Road" (from the Beatles *Let It Be* album), and even "Road to our Dream" (a minor hit for T'Pau in 1989). But it did strike home with me. And it did produce results.

Miss Babbington, having been sliced and diced in compliance with our whole carcass nose-to-toe philosophy, was duly replaced by Mr Wilson. The silently morose man who remained unapologetically taciturn to the end. Not even hearing those final words seemed to break his mood. He wasn't to know it but he was the last.

As Mr Wilson died and was prepared for butchering, so those still remaining waited to see who would be next. Listening for that first "What?" Watching for that first glance over the shoulder. But neither happened and it was soon realised that nobody was suffering premonitions of impending speech.

Though this was greeted with a certain relief, it also posed the question of future food source requirements. But in the meantime I passed the time listening to the various versions of Shrewhampton North-West put forward by the group and some of their plans for reaching there. Plans which seemed a bit premature to me since they couldn't even get to Shrewhampton North-*East*, which was supposed to be the town this station was attached to.

My mother and I had set out for Lower Mallerton. We had changed successfully at Little Haslop, but that had only entailed disembarking from one train and climbing aboard another. We had not actually seen Little Haslop, and I hadn't even considered the possibility of a Greater Haslop, any more than we had seen the previously unvisited and unheard of Shrewhampton North-East. The single difference being that I had wondered whether there might be a Shrewhampton North-West.

And now this oddball little group were plotting the digging of tunnels and the flying of hot air balloons to reach somewhere that might not exist. All to the accompaniment of a Welsh lyric tenor's soundtrack. Life might be boring but it wasn't dull.

The Hunt-the-Porter excursions fell away when it became obvious the impending speech situation had come to an end. If there were no longer anyone to be named at their moment of death, then did the second porter have any other function? So maybe he was no longer around. Hidden or otherwise. But he was.

There was not much in the way of edible flesh left on the remains of the morose and silent man. "The Lord will provide, and maybe show us the way to North-West," predicted the man from Wales.

"Or maybe we will starve," suggested the lady who resembled the second porter.

Our military-moustached main man said nothing, but I noticed he was becoming decidedly edgy. When there was no more raw flesh to eat, the rest would turn to him. Expecting leadership. Expecting him to provide. He glanced in my direction. Slyly. Weighing me up. Looking at the tender young flesh on my bones.

"Mother?" I called.

"Don't worry dear," she said, reaching out and patting my cheek. "Just stay by my side."

On the day that the last piece of raw flesh was scraped from Mr Wilson, the second porter put in another appearance. Standing in the waiting room doorway, he smiled knowingly.

"Trains are coming," he announced. "The tracks are coming to life again."

"About time too!" snapped the man with the military moustache, trying to maintain an air of authority till the end.

"The train about to pull in to platform one is a short hop special going to Shrewhampton North-West." Porter number two looked in our direction. "Mothers and sons only to board this one." He looked back to the others. "The train due in five minutes at platform two is your connection to Lower Mallerton." Then back to me again. "And before you ask: Yes, there is an Upper Mallerton."

"Come along. Come along," said my mother, taking my hand and hurrying the pair of us to platform one where a single carriage locomotive was waiting. We got aboard.

"I always like an empty compartment," she remarked. "Don't sit with your back to the engine."

I swopped to the opposite side.

It was, as expected, only a short journey and when we got out at Shrewhampton North-West a third porter was waiting to greet us. I quickly ran through the faces of people I remembered and yes, this latest railway employee was something like the man with a military moustache, only without the upper lip appendage.

"An honour, ma'am. You and the boy," he was saying as he led the way. "Oh what an honour for my humble station."

As we progressed towards the waiting room I became aware that my mother was gradually increasing in size. Becoming larger. More powerful. Even her features were changing in subtle but definite ways. I thought it best to say nothing, withholding judgement until I learnt more.

The waiting room, when we reached it, was more like a meeting hall. There were hundreds of people. Apparently waiting for us. As we moved through them, making for a stage at the far end, I picked up odd pieces of muttered conversation.

"Lilith, she comes…"

"Young Scratch!"

As we stood at the back of the stage my mother placed a mighty arm around my shoulders. "This place," she whispered to me. "This Shrewhampton North-West is for you and I to rule while we wait for your father. Under my guidance you will learn your true place in the universe. And when he comes your father will glory in you, his son and heir."

The third porter, the one who looked like the military-moustached man but without the moustache, stepped to the front of the stage and gestured for silence.

"At last!" he told the gathering. "The moment we have been waiting for. May I present to you … Mrs Fear."

He moved to one side and my mother heaved her bulk forward. Looking into the audience she snaked out a sudden tentacle, curling it around a man in the front row and dragging him to her. Mother bit off his head, chewing hungrily, and threw the rest of him back to me so that I could feed. Then she faced the waiting crowd.

"I am Mrs Fear," she told them, "but you can call me Lucy!"

The place went ballistic!

AFTERWORD

Johnny Mains first rang me not long after my son died. He was tracking down old Fontana authors for something he was planning to write on Mary Danby. For a few brief minutes I was transported back to the 1970s and away from the tragic madness of Jim's murder. I will always be grateful for that phone call.

Life got in the way for Johnny. He didn't follow through with what he had intended to write, but four years later Mary Danby was due to be interviewed by him at the 2012 FantasyCon at Brighton. So he rang again, hoping that some of the lost writers Mary had published might be cajoled into making an appearance.

The four years had not been good for me. Maddalena, my wife, never recovered from the loss of our son, gradually deteriorating until she too had died just before Johnny's second phone call. Once again, an enthusiastic revisit to my personal moment as a brief footnote in the history of British horror short stories was a welcome diversion.

Having been more involved with poetry than fiction for a number of years, and having written poems for Jim when losing him, I wrote more when Maddalena died. Her death also released a deeply realised grief for our son, which I had held in check while caring for her, and having poured my loss into words I felt written-out, poetry-wise.

It is sufficient for me to say that I was completely lost and without direction. But this time Johnny Mains did not disappear. He kept in touch and started encouraging me to start writing short stories again. He also put me in touch with David Sutton who was planning to reprint two of his 1970's anthologies as *Horror! Under the Tombstone,* and David told me about a couple of editors who were currently inviting submissions.

As my daughter, Maria, will happily admit, it would not have crossed her mind to suggest I should start writing fiction again. But when I did, and she saw the difference it made in me, she gave all the support she could. Being quite the bully when storyline-snags reared their heads and supplying endless cups of tea when the words were flowing.

The end result was that Jan Edwards and Jenny Barber accepted "Ithica or Bust" for *The Alchemy Press Book of Ancient Wonders.* I attended the 2012 FantasyCon at Brighton, taking part in the anthology launch and meeting Johnny Mains and Mary Danby, a special highlight. And I have kept on writing.

This collection is a mixture of old and new. Some flowed easily while others had to be dragged screaming onto the page. "Shrewhampton North-East" virtually wrote itself. I had not, at the time, written either about a child or in the first person. Inserting a sheet of paper into my typewriter I banged away at the keys, meaning it just to be a practise sort of thing. Five or six pages later I realised that a story was emerging and merely kept typing.

"Daddy" is my one and only story based upon a dream. A rather unpleasant nightmare I had not long after Maddalena died. After I started writing again Maria and my two granddaughters kept insisting it should be turned into a story. I finally gave in to their pressure.

Some stories have the occasional in-joke. In "Nasty", for instance, I have a little gentle fun at the expense of my publisher, The Alchemy Press, and the sort of anthologies they are well known for. My protagonist in "Wordsmith" is named Piller Presavorrat, which translates as – Piller: to pillage, to *Rob*; Presa: to preserve, to *Hold*; Vorrat: a straight translation to *Stock*. Rob Holdstock and I were good friends at the time we were both making our first sales. By way of revenge he named a character Bryn the Merciless, a Dwarf Warlord in one of the *Berserker* novels he wrote as Chris Carlsen.

There was also a Rob Holdstock connection with another story. When I told him the rough outline to "Remnants" he stated an interest and we did talk about a collaboration, but Rob was Robert P Holdstock by then and the idea lapsed.

Jack Marsh was another good friend I would talk plot outlines with. He provided important input into "The Oscar Project" and the story was accepted by *SF Monthly* but the magazine folded before it appeared and at over ten thousand words I couldn't think of anywhere else to submit it. The story languished forgotten for years until I recalled the sad tale during a Facebook discussion about *SF Monthly*. Andrew Darlington asked if he could see the story and I sent him an old carbon copy. Andrew proceeded to modernise the outdated political segments of the story, which now owes much to Jack and Andrew for their substantial input.

"The Flier" is another with old origins. My son was always interested in UFO phenomena. We would argue often, him for and me against, and Jim would bring me details of any new sighting. One such case prompted me to outline a story, but it got shelved when my boy died. Years later, though, I remembered it when reading *The Alchemy Press Book of Pulp Heroes*. So I dug out the original, adapted and developed it into a fuller version and luckily Mike Chinn accepted it for *Pulp*

Heroes 2.

I took "Denton's Delight" to a writer's evening where I knew a pianist and bass guitarist would be providing a jazzy interlude. I wanted them to check my manuscript for any mistakes I might have made in musical references. I'd set the story in a Jazz Club I had frequented many years before, much to the amazement of Terry Hallett and Ray Turley who I asked to read it. They had been two thirds of the regular trio at that club and recognised themselves. Luckily their mentions had been complimentary and they both became good friends of mine.

My first version of "The Pawn Shop Window" was written before Louis Armstrong died and although I liked the idea, I knew the story lacked a certain something. After his death I looked at it again, bringing his passing and burial into the storyline. Making it, I hope, a more rounded and complete little tale.

"Shrewhampton North-West" came about when Johnny Mains challenged me, and others I believe, to write a sequel to a previously published story. Mine was not so much a sequel as *a continuation*. I had often wondered myself what might have happened to the people at that station.

Of the poetry, "A Taxi Driver On Mars" was placed first in the 2009 Data Dump Awards for science fiction poetry published in the U.K. It was Rhysling nominated in America the same year. "Siren Women Of Tremulan III" was Dwarf Star nominated in America in 2007. Both poems originally appeared in Atlantean Publishing titles. There are also some song lyrics, but don't worry – I promise not to sing them!

Johnny Mains, when submitting his Introduction, stipulated that I was not to see it until the book was published. So at the time I am writing this, I have no idea what he has said in his piece. He looked me up when searching for lost Fontana authors. He encouraged me to start writing again at a time when I was sorely in need of direction to fill my latter years. Through him, and Facebook, I am now communicating with so many interesting people. Johnny Mains is a man whose friendship I treasure. Thank you, Johnny.

My thanks also to Mary Danby, David Sutton and the late Ken Bulmer for those long ago acceptances, and to Mary again for the quote she kindly allowed us to use in this book.

A final word before I sign off, about my publisher. The whole business of putting a collection together has been both seamless and easy due to the expertise of The Alchemy Press. I felt we were going to be a good fit when it was discovered that Peter Coleborn and I shared a similar enthusiasm for what I describe as *quirky* elements of fiction.

It's been a gas!

Bryn Fortey, February 2014

Acknowledgements

Some of the work in this collection has appeared in the following publications:

Blue Danube (Romania), *Blue Frederick, Canine Teeth, Carillon, C.P.R., Dwarf Star Anthology* (America), *Horror! Under The Tombstone, Iota, Mineshaft* (America), *Never Get Out Of These Blues Alive, New Writings In Horror & The Supernatural, New Writings In SF, Outlaw, Poetry Cornwall, Poetry Monthly, Read The Music, Renegade, Rhysling Anthology* (America), *Saying Goodbye, Scar Tissue, Solo für einen Kannibalen* (Germany), *Spiders & Flies, The Penniless Press, The Seventh Quarry, Writer's Muse,* and various titles from Atlantean Publishing, Fontana Books and The Alchemy Press.

"Crossing the Snowline", "Daddy", "Nasty", "Remnants", "Shrewhampton North-West", "Skulls", "The Oscar Project", "Therapy" and Poems #4 ("A Solitary Dream", "These Autumn Days", "Let Me Journey", "Nightfall") all appear here for the first time.

I would also like to acknowledge the substantial input made by Jack Marsh and Andrew Darlington into the writing of "The Oscar Project". My thanks to them both.

Bryn Fortey

Lightning Source UK Ltd.
Milton Keynes UK
UKOW03f0859290414

230775UK00001B/38/P